SCHRUMMSCHRUMM

SCHRUMM SCHRUMM

or

The Sunday Quicksands Excursion

FERNAND COMBET

FOREWORD BY ÉRIC DUSSERT

TRANSLATED BY K. E. GORMLEY

WAKEFIELD PRESS

CAMBRIDGE, MASSACHUSETTS

Wakefield Press, P.O. Box 425645, Cambridge, MA 02142

Originally published in French as *SchrummSchrumm ou l'excursion dominicale aux sables mouvants* by Jean-Jacques Pauvert in 1966, and then in a revised edition by Éditions Verticales in 2006.

Cover image: Albert Pinkham Ryder, *The Canal*, 1890.

This book was set in Garamond Premier Pro and Helvetica Neue Pro by Wakefield Press. Printed and bound by Versa Press in the United States of America.

ISBN: 978-1-962728-07-2

Available through D.A.P./Distributed Art Publishers
75 Broad Street, Suite 630
New York, New York 10004
Tel: (212) 627-1999
Fax: (212) 627-9484

10 9 8 7 6 5 4 3 2 1

FOREWORD

Forty Years Later . . .

For Onuma Nemon
and Dominique Poncet

"In the morning, I bought an empty bottle from the concierge and then I, too, set off for the desert."
Georges Henein, *Une certaine poussière*

Sometimes one great book is enough to establish an œuvre. Sometimes one good book is worth a Mass, or a sterling reputation. Witness Arthur Cravan and John Kennedy Toole. But a masterpiece often leads to nothing, or, to plagiarize Gherasim Luca, absolutely to nothing, and leads there so belatedly that one has to wonder who benefits from talent, genius, inspiration, and artistic ecstasies. Not Fernand Combet, certainly, who slipped away unnoticed and let the shadows cover him. For lack of planning ahead, for lack of scheming and striving, or simply for lack of fighting with the right weapons. But is there any other certainty in this life than that oblivion will soon engulf us all, and that, our places being vacated, others will come along to trample on our withered, dusty laurels? Combet knew he had an œuvre. What need had he to plan? Planning is for the unsure.

An unruly and uncompromising man, an opinionated writer—*temperamental* is what he'd be called by those timid souls frightened of a mood swing, scandalized by an iron will—Fernand Combet would come to know the torments of a chaotic literary career. Fame is as fragile as glass when anger is of marble. Let us put it plainly: Combet was not made to schmooze his way along the royal roads of success. He was born to write, not to get his work into print. There remains the mystery of his fate, and of this rare refusal to participate in the farce. He confined himself to five published works over a span of twenty years, a brief bibliography inaugurated by a masterpiece.

Born in Croix Rousse, a hilltop district of Lyon known for its hard-headed personalities, on 1 April 1936 (what a date), he was a rambunctious child who attended every secondary school in the area one after the next. His father, the owner of a small dye-works, died when he was sixteen. Three years later, Fernand would leave his young bride and eventually, it's unclear how, wind up in law school, then at Sciences-Po (with a focus on foreign policy) in 1956. He proved to be a brilliant student, but before he earned his diploma a more urgent goal claimed precedence. What he wanted to do was write. And so he abandoned a promising career on the eve of his second-year exams and enrolled in Langues-O, which also promised travel. To make ends meet, he wrote a food column for the magazine *Bien vivre* and did so with great erudition. He soaked up culture like a sponge, devouring everything: literature, music—all kinds of music—sculpture, painting, life. After living for a while on rue Saint-Jacques, he settled down on rue Saint-Séverin, near the Fontaine Saint-Michel, just above Marcel Béalu's bookshop and not far from François Maspero's. His top priority didn't change one iota. He wrote, and well. Gallimard's interest was piqued by the quality of a text Combet had wrestled with for five years, but the young man was wary of that institution. It was to Pauvert, the publisher of the moment, that he entrusted his manuscript, on the advice of friends. And when, in February of 1966, *SchrummSchrumm, or The Sunday Quicksands Excursion* appeared under this imprint, it made a splash. An enthusiastic press braided him laurel wreaths from leaves the size of palm fronds. Leading critics sang the praises of his stunning novel. From Matthieu Galey (*Arts*) to Kléber Haedens (*Candide*), not to mention Luc Estang (*Le Figaro littéraire*) and Georges Anex (*Le Journal de Genève*), *SchrummSchrumm* was at once placed "between Kafka and Chrétien de Troyes" and featured prominently, thanks to an article by Marie-Claude de Brunhoff, in the table of contents of the first issue of *La Quinzaine littéraire* on 15 March 1966. That was forty years ago. It was even likened to "Kafka through the lens of Dostoevsky." All this from a writer with "the physique of a Mongol conqueror."

A conqueror, yes: Fernand Combet had been battling tirelessly for five long years to finish his book. Five ascetic years spent purifying, paring down, and shaping a pull-no-punches form that was to stamp its mark on the era. For when *SchrummSchrumm* burst onto the scene, at a moment uniting the postwar years, *Les Trente Glorieuses*, and the Cold War, it was as a weighty, knotty, terrifying book. The apparently bureaucratic madness it describes—there's something that should ring a few bells—was that of a century spinning out of control, a century whose aftershocks still shake us to this day.

SchrummSchrumm is, of course, a book about oppression and death, a haunting book open to several readings. Even if the author intended it as a work of fiction on the subject of free will, it can also be read as a statement on blind, senseless cruelty, on Absurdity with a capital A, on the walls that hem in every human life. Others will see it as a fable of totalitarianism, while readers of Sergei Chakhotin's *Rape of the Masses* (1939) or Jean Norton Cru's *Témoins* (1929) and *Du témoignage* (1930) will find echoes of the manipulation to which entire peoples were once subjected, manipulation to which we ourselves now meekly submit on a daily basis because it goes by the name of "PR campaigns," "marketing," and "publicity," though it is in fact propaganda, plain and simple. True, we don't yet have backroom tourist offices offering us mandatory "Sunday excursions." Or so we think.

For all these reasons, *SchrummSchrumm* is without a doubt one of the great novels of the twentieth century, one of those books that will never cease to astound us: Combet's *Abocketaback*, that supreme Rule that commands every citizen of Misunderstanding to refrain from seeking logic in the sequence of events that befalls him in that city, this Abocketaback synonymous with lies and banal, everyday horror, two things that, in 1966 as in 2006, govern consciences, in the apparent innocuousness of the Great Iron Gate, the Original Pissoir, and the Primordial House.

The most striking take on *SchrummSchrumm* was given on 16 March 1966 by André Hardellet in a letter to Jean-Pierre Castelnau, Pauvert's collaborator. The author of *La Cité Montgol* could disguise neither his admiration nor his emotion: "Combet has written a fine, calmly ferocious book. . . . An important book, too, whose meanings and mines have yet to be exhausted. . . ." Admiring and enthusiastic, he lauded this "Book of Doubt," its rigorous logic that leads to false explanations, symbolic abstractions, and endless planning designed to "drown out" the real objectives of a system, of a society, of a machine for human beings. "If I should meet Combet someday," added Hardellet, "I'll ask no questions about his work: it's enough for me that it exists. It all became TRUE the moment he created it in black and white. . . ."

André Hardellet didn't know how right he was.

Fortified by his author's *succès d'estime*, Pauvert pushed him to "produce" another book. Combet complied . . . or so it seemed. It's now 1968. Combet gives him *Factice, ou les Hommes-oiseaux* (Factitious, or The bird-men), a slapdash effort that comes out in September. Equally hallucinatory, this allegorical tale was obviously inspired by the events of that year he'd witnessed firsthand, forced to seal his doors against the tear gas, but it preserved—was this mere accident?—a slight flavor of buffoonery even within the prevailing tone of the era, unless it was just that the booze, hash, and coke were doing their job a little too well. Was Fernand Combet laughing up his sleeve at his publisher? You can never put anything past a free spirit. Pauvert accepted the book nonetheless and published it, but he'd learned his lesson and next time would give his author time to work.

His third novel, *Mort et passion de Félix C. Scribator* (Death and passion of Félix C. Scribator), originally titled *L'Éventail plié* (The folded fan), Pauvert published in a format unusual for the retail book trade of the 1960s and 1970s: a generous quarto with an imposing black cover. In it one finds Fernand Combet at the top of his game, narrating, in language more exuberant than ever—newer as well, and more muscular—the adventures of Félix C. in the city of TutiNova. It's another allegory: Félix C. Scribator bears too close a resemblance to his creator, "with his collars, his long hair, his orange-and-brown hippie getup" not to run up against the same obstacles in his social trajectory.

But his heyday of success was over. Fernand Combet withdrew from the literary scene and began traveling, attracted by Asia, its peoples and its philosophies. In the 1980s, he even went so far as to open a shop in Paris selling Indian miniatures and antiques, stocked with finds from his periodic wanderings along the Ganges. The store was a passing fad he abandoned after three years. But the traveling continued apace, and somewhere around 1984–1985 he grew consumed by a new passion: computers. From that point onward he would never be without them, nourishing himself on music (he and his partner Renée regularly attended the Chennai Music Season) and extensive reading. It took an encounter with publisher Christian Laucou for a few rare pages of his to find their way into print: *Contes de l'Ambre et de l'Opium* (Tales of amber and opium) in 1985, and a poem, *Chanson* (Song), in 1988. After which, Fernand Combet fell silent.

Increasingly reclusive, intransigent in his desire for seclusion, Fernand Combet eventually exiled himself from the world of letters, as well as from the world in general. Nevertheless, he was still writing relentlessly.

On 3 August 1994, a stroke left him paralyzed. Now glued to his computers all day, he would be slowly worn down by amphetamines, alcohol, and those pesky words that chained him ever more agonizingly to his keyboard. His calvary would last nine and a half years.

There can be no doubt that reissuing *SchrummSchrumm* will earn Combet the lasting acclaim that has hitherto eluded him. For, by refusing petty compromises out of a sense of dignity and shunning worldly society out of a clear sense of his priorities, Fernand Combet was always conscientiously pulling the rug out from under his own feet. Henceforth, readers of Poe, Lovecraft, Flann O'Brien, Borges, Arno Schmidt, or Philip K. Dick will know that there exists, here and now, another writer for them to discover. Jean-Jacques Pauvert himself admitted in his memoir, *La traversée du livre* (Viviane Hamy, 2004), that *SchrummSchrumm* was the best *livre de feu* in his catalogue and the one of which he was proudest. The book is, in fact, the most unsettling novel ever put out by his press—the one, most importantly, that is like no other French book of the last century.

"I would like to make a book that dreams," wrote Lawrence Durrell, and, like Loys Masson maneuvering his *Tortoises*, Fernand Combet created this book and this dream that lead us over the edge. Utterly forgotten by those in his field, he died in Renée's arms on 29 December 2003, all too uncertain of his œuvre's place in posterity. With a slight delay, which is regrettable, posterity will nonetheless show that a hard-headed man can be a man of genius.

Éric Dussert

SCHRUMMSCHRUMM
or
THE SUNDAY QUICKSANDS EXCURSION

I

One morning, someone came to tell SchrummSchrumm that the Sunday Quicksands Excursion Company bus was waiting for him outside his building. SchrummSchrumm replied that surely there must be some mistake. Aside from the fact that he hadn't submitted an application to go to the Quicksands, the bus in question had never—within living memory—stopped at his building. But he was told to look out the window and see for himself. It was true: the bus was parked right out front. It was the same bus—legendary, lurid, and sinister—that had often thundered past at dizzying speeds in a halo of purple flames ... The driver could be seen behind the wheel. Two youths had descended from the vehicle. They were propounding the following publicity slogan, which was picked out in gold letters on a large banner of black cloth: "The Quicksands Excursion: More than a match for the strong, sends the weak on to glory. Don't resist your calling! Take the ultimate trip!" They were distributing candy to the children and hot sausages to the adults. They were not, however, having much success. Every so often they'd throw back their heads and cry out for all to hear: "We're waiting for the excursionist SchrummSchrumm!" As a result, all the neighbors at their windows turned to face him and wished him bon voyage. The semi-wholesaler in small hardware supplies—who himself was preparing to set out for the city of Acupuncture, as he did every day—wished him bon voyage and a happy excursion. The elderly couple who took daily walks pushing a dead baby in a pink stroller wished him bon voyage. Even total strangers, on this particular morning, wished him bon voyage. The Dispatch and Receiving Department men—who were toting three iron-banded wicker trunks on their brawny shoulders—smiled at him and wished him a happy excursion. A group of villagers—who'd come for a wedding and were brandishing golden scissors—wished him bon voyage. He protested in vain that he wasn't going on any excursion; they only nodded knowingly ... He was beginning to wonder, with some degree of anxiety, whether he might possibly have submitted an application he no longer remembered. And how long had it been since he'd gone on a Sunday excursion? Ah, he couldn't remember that, either ...

When he reached the bus, he noticed that all the neighbors had suddenly disappeared. The semi-wholesaler in small hardware supplies, the elderly couple who took daily walks pushing a dead baby in a pink stroller, as well as the others he didn't know—the Dispatch and Receiving Department men and the villagers in wedding attire—had also disappeared. All the windows were now shut and their curtains drawn.

The two youths stepped forward smartly to meet him. Their eyes were delicately embellished with shadow, their lips and nails painted. Once they'd verified that he was indeed Schrumm-Schrumm, excursionist first class, they said:

"Your registration application has been accepted by the high authorities of the Excursion. Accordingly, we have come to collect you. Mr. Prestige is waiting."

"Who's Mr. Prestige?"

"Mr. Prestige is the procession director. We report to him. Mr. Prestige ensures that the journey proceeds under optimal conditions and that the ritual is scrupulously observed."

At the word *ritual*, SchrummSchrumm was unable to conceal his embarrassment. As it happened, the legends also spoke of a ritual. He had, moreover, done some research on this subject and corresponded with various specialists. He'd even delivered a lecture on it. But now he was racking his brains for the formulas with no result. Fortunately, he had no time to agonize further. Mr. Prestige was approaching. He was tall. He was broad. He was laughing in a way that displayed every tooth in his head and carried a long whip that began at a hard, thick handle and tapered to a fine point. This he wielded with extraordinary dexterity, sending the lash whistling and snapping within an ace of the youths' ears as they stood stock-still, unflinching. By contrast, when the leather whip was cracked in SchrummSchrumm's face, he couldn't help but jerk backward, much to the others' hilarity.

"Please pardon my jumpiness," he said. "I'm a little on edge."

"That's always the way," nodded Prestige. "You weren't expecting us so soon, were you?"

"I wasn't expecting you at all," replied SchrummSchrumm. "I don't recall putting in an application."

"Did you hear that, Mr. Prestige?" shrieked the two youths. "He doesn't remember a thing! Isn't that simply incredible?"

But the procession director showed no surprise.

"Not to worry, Mr. Excursionist, these things happen," he said, motioning at the boys to settle down. "It's not strictly speaking a *normal* reaction, but neither is it any real cause for concern. Pay no attention to these two dunderheads. Here's how it usually goes: One day, a person submits an application. Then weeks, months, or even years go by, and he gradually forgets when and why he took that step. Maybe he was just in a blue mood. Maybe he wanted to see more of the world. But he's since put the whole thing out of his mind . . . So much so, that when finally, after all that time—all that *lost* time, you'll note, Mr. Excursionist—the Sunday Quicksands Excursion Company bus comes to collect the candidate excursionist, he claims he can't recall ever having signed an application. He expresses surprise, even manifests a certain hostility toward us, given that he's probably made other plans in the meantime . . . Now, tell me if I haven't put my finger on your very thoughts, eh? You see, we know all about it. The feeling will soon pass, believe me."

"What you've said is extremely astute and a testament to the sound instruction you've received as an Excursion employee," said SchrummSchrumm. "But it won't do as an explanation in my case. I, gentlemen, am a professional excursionist. Excursions, for me, are neither a pastime nor a mere pleasure: they are a vocation. In other words, if I'd put in a request, I'd certainly remember it."

"Don't go getting angry, Mr. Excursionist," said one of the youths.

"We talk in these terms to make things easier," said Mr. Prestige. "Anyway, whether you remember or not, you have to come with us now: we're behind schedule. What's more, we've already strayed quite far enough from the ritual. Is your house locked and shuttered, Mr. SchrummSchrumm? Are you ready, absolutely and entirely ready?"

In these last two sentences, SchrummSchrumm recognized, with genuine relief, the ritual formulas.

"My house is locked and shuttered, and I am entirely ready," he answered unhesitatingly.

"Perfect!" said Prestige, making a vague sign to his subordinates that they nevertheless appeared to comprehend. Quick as a flash, they pounced on SchrummSchrumm and pinned him down with a strength one wouldn't have thought they possessed. They stripped him naked and smeared him all over with stinking black catechumenal balm. In no way should he take offense at these measures, they explained. Quite the contrary. This was a ritual balm designed for hallucination protection during the journey to Misunderstanding.

SchrummSchrumm remembered the correct response just in time.

"What is Misunderstanding?" he inquired.

"Misunderstanding serves as seat of the Sunday Quicksands Excursion," they replied, steering him onto the bus. They sat him in front, directly behind the driver, who turned to give the newcomer a thoughtful once-over. The seat beside his was empty. Behind him, an elegantly dressed man of about fifty, wearing a flowered waistcoat and a huge pearl stickpin in his tie, was speaking quietly to a man in his forties with a stern, dour face. Apart from these two, all the other passengers were asleep and snoring prodigiously: neither the commotion of bundling SchrummSchrumm into the vehicle, nor the loud remarks that had just been exchanged, had caused them to open their eyes or turn their heads. "Strange bus, strange passengers," thought SchrummSchrumm, giving Boss Prestige an amiable smile. The latter pursed his lips ironically by way of reply and barked at the cosmeticized boys: "Get a move on, you two!"

The youths once again fell upon SchrummSchrumm. Ignoring his protests, they held him fast, put his wrists and ankles into manacles attached to the armrests and floor, and snapped them shut. "Stop making such a fuss! Everyone's chained . . ." said one, and SchrummSchrumm saw that, indeed, there were shackles on his fellow passengers' wrists as well. "Well done!" said Prestige when his two underlings had withdrawn to the back of the vehicle. He closed the door, sat down beside SchrummSchrumm, and gave the signal to depart.

"Away we go!" he said gaily.

"Away we go!" repeated the driver, equally gaily.

And the bus was off.

At first they traveled a route SchrummSchrumm knew well. The little houses they passed were those of peaceable, retired excursionists. These houses stood amid carefully tended gardens; wavering lines of smoke rose into the sky from their chimneys and checked curtains adorned their windows. Yet these houses very quickly began to grow sparse, the countryside became more arid, and the bus turned off in an unfamiliar direction. Now they were passing gypsies sitting in front of abandoned inns that must have once been fabulously opulent. They passed laughing children at the edges of murky woodland clearings, dancing with the blind, the crippled, and the simpleminded. And now the telephone poles on either side of the road had been converted into gibbets. Men hung from them with their blackened tongues protruding. Villagers in wedding attire had mounted ladders and were snipping off the hanged men's tongues with golden scissors while singing bawdy verses . . . The procession director waited till they'd left the hanged men behind before rising from his seat. He'd carefully laid aside his whip and taken out a small, artistically crafted hammer from a buckskin case. He then set about making a painstaking inspection of the passengers' chains. He rapped his hammer against each metal link in turn and nodded in satisfaction when it rang with a clear, crystalline sound indicating that it was in good condition. As SchrummSchrumm watched—despite his manacles, he was still able to turn his head far enough to see to the middle of the bus—he was struck by a detail he hadn't noticed on boarding: there were no women or children among his traveling companions.

"Odd duck this Prestige, eh?" murmured the nattily dressed fifty-year-old behind him. He had clearly waited until the procession director was at the back of the bus before striking up a conversation. SchrummSchrumm agreed:

"Awful man," he said. "As for our fellow passengers, they're remarkably sound sleepers!"

The two men nodded.

"Allow me to make the introductions," said the elegant man. "This is my friend and secretary, Mr. Broadway. I am Basil, an industrialist based in Acupuncture. We're here on our maiden excursion and this is all quite thrilling for us. We've heard a lot about you, Mr. SchrummSchrumm. Your feats are celebrated."

At that moment, a voice broke in and startled them. "Silence! No chit-chat on Sunday Quicksands Excursion Company buses!" It was Prestige, who, having completed his inspection, had returned to the front of the bus to issue the rebuke. This done, he heaved a loud sigh and was about to take his seat again when, for no apparent reason, the driver veered off onto the shoulder and slammed on the brakes, pitching the excursionists forward—which would have undoubtedly resulted in serious bruises had they not been restrained by the manacles. Everyone was instantly wide awake and a chorus of protests rose up, all the more indignant for the fact that Prestige was stretched out full-length on the floor. He'd suffered a violent tossing and it seemed impossible that he could have escaped without broken bones. The two youths were already kneeling beside their leader, taking turns licking his face and moaning at the top of their lungs:

"Oh, poor, *poor* Mr. Prestige!"

After a few moments, the procession director seemed to have recovered from the shock and realized what had happened. He grunted an expletive and slowly got to his feet, wincing, supported by his subordinates. The excursionists, reassured, hurled even louder recriminations at the driver. There was no small astonishment when the procession director interrupted them and came to the driver's defense:

"My dear excursionist friends," he said imploringly. "Please don't judge my colleague Illustrious too harshly. This was not the idle prank you might imagine. If it had been, I would have smashed in his skull with my silver hammer. On the contrary, it was an incident that may well have ended in catastrophe, and for which I am partly to blame. I forgot to blindfold you and close the metal window shutters as the Regulations stipulate. There can be no doubt that, having discovered this regrettable oversight, my colleague Illustrious wished to stop the vehicle as quickly as possible. You see, he's put in a Herculean effort on behalf of the Sunday Excursion Company. For nigh on twenty years he's guided this vehicle along this terrible route, day in and day out. At times he suffers dizzy spells akin to what you've seen today. I ask you to bear with him, and I thank you in advance for your understanding. And never fear: in just a few short minutes he'll be ship-shape again and ready to go."

This speech had its effect. Everyone saw that the driver was, in fact, in a pitiable state. He was babbling incoherently, shaking from head to foot, and a string of spittle hung from one corner of his mouth. Looking out at the road, they could also see that the catastrophe mentioned by Prestige had indeed been avoided by a hairsbreadth: the bus had come to a halt in a sinister-looking gorge between two chalky cliffs. The glare was intense, the heat stifling. The passengers began to discuss their situation and, now that they could appreciate the danger, someone piped up to express their unanimous opinion in heartfelt tones:

"You're a brave man, Mr. Procession Director, sir. I say this to you in plain, simple words on behalf of myself and all my companions."

Prestige nodded his thanks. He declared himself unhurt and told the two boys to tend to Illustrious with all due speed. Meanwhile, he cracked a window for some air because they were all beginning to feel suffocated. The youths, for their part, seemed to know exactly how to bring the driver out of his fit: one of them administered a series of resounding slaps to the face while the other plucked hairs from his beard with a pair of tweezers. When this treatment failed to produce any noticeable results after a minute or two, they pulled down his trousers and began to spank him with gusto. Everyone laughed at the twitching and jerking of the still-unconscious Illustrious. They no longer felt inclined to dwell on what might have been and were very much relieved.

Such was the state of affairs—the two assistants energetically smacking the driver's hindquarters and his return to consciousness imminent, judging by his groans—when the elegant excursionist Basil spoke up:

"With your permission, Mr. Procession Director, I'd like to ask a question."

"It is your right," conceded Prestige. "What do you want to know?"

"Just this: You've said you intend to blindfold us and close the shutters on these windows. Setting aside the latter operation for the moment, is it not enough to have put us in shackles? Is it really necessary to blindfold us?"

"It's part of the Regulations," said Prestige.

"Perhaps. Yet we haven't a shred of evidence to prove it. Admittedly, my experience of excursions is far from vast.

Nonetheless, I have never—and I mean never—heard of excursionists being chained or blindfolded on a journey. If such extraordinary measures are in fact mandated by the Regulations, there must be some method by which we can verify this. Are you not of the same mind, Mr. SchrummSchrumm? It's safe to say this isn't your first excursion! What ought we to do?"

Being thus solicited for his opinion, SchrummSchrumm offered it with pleasure, especially since he felt little sympathy for Prestige.

"My companion is quite right," he said. "What's more, checking the rules should be an extremely simple matter. A copy of the Regulations is supposed to be posted in every Sunday Excursions vehicle."

"We demand to see this copy," said Basil. "And should we learn that these indignities are unjustified, not only will we file a formal complaint as soon as we arrive in Misunderstanding, we shall insist on being unchained instantly, every one of us."

"Keep your voice down," said Prestige. "The others will hear you. There's no need to cause a scene."

But this was a futile request. The others had in fact been paying close attention to the discussion and now loudly voiced their support for Basil. Broadway, his secretary, had thus far not said a word. He chose an opportune moment to break his silence, announcing that he'd discovered where this all-important copy of the Regulations was posted. It was behind a sheet of mica above the driver's seat.

Faced with such a show of solidarity, the procession director thought it wise to be conciliatory, though it certainly went against his first impulses.

"All right then," he said with as much friendliness as he could muster. "I'll show you the Regulations and you can read, right there in black and white, that I have a positive obligation to chain you, to blindfold you, and to close those metal window shutters. But before I do, listen to me for a second, because there's something I want to make clear. Do you hear me, all of you?" This last sentence was directed at the few excursionists still talking, and they promptly fell silent. "You're aware that from the moment you set foot on a Company bus, the Company is responsible for your safety. You've had ample opportunity to see for yourselves, moreover, the uneven and dangerous state of the roads. Well, it's precisely for this reason you're in chains. The Company doesn't want to risk having of one of you tumble from the vehicle because you were leaning carelessly out the window, or because the bus was rounding one of these treacherous curves. I'll give you some food for thought. Years and years ago—excursionists weren't shackled back then—I was a rookie procession director on this very line, and would you believe it? I witnessed no fewer than two to three accidents a day, often fatal ones. This disastrous state of affairs eventually started causing alarm among the higher-ups. About ten years ago it was decided, first and foremost in order to keep our excursionists safe—in spite of themselves, if need be—but also because the Company was being forced to make an ever-increasing number of insurance policy payouts to victims' families, to start chaining the passengers. Since then, there hasn't been a single unfortunate accident . . . I hasten to add that one of the chief reasons for the success this Excursion has found with the public consists in the fact that our travelers enjoy the benefit of total security, both during their journey and on the Excursion itself. So there you have it: our job in a nutshell! What do you say to that, Mr. SchrummSchrumm?" he concluded, slapping the young man jovially on the shoulder. "I hope you're satisfied now and understand that these measures—unpleasant though they may be—are for your own good."

"You said the roads were excessively dangerous," said SchrummSchrumm. "I didn't notice any such thing."

"That's because our journey has only just begun," answered Prestige, standing on the driver's seat and, as evidence of his good faith, obligingly unscrewing the sheet of mica over the Regulations. "When the going gets rough, it'll take all the driver's skill to keep this bus from careening over the edge of a ravine . . . Isn't that right, Illustrious?" he added, turning around.

"True enough," said Illustrious, who'd managed to pull himself together during the procession director's lecture.

Prestige stepped down from the seat and handed the Regulations to SchrummSchrumm, who read over them carefully. It was true: they prescribed that the excursionists be blindfolded, their hands and legs shackled, and the metal window shutters closed.

"Well?" said Prestige. "Satisfied?"

SchrummSchrumm duly apologized. Basil, Broadway, and the others did likewise.

"So you see, then!" said Prestige, in a dignified tone. Upon which, with the kind of adroitness only years of practice can confer, he set about blindfolding SchrummSchrumm. The two youths followed suit, tying cloths over the eyes of Basil and Broadway while Illustrious resumed his place at the wheel. A few minutes later, metallic rattling noises could be heard: the window shutters were being drawn down. "Away we go!" said Prestige as he sat down. "Away we go!" echoed the driver gaily. And the vehicle was off once again.

"When will we be getting to Misunderstanding?" asked SchrummSchrumm.

"By midafternoon," answered the procession director.

They talked shop about excursions for a while. SchrummSchrumm recounted the sights he'd seen in Synonym City and the rear courtyard of the Chameleon Temple. He also described the famous Pigsties of Princess Hicciné. But fatigue was taking its toll on him, and he soon fell into a sound sleep. By the time he awoke, they must have arrived at their destination because the bus had stopped and there was a great bustling on all sides. The metal shutters were raised, the blindfolds and manacles removed.

He looked out the window at the surrounding landscape.

They were parked in front of a double iron gate with both of its gargantuan leaves shut, set in the middle of an imposing rampart wall. In the distance were the hinterlands they must have recently driven through: meadows, wheat fields, a few neat houses. Between the hinterlands and the wall stood a barbed-wire entanglement five meters high and at least ten wide, supported by metal posts in concrete footings securely anchored in the dirt. This entanglement ran parallel to the wall as far as the eye could see, unbroken save in one place: where it intersected the road the bus had taken. There was no sign of any sentries in the guard towers flanking the gate. No sign of the Quicksands, either. The area between the wall and the entanglement was crowded with multitudes of ominous noticeboards, and death's heads lined the road. High above all of this were gigantic black birds of a species unknown to SchrummSchrumm.

"Up and at 'em!" said Prestige. "Courage, men!"

He let loose a cry that sent the birds scattering in all directions, and as the excursionists filed out of the bus he approached the seemingly deserted stone edifice.

"Ahoy there!" he called, cupping his hands around his mouth.

To everyone's surprise, there was activity at the top of the wall. A rope ladder was flung out of a turret and a nimble figure began to descend, followed by a second figure whose appearance and manner of gripping the ladder were both extremely bizarre. When the two emissaries had leaped to the ground and walked over to Prestige, SchrummSchrumm saw that the first was a lieutenant. And in fact, he introduced himself as such: "Lieutenant Medullus," he said. The second was so wrapped up in a black cloak that nearly nothing could be seen of him but his eyes, nose, and mouth. He was very round and diminutive in stature, standing no taller than the lieutenant's knees. Both figures wore red leather caps, the little one's adorned with an artificial daisy. SchrummSchrumm could now see that the eyes, nose, and mouth of the little round man appeared to be painted on a translucent membrane, as if his head were an inflated balloon. The last thing he noticed was that Lieutenant Medullus had a proud, haughty bearing, while everything about the other figure denoted excessive humility.

"Who might you be?" demanded the lieutenant, addressing the procession director.

Prestige proffered his safe-conduct pass.

"I'm bringing in these thirty excursionists."

"Very good," said the lieutenant, and he turned to the little fellow in the black cloak, who began to speak in a strange, grating voice, vaguely metallic but perfectly intelligible:

"I am the messenger of my Master the Holy Director, King of the Quicksands and Prince of Misunderstanding. He sends you his compliments."

"Thanks," said Prestige, rather lamely.

"In the name of my Master the Holy Director, King of the Quicksands and Prince of Misunderstanding, I kindly request your attendance at the Grand Ceremony of Introduction."

"What is that?" blurted SchrummSchrumm.

He had addressed this to the messenger because he'd been the only one speaking; the officer had contributed nothing. But the question seemed to plunge the little fellow into a state of profound anxiety. A loud whirring issued from his head. He spluttered, tried to speak again, and failed. The lieutenant stepped in, but not before giving SchrummSchrumm a very sharp look.

"Have you recited well? Did you forget anything?" he asked the little messenger.

"I have recited in full," affirmed the latter. The motor noises in his head had stopped.

"Good," said Medullus, and took a notebook and pencil from his pocket. Then, regarding his miniature companion with an indescribable gleam in his eye, he asked gently: "Name and identification number?"

"I am Joseph. I am merely the little obese nudie Joseph, identification number 10014," answered the other humbly.

"Birth?"

"I was born this afternoon. I belong to the office of the Most Holy Excursion Director."

"Very good!" said Medullus, closing his notebook and stealing a glance at Prestige to gauge his reaction. Prestige was standing mouth agape, at the limit of stupefaction. "Are you ready?"

"I am ready, entirely ready, absolutely ready," replied the little obese nudie Joseph, in tones of gentle submission. "Am I going on my pleasant journey, officer?"

"Yes," said Medullus, smiling. "Approach!"

Like a bird taking wing, the little obese nudie rose off the ground and SchrummSchrumm thought the curious being was about to fly away. He was, however, only executing a gracious little leap which ended in a kind of curtsy; he was now directly in front of the lieutenant, whose smile had hardened into a nasty rictus of pleasure. The man made a lightning-fast motion. Prestige had to check an impulse to jump back. SchrummSchrumm caught the glint of something shiny. Then there was a sound like a balloon deflating. Little Joseph was shrinking with terrifying speed. SchrummSchrumm distinctly heard "Ah, yes! We have loved life!"—and he could have sworn it was the little obese nudie Joseph who'd uttered these words just before he disappeared. For Joseph had indeed disappeared. On the ground there now remained scarcely more than a black cloak, a red leather cap, and a bit of detritus that Medullus immediately set alight.

They all stood there a moment, thunderstruck. Everyone was gazing at the strange pile of ash at the lieutenant's feet. He continued in a calm voice:

"The act of penetrating the wall that shields Misunderstanding is an important and symbolic event. This moment, such a significant one in an excursionist's life, is always celebrated with solemnity. I would like to turn now to the Ceremony of Introduction—a particularly breathtaking ceremony, as you're about to see . . . Are you all paying close attention?"

They replied in the affirmative; curiosity was running high, though as yet there was nothing to suggest that a ceremony was imminent. A few minutes passed in a silence that grew thicker and tenser by the second. All of a sudden, a silhouette appeared some dozen meters away. The man must have been pressing himself flat against the wall, but they hadn't seen him because his clothing was of the same greenish color as the stone. Furthermore, he must have been standing in profile, because only one side of his face, half his torso, and his right hand were visible. He was looking in the excursionists' direction, and once he was sure they could see him clearly he raised a cigarette to his lips, sucked in a lungful of smoke, and then, tilting up his chin, blew a smoke ring. The ring ascended slowly into the air, expanding as it rose. Scarcely was this done before a second silhouette appeared a few meters from the first. This man, in turn, revealed only his face, torso, and right arm, and proceeded to blow his own smoke ring. Then a third silhouette appeared, a fourth, and many more . . . Within the space of three minutes, over a hundred men had peeled themselves from the wall to which they had been invisibly cleaving. Even more were rising from the ground, across an area that extended to the very edge of the barbed-wire entanglement.

When all the men had revealed themselves and stood ranged on either side of the completely dumbfounded excursionists, they began to take drags of their cigarettes at regular and frequent intervals with extraordinarily well-coordinated movements. As if falling in with a predetermined rhythm, they all (first step) looked directly at the excursionists, then all (second step) took a simultaneous drag on their cigarettes, a process they repeated again and again without pause.

Their technique was so virtuosic, and the ceremony itself so unexpected, that SchrummSchrumm had to wait until the hundred-plus smoke rings, exhaled by the hundred-plus mouths, had ascended into the sky several times over before he could be sure he wasn't seeing things. At the end of which time, he trembled with excitement: ten of the smoke-ring blowers were coming toward the group of excursionists. SchrummSchrumm wondered what on earth they could possibly want. Lieutenant Medullus stepped forward to meet them.

"In the name of the excursionists here present, who are you?" he asked.

"It is my great honor to be the one designated to officially explain the meaning of the splendid and unique ceremony you have just witnessed," one of them replied. "This splendid and unique ceremony symbolizes the sovereign power of our Holy Director, Lord of Misunderstanding and King of the Quicksands. It likewise symbolizes the impossibility of any excursionist gaining entry into the divine city of Misunderstanding save by obtaining this boon through either his own personal merit or the permission of the high authorities. In other words, we see to it that no one ever gains entry into the divine city of Misunderstanding without a pass.

"But," objected Medullus, speaking on behalf of the excursionists (and expressing SchrummSchrumm's own objection), "my friends present here are bound, not for Misunderstanding, but for the Quicksands."

"You raise an excellent point," said the man. "Hearken unto me. Our troops are deployed along the three obstacles separating Misunderstanding from the Quicksands. These three obstacles are, respectively, the wall, the barbed-wire entanglement, and the Enchanted Poplar Forest, which together bar entry to Misunderstanding as well as to the Quicksands. Thus you may infer that as it is with the latter, so it is with Misunderstanding, for those we grant entry into the one, we will, in due course, grant entry into the other."

"I hear and understand," said Medullus. "What is the nature of these poplars?"

"Eternal, colossal, sacred, they constitute the necessary and subtle boundary between the kingdom of nothingness, which lies beyond the Quicksands, and the kingdom of Abocketaback, whose capital is Misunderstanding.

"I hear and understand. But though we do in fact see before us a wall and a barbed-wire entanglement, we do not perceive the poplars. Where might they be?"

"Out there," said the spokesman, indicating the hinterlands with a circular gesture. The excursionists looked in this direction but saw nothing. One man who claimed to have very keen eyesight said he could make out some phenomenally tall trees. When asked to estimate their height, however, he gave such a patently exaggerated answer that everyone agreed no trees in the world could possibly grow to such a size.

Medullus, who had no doubt paused for the express purpose of allowing the excursionists to make these remarks, cast a final glance around to judge the effect that had been produced, then said:

"What is this directorial power you've told us is symbolized here?"

"The directorial power consists primarily in the fact that our Holy Director, Lord of Misunderstanding and King of the Quicksands, has full authority over those who, having applied for an excursion to the Quicksands, thereby depend entirely upon him. And this is for the very simple, very evident, and very just reason that the Holy Director, guardian and trustee of the Secret, must safeguard this divine trust and defend it from all who have not a pure heart or a valid pass."

"Very well. But what is this secret?"

"Regarding the Secret, I may tell you only that it is embodied in seven concentric circles, the meaning of which is inverted depending on whether one progresses from the outermost circle—the kingdom of nothingness—toward the innermost circle, ruled by the law of Abocketaback, or conversely from the innermost circle to the outermost."

"Truly, this is fantastically complex and wondrous strange," said Medullus. "Let us speak of it no further. Turning to a different subject, I can see neither the meaning nor above all the utility of your cigarette smoke rings. Would not a machine gun be more practical?"

Hearing these words, SchrummSchrumm could not help but marvel at the perfection of this dialogue, which was every bit as impressive as the technical dexterity of the smoke-ring blowers, for he himself, in Medullus's place, would not have ventured another question. What was more, during the whole time the spokesman had been delivering his explanations, his colleagues, still in place, had continued sending smoke rings aloft, adding to the dialogue's awe-inspiring effect.

"Your words astonish me," said the man. "Before I reply, allow me to offer a few clarifications. You are most assuredly unable to appreciate the difficulties inherent in the act—apparently so trivial—of gliding beneath the barbed-wire entanglement without rending one's flesh, an act we may be called upon to perform at any moment. Or of crossing the minefields in a single, fantastic, well-calculated bound. Or of blending into the stones of this wall, a feat of which you've had, only a few minutes hence, a most convincing demonstration. But let us take another example: the art of moving through the Poplar Forest unperceived, a skill essential to our success. In addition to the science of creeping over dead leaves without a sound, we must become proficient in all known tree-climbing techniques. We must master the thousand tiny details that render our surveillance impossible of detection (how to crack a hazelnut from time to time and thereby create the impression of a nearby squirrel, or how to imitate the nostalgic song of a night bird). No, you certainly cannot appreciate our difficulties . . . I will simply say that even our most gifted members take a full five years to earn their diplomas as Blowers of Cigarette Smoke Rings and Wardens of the Poplar Forest. It is true that the awarding of this certificate alone amply repays all their efforts: the Holy Director in person—appearing as a cloud of cigarette smoke—presents the laureate with his diploma, which depicts a guard, hand-drawn and embroidered by excursionists' widows, in the act of carrying out his duties according to the methods in which he was trained . . . But all this is neither here nor there. 'Why so many precautions?' you may ask. 'Why such prolonged training? Why blow cigarette smoke rings instead of using machine guns?' For the sake of stealth, pure and simple. Suppose one of us machine-guns a spy as he attempts illegal entry into the Quicksands: the sound of the firearm would immediately put any other potential spies on the alert. Instead of which, thanks to our smoke rings, the same result is achieved in perfect silence without anything that might betray the presence of the ever-vigilant guards. Here is a simple illustration to help you understand the extent to which such noisy demonstrations of force—like the aforementioned machine gun—have been rendered obsolete. Say a man is trying to cross the Poplar Forest with the intention of gaining unauthorized access to the Quicksands. One of our guards spots him. The first thing he'll do is launch a vigorous cigarette smoke ring into the air. (We have special cigarettes for nighttime operations.) The other guards see the signal. They converge, swiftly and noiselessly. In no time at all the spy is surrounded, run to earth, and captured. Note that the blowing of a smoke ring requires no superfluous expenditure of energy; we remain fresh and ready for action. Note, too, that our smoke rings, when enough of them ascend into the heavens, provide an instant proof of our numerical advantage. If we had to engage in battle, the enemy would need only to see these eloquent testaments of our strength expanding in the sky (one thousand smoke rings equal one thousand smoke blowers; ten thousand smoke rings equal ten thousand smoke blowers, etc.) for terror to overwhelm him. And consider this: our division leaders, to cite but one example, are capable of blowing not only circles but also triangles and squares. And our general, with a single lungful of smoke, can write in the sky: 'In the name of His Excellency the Holy Director, give yourselves up!' When spies get a load of that (it's been a long time since we've had to fight a regular pitched battle), they're ready to throw in the towel, believe you me . . . I should add that, approaching the question from an entirely different angle, our combat method is in perfect orthodoxical alignment with the metaphysical conception of the Holy Director. The smoke rings symbolize not only his limitless directorial power but also his mysterious nature. Just as the ring of cigarette smoke rises into the sky at first perfect and corporeal, then gradually dissolves into the atmosphere, so the directorial power, albeit quite tangible at times, is actually infinite and ineffable. To convince yourself of the truth of this statement, you need only consider how the theologians and ascetics among our ranks blow their cigarette smoke. The initial circle, after issuing from their lips, revolves for a moment in the air. But presently, by virtue of the many fasts and penances these men have undergone in the service of honing their incomparable skill, six new concentric circles split off from the original, forming seven in total. This dovetails very neatly with the symbolism of the Secret, which I sketched for you in its broadest outlines just moments ago."

The man was letting himself get carried away. It was clear he'd left the Ceremony behind some time ago. He might have rambled on like this for a good while longer if Lieutenant Medullus hadn't interrupted.

"I thank you," he said curtly. And then, in a louder voice: "Good sirs, blowers of cigarette smoke rings, please return to your places. The ceremony continues!"

The men darted back to their posts and disappeared into the wall. Medullus, addressing some person or persons unseen, shouted toward the Gate:

"We are ready! Absolutely and entirely ready!"

"We are ready! Absolutely and entirely ready!" responded a deep and terrible voice from the other side of the wall, a voice that seized the excursionists by the entrails. A viol, repeating one solitary note in a poignant rhythm, accompanied the riveting voice.

Then, as the two massive leaves of the Great Iron Gate began slowly to part in obedience to someone's order, there rang out what SchrummSchrumm took to be the Ceremony's ritual proper:

"We shall now recite Prayer Number One together," intoned the magnificent voice.

Lieutenant Medullus and, a little further off, the now-invisible blowers of smoke rings, recited Prayer Number One in unison with the voice:

"To the Excursion Director, we give thanks.
"For obscurity dispelled,
"For the tempest that is quelled,
"For this wall whose height is unexcelled, we give thanks.
"For the madness subjugated,
"For despair and pain abated,
"For the fairest Sands eye e'er beheld, we give thanks."

A few moments of silence followed. SchrummSchrumm studied Medullus closely: his eyes remained closed and his face expressed the most fervent devotion. Somewhere in Misunderstanding, a bell tolled eight. Did this mean Misunderstanding had churches and bell towers? The voice went on:

"... A reading from the Holy Gospel of Misunderstanding:

"'Those who wish to speak of Misunderstanding find not the words to describe it. And this is good, for the city is the image—though infinitely smaller—of that which passeth man's understanding. Even so, each excursionist enfolds, deep within his heart, the terrifying splendors of Misunderstanding.

"'Hearken, then, O ye who tend the flame of the vocation! Nastarz was the first man. No one created him: he descended from the heavens to replenish the depleted earth. And lo, he builded him a mighty dwelling place, and men rejoiced to shelter therein. It was called by them the Building. And thus Nastarz came to be called the Builder.

"'Misunderstanding is the name of the seat of the Ultimate Excursion. The heart of Misunderstanding is of quicksand. But Misunderstanding is merely one name among thousands, and all these names, devised by men according to their several tongues, do but describe the single and unique Building builded by Nastarz. Some call it Prison, others Hell; we, the excursionists, call it Misunderstanding. But all men belong to Nastarz the Builder, our Ancestor, and all men dwell within the Building.

"'And so this single and unique Building, called by so many diverse names, is no mere part within a more complex whole. Assuredly, it contains within itself a multitude of buildings and a multitude of building systems—each devoted to its own apportioned task—which themselves form a coherent whole. But though everything exists within the Building, nothing, in and of itself, *is* the Building.

"'No one knows where It begins and where It ends. It has no defined limits. And this is good. Thus, it is customary to say that the Building is infinite. To leave the Building or to enter It can never be but an illusion. No one ever enters the Building, nor does anyone ever leave; each human being is born, lives, excursions, and dies within the Building. Any man who falls prey to the illusion of entering or leaving knows terror and madness. Outside the Building there is nothing: neither space, nor time, nor logic. Only nothingness.

"'And yet Nastarz overcame this illusion. Thereupon he was filled with a supreme joy, his divine nature became known to him and he perceived that which lies beyond logic, that which drives men of the Building mad with terror. And lo, he was gathered up even to the heavens, his former and eternal home. Nonetheless, he left his Building to mankind, that men might shelter therein and contemplate its mysteries. Thus, Nastarz is also called the Initiator . . .'"

The voice fell silent. They had apparently come to the end of the Ceremony, for at this point a strange battle cry, repeated three times in succession, was heard from the invisible smoke-blowers:

"Holy, thrice Holy is Misunderstanding!
"When the earth was no more than a dream,
"Its cradle of walls was already dreaming!"

At the same instant, the heavy iron gates at last finished opening and came to a halt. “Forward, men!” said Medullus, beckoning to the excursionists.

Seized by an ominous foreboding, SchrummSchrumm took one last look back at the blue sky over the horizon, at the wheat fields, the green meadows, the neat little houses beyond the barbed-wire entanglement. Then he heaved a deep sigh and followed his companions, some of whom were shuddering just as he was. They found themselves facing a vast, walled courtyard whose far side abutted a smaller, rectangular, covered courtyard. There were so many people crammed into this smaller courtyard that they lay stacked on top of one another like cordwood. The walls were plastered with hugely enlarged photographs of the Quicksands. Some depicted fantastic creatures sprawled across the dunes in grotesque and frightening postures. Others showed these same creatures gnashing bloodied victims between their gigantic teeth. Still others showed excursionists fleeing in panic only to become bogged down in the sands a short distance away. But SchrummSchrumm found himself transfixed by one photo in particular. It showed a man sunk up to his breastbone in quicksand. His expression was one of genuine and unmistakable despair. He was plainly calling out for help. Yet just a few meters away on the nearest bank stood a group of people displaying the most serene indifference to his plight—some taking in the scenery as if deaf to his screams, the rest watching him die with smiles on their faces. A second group, consisting of three guards armed with long gaffs, instead of coming to the poor man’s aid, were using their implements to push down on his head and shoulders with all their might.

Obviously faked, thought SchrummSchrumm, and so he felt he should have laughed it off. But they’d done a masterly job making the photos look real. In any case, even if they were faked, these images—at once so preposterous and so horrible—must have been put here for a reason. Was it simply to warn excursionists of the dangers of getting caught in the sands?

"Grim, isn't it?" said SchrummSchrumm to the man beside him, indicating the billboard.

"Bah!" he replied, giving it a dismissive shrug.

Nevertheless, he plucked at SchrummSchrumm's sleeve to invite him to sit down, as his companions had already done, among the prostrate bodies under the roof of the covered inner courtyard. Glancing around, he again noted the absence of women and children. There were a few younger men, barely more than teens, but not too many, and these few were huddled together in a little knot looking lost and terrified. The population was predominantly middle-aged. He searched for Lieutenant Medullus amid the throng, but he had vanished, and it seemed no one was minding the group in his place. Having greeted his nearest neighbors, SchrummSchrumm began rapidly gathering as much information as he could.

The people already there had no idea why they'd been convened under the courtyard roof that day, he learned. It was the first time such a thing had happened to them, though most of them had been waiting to leave for the Quicksands for over three weeks. Some—fortunately not many—had been waiting for two to three months, or even longer. With tears in their eyes, they confided to SchrummSchrumm that they had been forbidden to send any mail. Nor could they receive any news from outside, and were consequently in agony, having no way of knowing what had become of their families. As they were telling him this, SchrummSchrumm noticed that everyone, with the exception of those few frightened youths, wore a circle of blue cloth sewn onto his chest and another on his back. He asked what these circles meant and was told that after orientation, all newcomers were given a physical exam and divided into two groups, the blues and the greens. Green was reserved for young men capable of strenuous climbs and long marches. These men were put on an accelerated training track and soon parted ways with their fellow travelers. By contrast, the rest (including themselves) had to undergo a much longer training regimen, and by extension wait that much longer for their departure. SchrummSchrumm questioned them closely about the frequency of these departures. They took place once a week: on Sunday, naturally. A fleet of sixty-seven buses would leave Misunderstanding for the Quicksands, which added up to a considerable number of excursionists. The departures were always in the small hours of the morning, and those who'd been selected were notified the day before, i.e., Saturday. Nothing more could be said about these people, though, for they were never seen again. This was probably to prevent them from coming back and leaking information about the trip. It was widely believed that, to this end, they were sent home by a different route from the one by which they'd come. In general, concluded his informants, the rules were draconian and strictly enforced. It was hard at first, but eventually you got used to it. There were supposedly two or three thousand excursionists here, distributed across several hundred hotels. These numbers seemed wildly inflated to SchrummSchrumm. The rest of what they told him, though, unhappy as he'd been to hear it, corroborated what little he already knew, and he made no attempt to conceal his disappointment.

"I'm relatively experienced as far as Sunday Excursions go, but I must confess that for once I'm at a total loss. What is this 'Secret'

I've heard tell of? And Abocketaback? And the Enchanted Poplar Forest, what do you know about that?"

They replied that the Secret was the sum total of the Excursion's foundational symbols as contained in the Gospels, which were a collection of all the traditions passed down in Misunderstanding from the beginning of time, which is to say from the time of Nastarz, the First Holy Director. In other words, the Gospels explained and elaborated upon the Secret. But no one apart from the Holy Director knew the Gospels in their entirety, owing to one of the principles of Abocketaback, which said, in a nutshell, that no one could or should try to find logic in the sequence of events that befell him in Misunderstanding. This was why only the younger excursionists, who were easily led and accustomed to swallowing stupid, puerile explanations without cavil, could live more or less comfortably under a rule so repugnant to both human nature and human intelligence. About the Enchanted Poplar Forest even less was known, and SchrummSchrumm could be sure that those who bragged about having seen the Forest or the Quicksands were either lying through their teeth or repeating second-hand information.

"Couldn't someone sneak off to the Forest or Quicksands without telling anyone, just to take a look around and get the lay of the land? Anyway, even if excursionists are technically banned, surely the guards must take their girlfriends out there all the time for romantic trysts. What do they have to say?"

The group stared goggle-eyed at SchrummSchrumm. Finally, one elderly man spoke up:

"You must be extremely new, and extremely naive, to imagine that anyone could sneak off to the Quicksands on the sly! No one, you understand—not the guards, not the excursionists (except in the course of authorized expeditions)—has ever reached the boggy, deadly wastes bordering the Quicksands. The only known route by which a traveler could make it there and back alive has been impassable and out of use for centuries, from what they say. The route is arcane and tortuous. Just to get out of Misunderstanding would require scaling the wall, then negotiating the minefield and the barbed-wire entanglement. And once you'd pulled off that trick, you'd still have to cross the Enchanted Poplar Forest, whose canopy sweeps the sky and which is guarded by trained professionals. Even supposing you reached the Quicksands—which is frankly impossible—you'd soon become lost without a guide to show you the way. Legend has it that anyone lunatic enough to make the attempt is condemned to wander in circles for all eternity. Such a foolhardy traveler would find madness at the end of his road, or at best death . . . I realize how strange all this must sound to you, but it's the truth. One last word of advice: take the utmost care from now on not to broach such subjects in front of strangers. There are spies everywhere, and they won't hesitate to denounce you to the authorities."

SchrummSchrumm made no reply. He was becoming more and more uneasy. It was about this time that several men appeared in the courtyard, led by a different lieutenant in full dress blues emblazoned with shoulder flashes. These were guards, someone explained, easily recognizable by the cords encircling their waists: white interwoven with gold threads. The lieutenant scrutinized the newcomers, while everyone else—both the men under the courtyard roof and in the outer courtyard—scrambled off into the furthest reaches of the enclosure as if desperate to avoid his eye. When a sizable area had been cleared around SchrummSchrumm and his companions, the lieutenant spoke:

"Valued excursionist friends," he began in a pompous tone, "you have attained your heart's desire: you are in Misunderstanding.

I have been commissioned with the task of furnishing you those practical details of which you will have most immediate need, and of communicating to you your first official orders. You've had a wearisome journey. Therefore, I will be as succinct as possible. Let me begin with a word on the people you've recently had the opportunity to observe groveling like animals beneath this very courtyard roof. Some of you, perhaps, have engaged in conversation with them. You may have heard them give vent to various gripes and grievances. Know that all of them, to a man, are incompetents, whiners, and mental defectives. Allow me to explain. The Quicksands Excursion is no walk in the park: it demands of its candidates exceptional physical fitness, fortitude, and a can-do spirit. The men you saw here possess none of these qualities; they are slackers and layabouts, incapable of performing the physical tasks necessary to navigate the Quicksands, and have failed in their examinations. Failed, despite our having lavished on them every possible encouragement and all the training anyone could ask for. After two months, there's nothing more to be done with them and we're obliged to send them home. To be sure, this in itself wouldn't be so bad, even if they do shower us with bitter reproaches for purposely delaying their departure. But the impression they produce on new arrivals like yourselves could not be more deplorable. In light of these circumstances, and for the greater glory of the Holy Excursion, we've been forced to take measures to shield you from these bad apples. From now on, you are absolutely forbidden to hold any communication with them. When you encounter one of them, you must avoid him like the plague. They all bear the distinctive insignia of a blue disk sewn onto their chests and backs. Such encounters, in any case, will in all probability remain a mere theoretical possibility, because you will never again—with rare exceptions—have occasion to mingle with this stupid, filthy rabble.

"Moving on to general rules and regulations. Point number one: our motto is 'Severity, Endeavor, Efficiency.' In a few short moments you will be conducted to your comfortable quarters after having been treated to a hearty repast. All we ask of you during the next few days is that you rest. We want our excursionists refreshed and in prime condition. You will, nonetheless, be expected to observe a few rules. The Bushido Hotel—where all of you will be residing during this initial stage—is your new home. You will have the run of the building. We have even provided a game room for your entertainment. There is only one restriction: leaving the Bushido Hotel without a pass is prohibited. One wing on the ground floor is likewise off-limits to you. Do not attempt to enter this wing; you will be sternly rebuffed by the guards.

"Point number two: each of you will be assigned a Misunderstanding staff member who will take over the more day-to-day duties involved in facilitating your adjustment. They are as charming as they are well-bred, and will heretofore serve as your valets, friends, and confidants. They will also be accountable for your actions, on which they must file daily reports—this is so we can learn more about you and better identify those who have leadership potential and the makings of elite excursionists. Therefore, do not be surprised if your guard follows you like your shadow, enters your room unannounced, searches your belongings, or checks under your mattress. It will all be done with the very best intentions. Besides, he'll be armed. But don't be apprehensive on that score, either: it's merely a precaution against the packs of ravenous wild dogs who roam the wide parklands on the outskirts of our fair city. I will add that the guards are duly sworn municipal agents. Any attempt to bribe or corrupt them would be futile, and making such an attempt would cause heavy sanctions to be levied against you, as these reprehensible acts would have to be included in their next report. I'm sure you'll draw your own conclusions when I tell you that among those pathetic creatures you saw in the inner courtyard, though the vast majority of them are indeed incompetents and slackers, there are also a few excursionists under sanction.

"Point number three: any discussion of the Excursion in general, or of the Quicksands in particular—either among yourselves or with the guards—is explicitly discouraged. One must not seek to learn the whys and wherefores of events in Misunderstanding. We have good reason for making it so, and, without encroaching too far on the symbolism and topography courses you'll be given later on, I can briefly outline our motives. Misunderstanding and the Quicksands are governed by the laws of Abocketaback and of paradox, respectively. I'm sure you'll agree that in jumping the gun and trying to comprehend these things before their time, you would necessarily form many preconceived notions which would turn out to be quite wrongheaded. This would render the task of your future instructors that much more difficult, and at the same time considerably delay your departure for the Quicksands. In short, the only conversations condoned will be those recounting your amorous adventures and recollections of your schoolboy days. You may touch upon personal matters with your guard, but you may not under any circumstances question him about Misunderstanding, its administration, layout, timetables, and so forth. These are all infractions which, depending upon their gravity and the number of times the offense is repeated, will send you on a more or less rapid trajectory toward joining those disgraceful, stinking swine of the inner courtyard. If you have the smallest complaint—by which I mean a complaint falling outside the sphere of your guard's competencies—you may submit it to us in writing. You will receive a response in very short order.

"I will close with a statistic that speaks louder than any admonition I could give you. Out of every hundred guards and every hundred excursionists, 98 percent of those who respect the rules—the guards by refusing to be bought, the excursionists by refraining from insidious lines of questioning—98 percent, I say, of guards and excursionists reach retirement age without incident, in the case of the guards, or leave for the Quicksands within three weeks of their arrival, in the case of the excursionists. There you have it: a word to the wise."

Things proceeded just as he had said. They left the inner courtyard, passed through several more courtyards, and then received, via serving hatches that opened out from kitchens, the promised "hearty repast," consisting of a dish of foul soup and a crust of rock-hard bread. They ate it standing up under the watchful eye of several guards, who told them to be quick about it and pretended to find the soup extremely appetizing. The atmosphere was tense, and SchrummSchrumm, despite being famished, was unable to swallow a single mouthful. When the meal was over, the guards told the excursionists they would be afforded a rest period. They were ushered through several more courtyards and finally emerged into something like a vacant lot.

"Here we are, the Bushido Hotel! You'll be taken good care of here," said one of the guards, pointing to a nondescript four-story building in rather bad repair hunkering on the far side of the vacant lot. There was one notable feature that stood out to them: its windows. Whether ogive or arched, with moldings or stained glass, each and every one was secured by thick and ominous-looking iron bars. As they drew closer, they saw at these windows weird, impassive silhouettes who silently observed their approach.

The lobby was no less disconcerting. It was cavernous and lit by twelve dozen gold candelabras. At the back was a staircase to the upper floors, and to the right of a small landing a short hallway was visible. This led into a large circular room lined with doors, all of them fitted with judas holes: some open, some shut. As the excursionists peeped into this circular room, not daring to set foot inside, a chorus of groans, hysterical pleading, and crazed laughter erupted from behind the doors. At this, a guard quickly stepped in to block the entrance with his bulk. He motioned for the excursionists to continue upstairs and not concern themselves with what they had just seen and heard.

"Remember what the lieutenant told you," said the guard gently. "At the end of this hall is the private wing. Off-limits."

"Why are they making those horrible sounds?" one man asked, pulling his head back into his shoulders as if expecting to be struck.

The guard only shrugged and they all proceeded to the second floor, where they were told the rooms set aside for new arrivals were the choicest in the hotel owing to their orientation, which permitted their occupants to enjoy the daily pageantry of the sunset over Misunderstanding, its light streaming through the city's spectacular boulevards. The news was greeted with a general silence. Perceiving this, the guards began to take roll. Everyone was present and accounted for, naturally, and the rooms were assigned. It was not an especially difficult task: the excursionists' names and identification numbers were already stenciled onto the doors. The guards insisted on showing each man around his new abode. The guard who escorted SchrummSchrumm to his room on the fourth floor asked him how he liked it.

"Oh, marvelous!" said SchrummSchrumm, suppressing a disappointed frown—the window, as it turned out, commanded a view of the vacant lot they had just come through. Worse still, the ground sloped upward from the hotel, obscuring the horizon. There were none of the "spectacular boulevards" evoked by the guards. There was no view at all.

"Good night, Mr. Excursionist," said the man as he took his leave.

SchrummSchrumm half-expected to hear a key turn in the lock, but no. He lay down and thought over the day's events, meditating on the many hardships inherent to the excursionist's calling. He soon dropped off to sleep. Twice in the night he was jolted awake: once around midnight, and again just before dawn. On both occasions he ran to the window to see what was happening. But though the sounds reached him quite distinctly, he could see absolutely nothing. He had to settle for trying to identify the noises as best he could. Around midnight, it had sounded like a large company of men marching past his window. The men must have been driven on by exceptionally coarse and brutal soldiers: there were whipcracks, curses, and groans. Accompanying this was a metallic clinking like chains being dragged along the ground. Just before dawn, the same sounds began again: feet trudging in lockstep over hard-packed earth, chains dragging, whipcracks followed by curses or stifled moans. Could it really be possible? Shortly afterward, as he was still in the midst of wondering whether he might have been dreaming, came another sound, one he easily recognized: that of a train pulling slowly out of a station a short distance away. Wheels grinding on rails, an engine chugging, the puff of a smokestack … The train picked up speed, rumbled through a valley, became progressively fainter, and finally disappeared.

SchrummSchrumm leaned out his window, straining his eyes to see. It was no use. He shrugged and returned to bed, defeated. He had trouble falling asleep again and had almost given up on the idea when he felt perfumed fingers smoothing his hair. He sat bolt upright: it was morning, and a magnificent specimen of young manhood was standing at his bedside.

II

His blond hair was powdered, his face made up, his nails painted. The muscles of his chest and arms bulged under his jacket. Around his waist was a white cord interwoven with gold threads.

"Good morning, Mr. Excursionist."

"Who are you?"

"My name is Krikri. I hold the rank of Sergeant."

Without saying more, he smiled and signaled toward the door. Two girls who'd been standing at the threshold entered, each carrying a tray of mouthwatering dishes which they laid on the bed. They couldn't have been much more than sixteen. They made little curtsies to him and stepped back, saying:

"We're Lucette and Lulu, your maids."

The handsome sergeant, with another dazzling smile, invited SchrummSchrumm to eat. He didn't utter a word during the meal.

"From now on, you're in my charge," he explained when SchrummSchrumm had finished. "I'm sure they filled you in yesterday. In particular, I'll be responsible for seeing to your comfort and doing whatever I can to ensure that your introduction to Misunderstanding goes as smoothly as possible in the first few days of your stay. Did you sleep well?"

"No," said SchrummSchrumm, watching closely for the sergeant's reaction. "I slept very badly. I was awakened twice by extremely strange noises."

"Strange?" inquired Krikri, as if not understanding.

"Yes, and I've been wondering about them quite a bit. I heard noises, undeniably. But I saw nothing. And so I don't know quite what to think."

The guard seemed to suddenly realize what he was talking about.

"Excursionists always hear—or think they hear—strange sounds during their first few nights in Misunderstanding," he said, fluttering his eyelashes like a girl. "Don't worry, though: you'll soon get over it."

He laughed, displaying rows of pearly teeth between candy-red lips. Then, without waiting for a response, he set about making a systematic inspection of the room, rummaging through the wardrobe, lifting the mattress, and checking under the bed. Yet the very manner of this inspection seemed to prove that it was nothing too serious, as he was careful to avoid disturbing any personal papers. In fact, the whole thing was over in a matter of minutes and SchrummSchrumm was left with the impression that the young man had been thoroughly charming and faultlessly polite. Krikri headed toward the door, announcing that he'd be back to conduct a second search after lunch and then a final one that evening.

"Don't forget, there's a recreation room for guests on the ground floor," he said before leaving. "They hold games, contests, and charades on a regular basis, with every amenity you could possibly desire for your leisure and relaxation. You are most cordially invited to participate."

"Will you be there?" asked SchrummSchrumm eagerly.

"Unfortunately not," he said with apparent regret. "We have our own staff lounge. But anytime you need me, all you have to do is send for me; we're right beside you . . ."

With that, he was gone.

SchrummSchrumm dressed with meticulous care. He reasoned that it was still early and there would likely be no one downstairs yet. But when he emerged onto the landing, which was open to the lobby atrium on one side and had a view down into the community room opposite, he saw a dozen or more domino-players already gathered at the tables. Perhaps his companions had slept no better than he had . . . Three guards were playing with the excursionists. A fourth, standing a little apart, was idly supervising the group and presently raised his head to look up: SchrummSchrumm realized that someone stationed below could easily keep an eye on all the upper floors. He gave a little wave to the guard (who immediately looked away) before proceeding downstairs, dragging his feet. He pretended not to see the sentry with a submachine gun discreetly posted near the entrance to the hall of the so-called "private wing" and went to join the others in the game room. He noticed right away, to his immense surprise, that the regulations were not being strictly observed on either side. Some of the excursionists were chatting openly about their previous excursions and even airing their views on the Quicksands and the symbolism thereof. Those indulging in this banter—to which the guards were listening with half an ear—must have arrived in the city at least a day ahead of him, because they exhibited a casual, undisguised contempt for the newer guests. Nonetheless, there was one subject everyone scrupulously avoided: the private wing.

SchrummSchrumm listened but refrained from joining in any of these conversations. Once and only once was he solicited for his opinion. The person who did so was a small, thin, hunchbacked man with a rank, goatlike odor about him. His face was wrinkled and hypocritical, his eyes bloodshot. He stopped all of a sudden and looked up, toying with his domino.

"What are your first impressions, young man?" he said, turning very pointedly in his chair in order to make SchrummSchrumm the focus of the room's attention.

SchrummSchrumm hemmed and hawed, trying to evade the question.

"Don't give us that, Mr. SchrummSchrumm!" continued the little man. "We know what a celebrated and seasoned traveler you are: the Pigsties of Princess Hicciné, Synonym City, the Chameleon Temple . . . Those are some sensational exploits right there! Even we, your elders with thirty years' excursioning under our belts, can't boast of anything half so glamorous. Your opinion is worth more than the rest of ours combined. Give it to us straight: what do you make of all this?"

SchrummSchrumm's eyes widened.

"Of all what, exactly?"

"Oh, anything and everything," said the man, suppressing a nervous tic. "This and that. These nocturnal noises, for instance, what do you make of them?"

"So you've been hearing nocturnal noises! Of what nature?" asked SchrummSchrumm, nodding sagely to himself as if he'd been given much food for thought.

"I didn't say that!" protested the man. He tried to cover his agitation by playing his domino, but his hand shook as he placed it on the table.

"Well, in that case I take it you haven't heard any nocturnal noises, and since I haven't heard any either, there have been no nocturnal noises after all," said SchrummSchrumm calmly.

"I didn't say that, either!" the man burst out. "Ah, you're a sharp one, Mr. SchrummSchrumm. One doesn't meet many excursionists as devilish clever as you are." And he gave a nervous laugh. Neither the guards nor the other guests seemed to be taking much interest in their verbal sparring. Yet the former were all stealing glances at SchrummSchrumm whenever he turned his head.

"Listen," said SchrummSchrumm. "I have to wonder why you're even asking me such questions. Have you forgotten our instructions? We're supposed to be behaving ourselves and holding our tongues!"

At the word "instructions," the guards scowled. But the conversation was already over.

"Hats off to the younger generation!" said the man. "Bravo!"

Paying no one any further mind, the man returned to his domino game, and SchrummSchrumm was not drawn into any new discussions. Minutes passed. Every so often someone shot him a dirty look. A few excursionists whispered among themselves.

Then the guards began to get antsy, and it was clear a shift change was approaching. Soon Krikri and three new guards appeared; their comrades left. Krikri stood out in sharp contrast to his colleagues. He walked directly over to SchrummSchrumm and laid his hand on the excursionist's. He was as immaculately made-up as before. SchrummSchrumm pulled him aside.

"Who is that man?" he asked, nodding toward the little hunchback with the goaty smell.

Krikri hesitated imperceptibly.

"That's Leopold," he said. "I must warn you, Mr. SchrummSchrumm, he's one to watch out for."

SchrummSchrumm didn't press him for further details, but glanced around the room and said:

"Could I step out for a minute?"

Krikri hesitated again. Then a twinkle of friendly connivance came into in his eye. He pointed to a hallway directly across from the game room, facing the stairs to the upper floors.

"Go down that hallway," he murmured with a mysterious smile. "You'll see seventeen doors. All are off-limits except for the third, which is the one you want."

SchrummSchrumm had the disagreeable impression that he was still being watched by Leopold, and that the guards huddled together in conference were talking about him. He heard his name spoken quite distinctly once or twice. Nevertheless, he headed toward the hallway indicated. It was very dimly lit. He counted off one, two, three doors and stopped. But that long row of doors—all off-limits, all on the right-hand side—exerted an irresistible pull. He walked on. The hallway grew darker and darker, and he gave a little cry of alarm when he eventually collided with a large, warm mass. It was a man—a guard, to all appearances—seated on a stool outside the fifth or sixth door, upright but sound asleep. SchrummSchrumm had bumped into him fairly hard and the man seemed to be making an effort to rouse himself. Though still no more than half-awake, he was comically rubbing his eyes with his fists and saying, "OK, up and at 'em! Duty calls!" Then sleep once again gained the upper hand and his head drooped. Soon he was snoring. SchrummSchrumm pushed open the door without difficulty and found himself on the threshold of a long, dark, musty library. No one was reading here. The only men present—five or six in all—were seated around a hearth containing a crackling wood fire. The room was, in point of fact, rather cold and damp. SchrummSchrumm lost no time in accepting their wordless invitation and sat down beside them at the fire. He let them look him over for a minute; there was nothing malevolent in their interest.

Finally, turning to face them, he asked if they were all excursionists. They replied in the affirmative.

"I'm lost," he lied. "I was looking for the way to the covered courtyard, where my friends are waiting for me."

"Do you have a pass?" asked one of the men matter-of-factly.

"No," admitted SchrummSchrumm.

A look of utter incredulity appeared on the nameless questioner's face. Another man opened his mouth to speak, but one of his companions stopped him before he could make a sound. As if the act needed no explanation, they all rose as one with eerie synchronicity. The man who'd spoken said hurriedly, "Let's get out of here!" and they decamped, leaving SchrummSchrumm alone in stunned silence. Before he'd fully recovered from his shock, the man who'd been napping on the stool came in, having likely been awakened by the others on their way out. He made a beeline for SchrummSchrumm and looked him up and down as if he, too, were unable to believe his eyes.

"I'm the monitor of this library. Do you have a pass?"

"I was just asked that same question," answered SchrummSchrumm, "and I'll repeat the answer I gave before: No, I don't have a pass! Why do I need one?"

"Because a pass is required to enter any of these rooms, young man!" said the guard almost angrily. "How long have you been in Misunderstanding?"

"A day and a half."

"Humph! I see. In that case, kid, you should do as I say. First, let's go somewhere we can talk."

He led SchrummSchrumm behind an enormous table in the darkest corner of the library, piled high with ancient-looking tomes. Once there, he continued: "Now tell me how the devil you managed to get in here," he whispered, glancing nervously at the dormer window just over their heads.

"Simple," said SchrummSchrumm, and proceeded to explain that he must have miscounted and chosen the wrong door . . . but that his overwhelming curiosity had also played a role in the error. ". . . I do beg your pardon, Mr. Monitor, sir," he concluded. "It would never have occurred to me that I might need a pass to visit this room, where, apart from this cheerful log fire, there's hardly anything to speak of except some moldering old books. I'll be on my way now."

"Not so fast," said the monitor, grabbing his arm. "You seem so hopelessly naive that I can't let you go without giving you a few pieces of advice. First, the punishments meted out in Misunderstanding are harsh, and someone should've warned you that they don't fool around when it comes to the Regulations. Second, there's a very good reason why this library is strictly off-limits to anyone without a pass. It contains the annals of the Seat of the Sunday Quicksands Excursion going all the way back to its founding. Some of these books you've been sneering at date from the time of Nastarz the Builder himself."

"Is that so! Then why did those other men, who were excursionists like me, seem to have permission to be here? Did they have passes?"

"Only *official library sweeper* passes, that's all!" said the monitor with sarcasm.

SchrummSchrumm nodded thoughtfully.

"But as for yourself, could you potentially land in hot water, too? Would it count as a serious infraction if they found me here?"

"As serious as they come, kid. I have this library monitor job and I want to hang onto it more than anything in the world. That's the plain truth! 'Cause if I don't keep a good watch, *whammo!* I'll be shipped right out on the next excursion!"

"Does that mean you were an excursionist before you took this position?" asked SchrummSchrumm, astonished. "Do you mean to tell me you gave it all up for this dismal occupation?"

"Darn right I did!" said the man. "And with any luck, I'll be doing it for a long time to come."

SchrummSchrumm sank into the nearest chair.

"It's inconceivable," he murmured. "I've gone on my share of excursions and seen my share of amazing sights, but this! This goes beyond anything I could have imagined. You, for instance, Mr. Monitor. You tell me you started out as an excursionist? And who's to say your zeal wasn't every bit as intense as mine! What could have happened to change your mind so completely? What unseen danger hangs over us?"

"Kid," said the big man, "this talk of ours has gone on long enough. Besides, it can lead to no good. It's in the nature of this place that if you stick around long enough, you'll understand everything. All I can tell you is that guards are constantly patrolling this area, and if they catch you here it'll be just as bad for you as it will be for me . . . Now go! Scurry on back to your friends, don't talk to anyone along the way, and try not to draw any attention to yourself. Farewell!"

"Farewell," echoed SchrummSchrumm.

Unfortunately, no sooner was the word out of his mouth than they heard a door slam nearby, closely followed by the sound of footsteps. The monitor peered out the dormer window and an expression of blank terror spread across his face. SchrummSchrumm rushed to the window to see for himself. He saw a long, narrow rear courtyard and an old-fashioned horse cart, but the man they'd heard must have already entered the hall. From the way the monitor was trembling, SchrummSchrumm knew it had to be a guard. And there was no chance the man's destination was anything but the library: his footsteps were coming inexorably closer. There was a slight pause between each step, however, as if the guard needed to look carefully to see where to put his feet. SchrummSchrumm, recalling the poor visibility in the hallway, felt a sudden surge of hope:

"Is there a back exit?" he asked hurriedly.

The monitor nodded mutely, too terrified to speak.

"Where?" demanded SchrummSchrumm, but it was too late: the footsteps had stopped at the library door. SchrummSchrumm ducked behind a bookshelf. The monitor merely shook SchrummSchrumm's hand in acknowledgment of the catastrophe that was about to descend on them both.

"My God! What a disaster!" he moaned.

"Look out! He's coming in!" whispered SchrummSchrumm.

At that instant, the door flew open and an imposing figure stood framed in the doorway. SchrummSchrumm had been prepared for a colossus, given that all the guards in Misunderstanding seemed to have been chosen for their strength, but this man was even more impressive than he'd anticipated. His undershirt was shiny with grime and wear beneath a patched black jacket and a shabby silk hat of the same color. At his belt—which further accentuated his powerful torso—hung a short riding crop and a dagger with a wrought metal handle. He squinted into the library, evidently unable to see much, since he growled a doubtful "Anybody there?" before turning as if to leave. He thought better of it, though, and asked again, more suspiciously, "Anybody there?" The monitor kept quiet. SchrummSchrumm didn't dare answer, either, but he cursed the monitor's cowardice all the same: the man should have taken cover. In desperation, he was about to emerge from his hiding place and explain his situation to the brute, when the monitor beat him to it.

"Mercy! Mercy!" he whimpered, approaching the guard and taking him by his filthy hand, upon which he bestowed a deluge of smacking kisses punctuated by further heartrending repetitions of "Mercy! Mercy!"

If he'd been less apprehensive, SchrummSchrumm would have found the scene funny, with the guard, who hadn't yet spotted him, being at a total loss to understand why he was being supplicated in this manner. At any event, this misapprehension, together with the ridiculous spectacle the monitor was making of himself, predisposed the colossus to clemency.

"Fine, fine! That'll do," he said gruffly, extricating his hand as best he could from the monitor's grasp. Just then he caught sight of SchrummSchrumm, who thought for a moment that things were going to turn very ugly indeed. But the guard only chuckled and muttered to himself, "So that's it!" Then he added, in a tone that was almost reassuring:

"You're new to Misunderstanding and the Bushido Hotel, aren't you, Mr. Excursionist? And you came in here without a pass, am I right?"

"It's true! But have mercy!" pleaded the monitor.

The other man silenced him with a withering glance and waved him away. The monitor crawled off on all fours.

"I'm sorry to have to do this, Mr. Excursionist," continued the Hercules with a touch of sarcasm, "but I must ask you the routine question: Have you, or have you not, been put on official notice that you are never to speak to excursionists who have been here longer than yourself, and never to leave the hotel for any reason whatsoever?"

"I knew we weren't supposed to venture into the private wing, yes," admitted SchrummSchrumm. "But no one said anything about the library, and I didn't know it was off-limits. Also, as far as those other excursionists are concerned, I never got the chance to talk to them. They fled as soon as I came in."

"They did right," said the guard. "Look here, you seem like a bright young man. I'm amazed you've proven so incapable of understanding anything beyond the literal meaning of words. When we at the Bushido say 'the private wing,' we mean every area apart from the individual guest rooms and the game room. To put it another way, you have to extrapolate a little: even if the library isn't technically in the private wing, it falls into the same category, which means that for excursionists, entering the library is as strictly forbidden as entering the private wing."

"Then are you the *real* library monitor?"

"You're beginning to catch on," said the man with some satisfaction. "I am the real monitor of this library. The fellow you saw before was only second monitor. You can think of it this way, if you like: within these walls, I represent the Holy Excursion Director who, in the name of his Excursionary wisdom, forbids excursionists entry into this library. Please note, moreover, that this is no arbitrary prohibition. There's a very simple, very obvious, and very sound reason behind it, namely that excursionists should not be loitering in rooms where they have no business, and where they might see or hear things that are none of their concern. It stands to reason that excursionists should be either keeping to their rooms and resting up, or relaxing with their companions in the game room. And besides, let me ask you this: Doesn't our Holy Director, simply by virtue of the fact that excursionists have signed up for his Excursion, enjoy full and absolute authority over said excursionists? Of course he does! Thus, the excursionists must blindly obey every order they receive. There's no getting around it!"

"What are you going to do to me?" asked SchrummSchrumm, whose head was spinning from this line of reasoning.

"Nothing too bad," said the guard. But even as he spoke, something happened that could never have been predicted based on the guard's laid-back demeanor. SchrummSchrumm was literally lifted off his feet, held at arm's length by the back of his shirt-collar, and his face savagely slashed with the riding crop. The man must have had his crop at the ready for some time. All he'd had to do was pull his hand from behind his back and take a good swing. After hitting him, the brute dropped him on the ground and dealt him a powerful kick in the seat of his pants as he lay sprawled on the dirt floor. Then he sauntered away, immense and disdainful. SchrummSchrumm saw that he had landed next to a pile of books behind which the other "monitor" was cowering, shaking in every limb.

"Why didn't you tell me you were only Second Monitor!"

"There's no real difference between First and Second Monitors, you know."

"I'm leaving," said SchrummSchrumm, thoroughly disgusted.

"Wait! Some people want to see you in the rear courtyard."

"What people?"

"Just go," said the man. He pointed to a small door at the back, then disappeared into a dark corner of the library. SchrummSchrumm recrossed the room. As promised, the door at the back led out into the rear courtyard. At first he didn't see the men. His attention was drawn instead to the object he had taken for a dusty old horse cart during his brief peek through the dormer window, but which he now saw to be an old-fashioned hearse. Someone had removed the black curtains that would have normally hung on either side of the space reserved for the coffin. This area now contained two rows of multicolored chairs. A pennant hanging from the cart read, in gold Gothic script: "The Sunday Quicksands Excursion Company." At that moment SchrummSchrumm heard a faint call and saw three of the men who'd been sitting by the fire. They were motioning for him to come join them in their hiding place behind the hearse. When he was close enough, they pressed him flat against the carriage and whispered, "Careful!," pointing toward the library, where the Second Monitor's merry whistling could be heard.

"We're so sorry," they said. "We overheard your altercation with that big bruiser. What's more, we were afraid something like that might happen and desperately wanted to warn you, but it was impossible while Arnold the spy was among us."

"So it's true they've planted spies among the excursionists? Which one was Arnold?"

They described him. But SchrummSchrumm hadn't gotten a good look at the men around the hearth.

"Are there very many spies?"

"Of course! They all take orders from Leopold, the crippled, stinking, hunchbacked spy."

This time, SchrummSchrumm made no effort to conceal his astonishment and said he already knew Leopold.

"Arnold and his henchmen are only apprentice spies," they said. "Leopold is a real spy, maybe the craftiest of the bunch. You've got to watch out for him . . . He's going to come and talk to you. He won't be long now. He asked us to tell you he wanted a word."

"What! You say I should watch out for spies, especially Leopold, and yet you're collaborating with him? You're delivering his messages?"

"That's exactly what we're doing," they agreed. "And here he is." They bustled off, eyes averted, as the goat-smelling spy came hopping toward him like a wind-up Punchinello. When he reached SchrummSchrumm, he patted down the younger man's jacket, ran a finger over his nose, and tugged on his ears and beard.

"I like handsome excursionists, and it's always a pleasure to converse with a young man who's not only courageous but also extremely well-versed in the Excursion's symbology. Which you are, Mr. SchrummSchrumm."

"There are a number of details that intrigue me," said SchrummSchrumm, passing over Leopold's compliments. "Would you be kind enough to enlighten me on a few points?"

The hunchback smiled and nodded his consent.

"Firstly," said SchrummSchrumm, indicating the carriage, "I fail to see the purpose of this vehicle. It's an undertaker's carriage, yet the plate says it belongs to the Company and the chairs seem to suggest it's some form of public transportation. What does it all mean?"

"Oh, nothing too extraordinary. It's something of a museum piece. They used these horse-drawn vehicles in centuries past, before combustion engines. Also, the fact of its being a funeral wagon directly ties in with one of the most complex symbols of the Excursion. I'm not allowed to tell you anything more."

SchrummSchrumm shrugged.

"Be that as it may, Mr. Leopold, even though these vehicles have become obsolete, some of the guards are happily sporting equally outdated undertakers' attire. The fact has not escaped my notice. Why is that?"

"That's a different matter," replied the spy. "I can satisfy your curiosity there. The guards in Misunderstanding are strictly compartmentalized. Each group has a specific role, and each has been assigned a specific uniform. At least that's how it's supposed to be in theory. But oddly enough, despite the rigid discipline enforced everywhere else in Misunderstanding, the most outlandish sartorial extravagances are tolerated in the staff. For example, the training instructors who escort excursionists to the Sands wear a jumpsuit, black leather boots, and black leather gloves. The wall guards have unanimously adopted red leather caps adorned with a single artificial flower. The militiamen—meaning those who aren't active-duty military but were hired to work in Misunderstanding because they possess desirable skills of one kind or another—wear the undertaker's outfit you've already seen. This is because they're the ones most often called upon to perform the grimmer variety of tasks. There are other categories, too: officers, who are allowed to dress however they please, in uniforms or civilian clothes, but who can always be identified by their shoulder stripes; the guards in the strict sense of the term, who wear a white cord around their waists with either gold or silver threads woven in, depending on their level of importance; public officials, recognizable by their beards (dyed yellow) and their red velvet suits; etc."

"You've furnished me with a wealth of fascinating information," said SchrummSchrumm. "One final question, if you please, Mr. Leopold, and then I'll leave you in peace. Is it true you're a spy?"

Leopold faltered for no more than half a second. Then he said, with an aggressive smile:

"Certainly it's true! I, young man, am Leopold, one of the greatest spies in Misunderstanding!"

But even as he was smiling in this unpleasant manner, revealing his large, rotten teeth, SchrummSchrumm was himself making a horrible face and rendering it as irritating as possible by the addition of gobbling, clucking, poultry sounds. Gobbling and grimacing, he advanced on Leopold, kicking him and shoving him with all his might, even at the risk of knocking him over. The lame, evil-smelling hunchback understood at once which way salvation lay. "Whoa there! You're younger than I am!" he cried, putting his hand to his chest as if SchrummSchrumm had wounded him to the heart. Then, with a series of mechanical bunny-hops, he crossed the little courtyard and was gone.

SchrummSchrumm thought he would see him back in the game room—and, who knew, maybe even publicly humiliate him—but Leopold wasn't there when he returned. No one seemed to have noticed, let alone become concerned about, his absence. It was true, though, that a heated discussion was absorbing the general interest just then. Some half-dozen guards, including Krikri and another officer of lieutenant rank, were berating an excursionist on his knees before them. The other hotel guests had cleared out. SchrummSchrumm reached the group just as the kneeling man, giving the lieutenant a look of utter dismay, was saying:

"I don't know anymore! I don't! What more do you want from me?"

"Let's go over it one more time," said the lieutenant with a self-satisfied glance at his colleagues. "You have every right to file a formal complaint, either by addressing it to your valet or to the captain on duty, or, if you must, by referring it directly to the head office, which is under the command of Colonel Red-Bartlett and represents the Holy Directorate itself. The choice is yours! The minute you notify us in writing, everything is in order." (The lieutenant's *r*'s were rather guttural, and he seemed to be not so much instructing the man in this section of the Regulations as refreshing his memory on something he already knew. They must have been discussing it earlier, before SchrummSchrumm arrived.) "And yet the bare possession of this right—nominally granted to you by the administration—is not sufficient in itself to entitle you to file a complaint. It is also imperative, in the first place, that your criticisms do not rest solely on your own personal assessment; in the second place, that the proofs you rely upon are meticulously detailed and scrupulously documented. And so, I repeat: Are you, or are you not, prepared to furnish such proofs? If you are, then will you be so good as to state them without delay, as I've expressly ordered you to do? Otherwise we'll have no choice but to assume you've been lying."

This time the man spat scornfully and—in a voice that still held some faint, lingering hope in spite of everything—explained that the night before, while suffering from a bout of insomnia, he'd been puzzled and intrigued, first at midnight and later at dawn, by unmistakable noises which he'd likewise heard on several previous occasions, always at the same times. These noises were produced by a troop of people walking in step. When he'd gone to the window, he'd seen a large crowd marching toward an unknown destination, accompanied by an escort of guards and police dogs. Shortly thereafter, he'd heard a train pull away. And this morning, two of his excursionist friends who'd been notified yesterday of their imminent departure for the Quicksands were nowhere to be found. From this he'd deduced that they must have left on the excursion (their belongings were also gone). But these friends, though they'd been waiting more than two months to leave, had nonetheless arrived in Misunderstanding a full week after himself. For this reason he considered himself grievously wronged, since any administrative system worth its salt would have arranged its departures on a first-come-first-served basis. Which was to say that those who arrived first should leave first. In other words, he should have left before his friends.

"I am willing to overlook this injustice," said the man. "But I want a firm answer by the end of the day as to whether or not I'll be leaving on the next departure, and in the event I receive a reply in the negative, I intend to file an official complaint. I haven't ruled out demanding a refund of my ticket price."

The lieutenant had listened to the whole of this little speech without interposing a word. But at the concluding phrases, expressed as they were in a tone so rarely heard in that establishment, a smile crept over his lips.

"You're making two separate assertions there, Mr. Excursionist. Let's address the first. You must understand that it's altogether unthinkable that you could have been wronged in this way by the Sunday Quicksands Excursion Company. This is for the excellent reason that the Company always earnestly endeavors to honor its commitments, and indeed it is in its own interest to do so. On the other hand—conversely, I might say—you, for your part, are obliged to honor the commitments you've undertaken through the simple act of your enrollment. This means, as far as your responsibilities toward us are concerned, that once having paid the excursion's registration fee and entered Misunderstanding, it is no longer possible for you—according to the provisions of the Regulations you yourself have signed—either to demand a refund or to pass through the Iron Gate except in the course of a scheduled departure for the Quicksands. This also means, as far as our responsibilities toward you are concerned, that if there's been the smallest oversight, I'll do everything I can to secure you a place in the next departure for the Quicksands . . . That question, as you see, was easily sorted. And I would never lose my temper over so trifling an issue, if that were all there was to it. But it's quite another matter when you start telling stories about a troop of chained excursionists, guarded by attack dogs, being marched around in the dead of night toward a train loaded with iron cages. That's pure fantasy. First off, where is all this supposed to have taken place?"

The man rose to his feet and beckoned the guards over to a window that, like those on the landings and in SchrummSchrumm's room, faced the vacant lot. Once there, he pointed at something glittering far out on the horizon, which might have been taken for a line of telephone poles. SchrummSchrumm saw it, too. But even if, at a push, it bore some resemblance to train tracks and telephone poles, it could also have been any number of other things, and it was impossible to say anything about it with certainty.

The same thought must have occurred to the guards. The lieutenant broke in with, "You're all the same! Liars and more liars! This railway of yours doesn't exist. If there are no tracks and no telephone poles, it follows that there are no train cars and therefore no trains. Nor are there any iron cages, much less passengers. Besides, by your own account there would have been two departures for the Quicksands last night: one at midnight and the other just before dawn. That's even stupider than the rest of your story, for two reasons. First, because there's only one departure a week, on Sunday. Second, because no one would be fool enough to schedule a trip at night, when a man can't see his own hand in front of his face. If you don't want to meet your death in the Quicksands, you have to be able to see where you're going!"

It was then that the group noticed SchrummSchrumm standing in their midst.

"Who're you? What're you doing here?" growled a guard, raising a fist.

Fortunately, Krikri stepped between them. He must have outranked his colleague, because the latter grudgingly backed down. Krikri, incidentally, had not acted until the lieutenant, with a curt nod, had given him permission.

"I'd like to say a word, if I may."

"Yes, what is it, Mr. SchrummSchrumm?" asked Krikri in a cautious tone.

SchrummSchrumm paused for a moment as he considered whether he should speak exclusively to Krikri and the lieutenant or address himself to the group as a whole. He glanced around and saw that the expressions of anger had given way to those of polite interest. The lone exception was the lieutenant, who was dreamily smoking a cigarette.

"I'd like to speak in this man's defense. Purely on principle, of course: though he is a fellow excursionist, he doesn't do the profession enough honor to have earned my sympathy."

"Disinterested testimony, then?" inquired the lieutenant, rousing from his dream.

"Quite so. I desire justice. Simple justice!"

"Justice?!" said one of the guards, incensed to the point of apoplexy by the word.

"Justice?!" echoed the lieutenant. "What do you mean? Speak your mind."

"Thank you. What I mean is this: Have any of you actually *been* to the Quicksands?"

"Of course not," said Krikri. "We're bureaucrats. Our work is intended to be sedentary."

"I'll bear that in mind . . . Now, why is this man being reprimanded? You say he's lying when he claims to have heard a group of men on a forced march, escorted by brutal guards and howling dogs, toward a train that departs in the middle of the night, seemingly for the Quicksands. He's presumed to be lying for several reasons. Example? It would be completely idiotic to take excursionists to the Quicksands at night, that is to say when no one can see his hand in front of his face and when accidents would be inevitable. I won't dispute that this falls squarely into the category of plain common sense. But then again, how can you know that one's sight is absolutely necessary to navigating the Quicksands? You yourselves have just admitted that none of you has ever been there! Let's take another example. It's true that the nature of those glittering objects we see out there, in the direction my colleague was pointing, is very difficult to determine. We cannot definitively affirm that they are rails and telephone poles. But neither can we definitively deny that they are rails and telephone poles ... This brings us to the sole point of any real consequence. It is because of these train noises—whether he really heard them or only imagined he did, it makes no difference—that my colleague felt justified in interpreting those glittering objects as rails and telephone poles. By the same token, it is because of the doubtful nature of those same glittering objects that you gentlemen feel justified in dismissing out of hand his auditory impressions: groaning men, barking dogs, rattling irons, departing trains ... When you come right down to it, only one thing is certain: if there's a train running nearby, a person should be able to hear it. And you can't rule out, *a priori*, that he did hear it."

SchrummSchrumm thought this little oration of his would cause quite a stir. The effect was not at all what he had anticipated. The lieutenant burst out laughing, followed by the rest of the guards. Then he said, with an ironic glance at Krikri:

"I take it your protégé is attempting a joke?"

"What? I'm not joking in the slightest!"

"Of course he is," replied Krikri, giving SchrummSchrumm a look of reproof. "This excursionist is joking, lieutenant."

Krikri had for a second time taken it upon himself to enter the fray of this conversation—a conversation he seemed to consider dangerous, because as he went on, he gave SchrummSchrumm unmistakable signs that he should let the matter drop:

"Ah, Mr. SchrummSchrumm," he continued. "You don't know this kind of excursionist the way I do. Your ignorance both explains and excuses your intervention, which was courageous and unselfish. But I've spent a long time around his type, and I can tell you they're all liars, every last one of them. There is no railroad, the lieutenant's right . . . You were lying, weren't you?" he demanded of the man in desperation, taking him by the collar and giving him a hard shake. "Come on, speak up! Explain yourself! Defend yourself!"

"No! I won't say anything!" protested the excursionist.

For a moment, SchrummSchrumm didn't know what to think. He quickly reviewed the entire conversation, or what he had heard of it, and as far as he could tell, everything that had been said was perfectly logical. More than logical: irrefutable. Why was his fellow excursionist behaving this way? Was he conserving his energies for a later speech, or was he simply an imbecile? Either way, SchrummSchrumm had gone too far to back down now. Besides, like it or not, he had in some sense cast in his lot with his comrade, who, though perhaps less mentally adroit than he was, had shown undeniable bravery in deliberately opposing the guards.

"You see, lieutenant, he has nothing to say for himself!" crowed Krikri. "They never make more than a token effort to defend their allegations. Mr. SchrummSchrumm, on the other hand . . . I'll vouch for him with full confidence."

"It's no good, Mr. Krikri," said SchrummSchrumm quietly. "It so happens that I, too, heard the train depart last night. First at midnight and again just before dawn. The sounds were easy enough to recognize. A train in the valley was slowly pulling away: there was the grinding of wheels against rails, chugging, puffs of smoke from a smokestack; the train rumbled along so that I could almost have counted the cars. The sounds grew steadily fainter until they vanished completely. I heard everything, I tell you. Everything!"

The response that fell from the lieutenant's lips was so outrageous, so insolent, that SchrummSchrumm felt himself overcome with rage. He was close to throwing himself on the floor and screaming.

"Apparently, Mr. SchrummSchrumm," he said mildly, "you're just as moronic as this man is. Simply because one hears a train pass, must one conclude that a train has really passed? If such is your logic, I'm here to tell you that your reasoning is garbage and you'd better think again."

"I'll stand by it until there's proof to the contrary!" shouted SchrummSchrumm.

Had they been waiting for him to say these very words? The entire group turned as one to look at the lieutenant, who winked roguishly at Krikri.

"Follow the usual procedure," he said.

Then he addressed a stupefied SchrummSchrumm:

"We're going to give you your proof to the contrary, young man."

Krikri had already grabbed SchrummSchrumm by the arm and was now pulling him out of the room and down the famous hallway, where they passed yet more guards. SchrummSchrumm counted the doors; they went past the library and stopped at the ninth. This door led into a sort of semicircular indoor amphitheater where an armed guard, who'd been sitting on a chair beside a second door that apparently led into a second room, stood as they entered. They didn't say a word to him, nor he to them. Instead, he took a miniature key from a hook and, after flourishing it ostentatiously under SchrummSchrumm's nose, inserted it into a tiny slot hidden within a crack in the wall. Then he spoke into the keyhole as if it were a telephone, which perhaps it was:

"Coctus! Coctus!" he called, as SchrummSchrumm turned to see how Krikri was taking this.

The door opened just wide enough to permit a second man to stick his head out. He made an amiable face at Krikri.

"It's time," Krikri said. "Could we come in and watch, the two of us?" His gesture indicating SchrummSchrumm was almost paternal.

"Fine by me," said the man called Coctus with a little pout of acquiescence. Then, looking at his wristwatch: "You're right, it is time . . . Hey! It's time!" he shouted to someone who must have been behind him in the second room.

There was no reply, and his face betrayed a hint of panic.

"It's time!" he bellowed louder, opening the door the rest of the way.

Krikri and SchrummSchrumm followed him inside. The man who'd been standing guard in the antechamber closed a set of padded doors behind them. Coctus was conferring quietly with two other staff members who seemed to be his assistants. The room was empty except for a large box in one corner and a freakishly outsized gramophone horn dominating its center. Every available wall surface was covered with holes. SchrummSchrumm was immediately intrigued. These holes were about twenty centimeters in diameter, smooth and shiny inside. They couldn't be air ducts, but neither could they have been put there without some specific purpose in mind.

When their whispered conference was over, Coctus gave the others an affirmative nod—it was clear that his primary mode of communication was facial expressions—and one of them picked up the box, which must have been relatively light in spite of its size, so easily did he carry it. He brought it over and set it directly in front of SchrummSchrumm, as if to give him a front-row seat for what was about to take place. Coctus slowly approached the box. He looked inquiringly at the other two men, as if asking whether the honor of opening the box really fell to him. They must have agreed that it did: he ceremoniously lifted the lid.

Everything that followed happened with rapidity and precision, each man apparently knowing exactly what movements he had to perform. One took out a wire and connected one end to the enormous gramophone horn and the other to the bizarre apparatus Coctus had removed from the box. This appliance, small enough at first, grew larger and larger as more accessories were screwed onto it, until it was an imposing gramophone player mounted on a sturdy tripod.

"Hut-hut!" said Coctus in a voice of command. They immediately took up positions on either side of him, facing SchrummSchrumm and Krikri. All three had assumed a martial attitude; they had donned their red caps and put their left hands firmly on their hips. At the base of the apparatus, on a copper plate, SchrummSchrumm read: "Obedient and depraved machine that sends out in all directions—and into the foolish hearts of excursionists—deceptive and dangerous sensations."

"Are you ready? Are you absolutely and entirely ready?" said Coctus in a changed tone.

They were. One of the two energetic young men turned the gramophone crank; the other produced a disk from his inside breast pocket and set it on the turntable. Coctus, having consulted his watch one last time, delicately raised the arm and placed the needle on the disk, which was already spinning.

"What sort of joke is this?" muttered SchrummSchrumm. But at the same time such a horrible din erupted that even Krikri and the other three guards, who were evidently used to the machine, jumped as much as he did. Dumbstruck, he finally understood what was happening. From the titanic gramophone horn emerged sounds that were growing louder by the second. Anyone would have sworn that a troop of men was approaching. The men were marching in step; they were dragging heavy chains. Curses rang out, then whipcracks, followed by stifled groans of pain. Shortly thereafter, a train pulled out of a station. Yes, it seemed to be passing very close by, down in the valley. SchrummSchrumm could have counted its wheels ... Grindings of metal on rails, chugging noises, puffs from a smokestack: everything was just as it had been last night. And this uproar, amplified by the holes in the walls, must have been reverberating throughout the building, truly sending deceptive and dangerous sensations into the bruised and battered hearts of excursionists. The train rumbled past. The noise died down, faded, stopped altogether. The record had reached its end. The machine switched off automatically.

"The night train taking excursionists to the Quicksands has just gone by!" laughed Coctus. All of them guffawed, and Krikri did likewise. Already, as methodically as it had been assembled, the machine was being disassembled and put neatly back into its case. But Coctus was no longer part of the proceedings. He'd gone to lean against the oversized horn, and SchrummSchrumm perceived on his oafish, ruddy face a smile that was no longer sarcastic, or even slightly ironic: a smile expressing satisfaction in a job well done. Then the two others asked their boss if they could go, since their work was now over until midnight. He gave them his permission and they went. Krikri and Coctus held a short conversation in hushed tones, during which SchrummSchrumm saw them turn around several times to look at him and smile. By the end they were openly laughing. Then Krikri motioned for SchrummSchrumm to follow him.

"Where are we going?"

"Things are taking their course," answered the guard, deliberately evasive.

But seeing that SchrummSchrumm was uncertain, perhaps because of what he'd just witnessed, he added:

"That was a fine mess you got yourself into, Mr. Smart Guy. Didn't I warn you? This is the last time I intervene on your behalf. You're a loose cannon."

This said, he led him back through the hall of seventeen doors. When they reentered the lobby, the other excursionist was still having it out with the lieutenant and remaining guards. SchrummSchrumm turned his head and tried to avoid meeting his eye, but the man must have been watching for him. He called out triumphantly:

"Thank you, Mr. SchrummSchrumm! Thank you for the lesson in courage you've given me! I've just heard the train go by again. From now on I'm sticking to my guns and never backing down!"

SchrummSchrumm would have liked to offer some sort of reply. These words disturbed him, and they filled his soul with extreme agitation and revulsion. But Krikri, with a look that seemed designed to freeze the marrow in his bones, pinched his arm so hard he cried out in pain. Then, with a brutal gesture, he shoved SchrummSchrumm toward the stairs.

"I'm warning you one last time not to leave the Bushido Hotel without my express authorization," he said when they were back in SchrummSchrumm's room. "I don't know exactly what the repercussions of your initiative today will be, but I don't want to see this behavior again. If you need to go out, call me; that's why I'm here. Believe me when I say I'm not kidding around. If you repeat this little stunt, you'll be in for some very severe penalties!"

Without another word, he turned on his heel and left.

III

On that night and the nights following, SchrummSchrumm slept soundly and heard no suspicious noises of any kind, either at midnight or at dawn. He was awakened each morning by the crackle of the loudspeaker that hung from the ceiling of his room: "Rise and shine! Rise and shine!" a gentle voice would say. "Attention! Attention! We shall now recite Prayer Number One together." Next came a reading from the Gospel of Misunderstanding, followed by some thoughts for the day, after which his door would be cautiously opened a crack, he would hear a volley of giggles, and the two maids would enter, accompanied by Krikri. This was, by far, the best moment of the day.

One morning, however, Lucette and Lulu were unnaturally quiet as they brought him his breakfast. They scampered quickly from the room as soon as they had set it down, and Krikri told SchrummSchrumm he would have to eat quickly.

"What's going on?" he asked as he swallowed his last mouthful of food.

Without replying, Krikri clapped his hands and three men appeared. These were no guards. The leader of the group was a little old man in a red velvet suit with a yellow beard reaching to his navel.

"Are you SchrummSchrumm, excursionist first class?" asked one of the men.

"Yes, of course he is!" said Krikri.

The little man with the yellow beard gave Krikri a look that seemed to make him want to sink into the floor.

"We require verbal confirmation from the excursionist himself," he said in a dignified tone, at the same time giving SchrummSchrumm a wink.

"Yes, of course I am!" replied SchrummSchrumm.

"Good," said the little man, coming forward to take him familiarly by the arm.

"Good! Very good!" said the two others.

SchrummSchrumm was beginning to lose patience. The two men approached, felt his nose, pulled his ears, examined his teeth, and were apparently satisfied with the results. They gave several little nods of approval and went away again, leaving the door open behind them.

"We'll be right back."

A few seconds later, several thuds were heard out on the landing and the two men reappeared, red-faced.

"Where should we put them?" they asked.

"Put what?"

The men replied that they were delivering the trunks and wanted to know where to leave them . . . "obviously!"

"Obviously!" said the old man, still hanging onto SchrummSchrumm's arm.

"Who are you?"

"We're from the Dispatch and Receiving Department."

"And what trunks would these be?"

"Why, *your* trunks, Mr. Excursionist," they said, taken aback. During this whole exchange, the old man with the wispy yellow beard had been nodding his approbation and liberally distributing winks to everyone present.

"You shouldn't leave them anywhere," declared Schrumm-Schrumm politely, "for the simple reason that I'm not expecting any trunks."

His words cast the two men into a state of complete bewilderment. They went back out to the landing and called for the little man with the dyed beard to join them. A very animated discussion in hoarse whispers ensued. When they returned, the men looked even more disgruntled.

"We don't understand, Mr. Excursionist-First-Class Schrumm-Schrumm. Your name's on every one of these trunks, nothing could be clearer . . . Maybe the best thing would be for you to take a look at the trunks in question. If you'd be good enough to come and examine them yourself . . ."

SchrummSchrumm consented and followed them onto the landing accompanied by the old man, who had once again taken his arm. There he saw three wicker trunks of generous proportions bound with iron bands. SchrummSchrumm studied each of them at length; he ran his forefinger over the wickerwork, he bent down to inhale their odor, he even flicked the third trunk and listened to the resulting sound. Then he said:

"These are not my trunks."

"The excursionist does not recognize his trunks?" inquired the old man.

SchrummSchrumm turned to look at him just in time to catch a hopeful gleam in his eye.

"I didn't say that," he hastened to explain. "I said, 'These are not my trunks.' For the simple reason that I'm not expecting any trunks, as I've already told you. It would seem there's been some mistake. You'll have to take them back."

"Bad!" said one of the Dispatch and Receiving Department men, mopping his brow with a checked handkerchief.

"Very bad!" agreed the other. "Will you at least sign the slip?"

SchrummSchrumm took the little slip of red paper the man held out to him. It stated that the undersigned hereby affirmed the occurrence of a "highly anomalous and isolated" error regarding the delivery of his luggage. SchrummSchrumm thought for a moment. It was he who had the upper hand in this situation. He decided to make the most of it:

"Why should I sign this slip? It would apply to me only if I were expecting three iron-banded wicker trunks and the trunks you delivered were not mine but someone else's. I'm not expecting any trunks, however, and therefore won't sign any slip. Good day!"

With this, he unceremoniously hustled the two men out of his room. The old man preceded them, laughing like a madman and whooping with joy. Krikri, the last out, closed the door without venturing even the briefest remark. SchrummSchrumm flopped down on his bed and thought over this extraordinary mix-up. Ah, he would definitely have to watch himself from now on, one could never be too careful on an excursion . . . Less than half an hour later there came another knock. The two deliverymen barged in. The little old man was still with them, of course. Who could he be? SchrummSchrumm still had no idea. There was a fourth intruder, too, a lieutenant in civilian clothes.

"We apologize for disturbing you a second time," said the officer genially, "but a formality of the highest order is at issue here. These gentlemen" (he gestured toward the deliverymen without bothering to look at them) "visited you half an hour ago to deliver three trunks, which you refused to accept on the grounds—and wholly legitimate grounds they are, too—that they didn't belong to you. Let's see if we can't tackle this problem from another angle. It is my duty to inform you, Mr. SchrummSchrumm, that the three trunks in question still—as far as concerns the Dispatch and Receiving Department, where I serve as Inspector—bear every sign of being items intended for you. For one thing, the dispatch slip included in your file leaves no room for doubt: the trunks match its description in every respect. In addition, all three are labeled with your name. Given this state of affairs, I feel confident that if we put our heads together we can get to the bottom of the matter."

"Not this again!" broke in SchrummSchrumm. "I've already told you how things stand, and your reasoning makes no sense to me. I hope, at the very least, you haven't dragged those three silly trunks all the way back up here."

"They're right on the landing," said the men, looking thoroughly delighted.

And, as in a well-choreographed ballet, they stepped nimbly aside, asked SchrummSchrumm to please follow them, and conducted him out onto the landing where three iron-banded wicker trunks, indisputably the very ones they had brought him half an hour earlier, were sitting large as life. SchrummSchrumm sighed and asked what they wanted him to do.

"I'm hoping we can have a calm, rational discussion about this without getting ourselves worked up," said the inspector. "In other words, Mr. Excursionist, sir, I cannot overemphasize my sincerest wish that we both abandon our attempts to come at the problem from the standpoint of what is evident. We'll never reach a resolution using that approach: however evident it may be to you that these trunks are not intended for you, it is equally evident to us that they were sent to you. In still other words, I'd be most grateful if you'd be so kind as to examine the trunks with meticulous care and make sure there's not even, let us say, one chance in a million that they might be yours, or that they might have been sent to you."

SchrummSchrumm looked at the man. He was smiling in a way that seemed to beg pardon for having to be so insistent. Then he turned and looked at the trunks. He ran his left forefinger along the wickerwork, he bent down to inhale their odor, he even lightly flicked the side of one trunk to demonstrate the extent of his good faith.

"They do resemble them!" he said after a minute. The idea had also crossed his mind that they might, after all, be empty, though the fact that they hadn't sounded hollow, as well as the sweat dripping down the deliverymen's faces, was sufficient proof of the contrary.

"They do resemble them!" repeated the officer with a hopeful gleam in his eye—an expression identical to that of the old man half an hour before, and no doubt just as dangerous.

"I mean they resemble some trunks I had back where I came from," SchrummSchrumm quickly corrected himself. "But these can't possibly be mine."

The man made no effort to hide his disappointment but seemed to be thinking deeply. Finally he murmured, with his eyes half-closed and in his wisest voice:

"If I understand correctly, then, you are ruling out the possibility that these trunks have been sent by you. This tallies with your previous statements. In other words, you rule out the possibility that you were expecting these trunks. From which one may infer that you were expecting no trunks at all!"

"You've hit the nail on the head," said SchrummSchrumm, regarding the inspector with a new interest. He was now rather pleased with the man, in fact.

"Good!" he said. "You have indeed come here from M----?"

In order to avoid any hint of indiscretion on so personal a subject, the inspector had asked this question in an undertone with his mouth close to SchrummSchrumm's ear. SchrummSchrumm appreciated his delicacy and promptly confirmed this piece of information.

"The trunks also came from M----. An odd coincidence, don't you think? And you indeed arrived on the --th? That was the date listed on your arrival form, and it was corroborated by Prestige, the procession director on the bus that transported you to Misunderstanding, as well as by the sworn testimony of Sergeant-First-Class Krikri."

SchrummSchrumm confirmed this, too.

"Well now, the trunks were expedited on the --th," the man went on. "Which means, allowing for travel time . . . that the trunks were sent the day after your departure from M----! What do you say to that?"

"No! No! No!" exclaimed SchrummSchrumm, making all the men jump except the inspector, who continued to show his perspicacity. "May I have a word with you alone?" he asked the inspector brusquely.

The officer agreed, visibly flattered by the request.

"Please understand my thinking, Mr. SchrummSchrumm," he began when they were out of the others' earshot. "I'm not saying you sent the trunks in question. You've given us a categorical denial on this point, and what's more, the idea has been conclusively disproven by the date on which the trunks were sent from M----, namely the day after your departure. Therefore you are not the expediter of these contentious pieces of luggage. Which accounts for your saying, 'I wasn't expecting any trunks.' But to leap from there to the conclusion that these trunks aren't yours! That involves skipping a step in the chain of reasoning that ought not to be passed over quite so lightly. I'll tell you my personal hypothesis, if you'll permit me: either you had someone else send the trunks for you—but this possibility seems implausible to me, because you would have remembered doing so—or, what's far more likely, someone took it upon themselves to send them without your knowledge, the day after you left. Your mother, for instance, or some other family member. Perhaps a domestic servant or a friend. This would account for the fact that you weren't expecting any trunks, while simultaneously accounting for the presence of said trunks."

"So it would," conceded SchrummSchrumm. "Your theory is an attractive and compelling one. Alas, it won't hold up under scrutiny: my mother is dead, I have no family, I employ no domestics, and I don't know a single person in M----."

"That's too bad," said the inspector. "All the same, you must admit that such a conjunction of circumstances—another person named SchrummSchrumm, also residing in M----, leaving M---- on the same day as yourself, traveling to Misunderstanding just as you did, to take the very same excursion to the Quicksands—all this seems most incredible. Everything has happened as if you and this other SchrummSchrumm were one and the same man. In any case, from the point of view of our Department, I'm afraid that's how it looks."

SchrummSchrumm scratched his head as he thought this over.

"Let's try another tack," he said at last. "Where do I stand as far as your Department is concerned? What would happen, for example, if I formally disavowed these trunks? In other words, what does the Sunday Quicksands Excursion Company do when they find themselves in possession of ownerless objects? I assume, of course, that this doesn't happen very often. It must be an extremely rare event, am I right?"

"Not a bit of it!" said the man, who seemed wounded to the quick by the question. "Not a bit of it! On the contrary, we deal with a great number of such objects, and we put them up for sale if their owners haven't come to claim them after a year and a day. Now, are you perchance just a little bit curious about what we do with the proceeds?" he asked hopefully. SchrummSchrumm said the question was of the highest interest to him. The inspector, after stepping a few more paces away from the others and dropping his voice even lower, as the conversation was about to venture into territory that would be over his associates' heads, continued: "We build new buildings, buy new shares of stock, acquire new plots of land, and the fruits of these transactions permit us not only to expand our services and even broaden our service network, but also to contribute to the development of the Company as a whole."

"How marvelous!" said SchrummSchrumm, feeling he'd just made a friend.

"My dear Mr. SchrummSchrumm," said the officer (and this term of address spoke to the altered tenor of their relationship), "unfortunately, I must point out to you that this arrangement is not among the options available in your case. Objects are sold at public auction only when their owners cannot be located. But we *have* located you: notwithstanding that little red slip you refused to sign, we still have the original shipping form. Which is to say that you, like it or not, are officially the owner *in posse* of these three trunks. Which is further to say, of three other trunks if not of these particular three. At least, should it be proved that these particular three aren't yours. In that eventuality, our Search and Investigation Department for Hard-to-Locate Owners will not rest until they bring you, within the shortest possible delay, your three *real* trunks."

"You're telling me that if I don't accept these three trunks, I'll be forced to accept another three?"

"Precisely. There's simply no way around it. And it may well turn out that, despite all our diligent efforts, the search takes us quite a long time. Which would correspondingly push back the date of your departure for the Quicksands."

"A terrible thought!" said SchrummSchrumm, not daring to imagine what disastrous consequences such a delay might entail for him. But just then, Krikri took the liberty of approaching them to interrupt. For the past two or three minutes he'd been conferring with the two deliverymen and the little bearded man. He came to report their unanimous opinion, namely that if the trunks in question belonged to SchrummSchrumm, they would necessarily contain his personal effects, effects he could easily identify as such . . . This idea had come to them while they were looking at the trunks' padlocks. Perhaps he might try his keys to see if they fit?

"What keys? I have no keys," said SchrummSchrumm disingenuously.

"Those!" said Krikri, pointing to a bunch of keys hanging from a solid silver ring on SchrummSchrumm's belt.

"There's no point," protested SchrummSchrumm. "These are very old keys that have never opened anything."

"Let's give them a try anyway," the four men suggested with knowing smiles.

"At any rate," said the inspector solemnly, "once the trunks have been opened in my presence, since I am a duly sworn agent, you will be relieved of all responsibility, Mr. SchrummSchrumm, in the event that they are found not to contain your personal effects. In the event that they do, of course, the question will be conclusively settled and the problem solved. I think it's an excellent suggestion. Open away!"

SchrummSchrumm suppressed a shiver of fear. Then, grudgingly, with much grumbling and sighing, he approached the first trunk. His hand shook a little as he tried the first key, then the second: they didn't fit the lock.

"What did I tell you? There's no point!" he said, trying to rise to his feet again.

But they insisted he try the third key. He shot them a desperate, hunted look, but they were watching his every move with greedy interest: there was no getting out of it. He tried the key, and a cry of victory rose from the group: it fit the lock perfectly.

"Now the others!" said the inspector. They worked equally well. "There remains one final formality," he said. "Will you please ascertain whether or no these are your personal effects?"

SchrummSchrumm opened the three lids. The trunks contained excursioning gear, books on excursioning, various items of excursioning apparel—in short, everything a seasoned, well-prepared excursionist brings with him on a journey. Nothing he wouldn't have packed for himself, but also nothing he could formally identify as his own personal property. While rummaging through the contents, he suddenly stopped short and an exclamation of surprise escaped him. He'd just spotted an old photograph at the bottom of one of the trunks. There it was, cracked and yellowed, and he picked it up gingerly between thumb and forefinger as if afraid it might crumble into dust. Was it possible? His hand trembled, his heart pounded in his chest. Meanwhile, the two deliverymen and the inspector were shamelessly craning their necks over his shoulder, trying to get a better look at the picture. SchrummSchrumm hastily tucked it into his jacket pocket.

"A family memento, I presume?" said the inspector.

SchrummSchrumm merely pointed at the trunks and said, decisively this time:

"These are indeed my personal effects. I formally recognize the contents of these trunks."

"Good man!" said the officer, slapping him on the back. "I can tell you now—now that there's no longer any risk of prejudicing your decision—that I didn't for one second doubt you'd eventually come around and recognize these trunks as your own. Don't get me wrong, I understand why you acted as you did: one has to be absolutely sure before committing oneself. It's becoming second nature to me! And now, farewell. I'm very glad this was sorted out so quickly."

He bowed, and everything in the demeanor of the Dispatch and Receiving Department employees seemed to imply that the business was settled, when the old man with the yellow beard interposed for the first time:

"If you don't mind," he said to the inspector, "I realize that on the face of it there can be no reason to call Mr. SchrummSchrumm's honesty into question. The photograph doubtless belongs to him. But I must proceed with the mandated verification all the same. It's my job. You're aware of that, aren't you, Lieutenant?"

The officer made no reply; his silence seemed to signify assent. Who *was* this man? SchrummSchrumm still had no clue. The man sensed, perhaps, what was in his mind. He promptly introduced himself:

"I am Director Bushido. It is I who manage the hotel of the same name. I'm also a distinguished archaeologist specializing in graffiti and old family photographs."

"I've never seen you before," said SchrummSchrumm.

"That's because my work as a specialist in graffiti and old family photographs takes up so much of my time," explained the old man. And, to the officer:

"Of course, you understand that I need to authenticate the photograph he slipped into his pocket. Everything hangs upon it."

SchrummSchrumm broke in:

"The photo can't possibly be of any interest to you. It's a family snapshot. I'm not going to make an exhibit of it."

The little old man didn't answer at first. Then a malicious smirk crept over his face and he took a paper from his pocket which he gave to the lieutenant, who studied it, nodding, and passed it to SchrummSchrumm. It read:

"On this day, to our feal Director Bushido: order to subject the excursionist SchrummSchrumm to Psychological Aptitude Test #4."

The message was signed, "Burns, on behalf of our Holy Director, blessed be his name."

"What does this mean?" asked SchrummSchrumm, handing back the note. "In the first place, who is this Burns?"

"Mister Burns is Deputy Director of Misunderstanding and Chief of the Secret Police," said the old man quietly.

SchrummSchrumm shrugged.

"Then I suppose I'll have to take your test," he said, exasperated. "Still, considering that this is a personal keepsake, I insist that these two underlings excuse themselves first. I'll explain myself to you and the lieutenant only."

His request was granted and the two deliverymen left the room, visibly disappointed.

"Would you now please produce the photograph? We'll examine it together."

SchrummSchrumm carefully drew the yellowed snapshot out of his pocket and they all three bent over it.

It was a picture of Allright, Mayor of Mahasky, standing between two of his assistants on a rise overlooking the city walls. The photograph was quite old, as its state of deterioration attested, and the trio looked decidedly old-fashioned, even a little ridiculous—especially Allright, with his top hat, his bow tie knotted around a high starched collar, and his baggy trousers puddling in folds around his down-at-heel shoes. The two assistants were smiling in a smug, affected manner, so great was their satisfaction at being photographed in Allright's company. They leaned familiarly on the mayor's shoulders. The mayor, too, wore a smile, though his was somewhat enigmatic, which was entirely in keeping with his character. It was a genuinely touching photograph. And not just touching, but extremely well composed, because if it hadn't been so familiar to SchrummSchrumm, if he hadn't known that the little man in the center was none other than Allright, Mayor of Mahasky and person of very noble lineage, he would have been perplexed by it.

"Well?" said the director.

"A singular photograph," remarked the inspector.

"Even more than you realize," agreed SchrummSchrumm. "And I can't deny myself the pleasure of showing you why. Take a good look at this trio, gentlemen. You'll notice that the central figure is appreciably smaller than his companions, who lean familiarly on his shoulders, smiling their smug smiles. What's more, his features can't quite be made out, while those of the others are perfectly sharp. Finally, though the little man is also smiling, he does so in an enigmatic, diffident way . . . What conclusion does this seem to impose on us? Obviously, that the photographer has deliberately redirected our attention from Allright to his two companions. In other words, we must conclude that these two are the little man's superiors."

"Quite so," agreed the inspector. "That seems plain enough."

"And yet what's actually going on is precisely the opposite," said SchrummSchrumm exultantly. "At least to the eye of an informed viewer . . . Take a closer look at the two companions' smiles, gentlemen. It would be impossible to say, based on these smiles alone, whether the men's self-satisfied expression derives from their instinctively holding themselves aloof, being the little man's superiors, in which case they're placing their hands on his shoulders as a way of emphasizing his subordinate status, or whether, inversely, they're extremely proud to be photographed in his company, being his inferiors, in which case they're assuming a false air of casual intimacy with him . . . Here's where all sorts of interesting considerations can be brought into play. Indeed, by positioning himself between his companions, the little man in the center is indicating to those in the know that, despite his small stature, he's the true center of the group, an idea further strengthened by the posture of the two others who, by leaning on his shoulders, are not expressing familiarity, as might be supposed at first glance, but on the contrary indicating that the little man is their sole support. By the same token, the act of dissimulating his features, far from diverting the attention of the intelligent viewer, actually captivates him. One immediately wonders, 'Why is he hiding his face? Why does he show us only his smile?' With this thought, one grasps the momentous significance of that smile. What can we say about it, except that it's the perfect emblem of this extraordinary personage? Just look! His smile is at once world-weary, compassionate, and serene. Yes indeed, I can tell you from personal experience, gentlemen, there's no other quite like it. But we need to interpret it correctly. This, in the end, is why the central figure, instead of showing us his eyes, his hands, or the rest of his face, shows us only his smile: to give each and every viewer an equal chance."

"Bravo!" cried the inspector. "Your exposition dazzles me, Mr. SchrummSchrumm."

"I wholeheartedly agree," said Director Bushido. "Hats off to your analytical powers. Nevertheless, it doesn't advance us much in the matter at hand. For, though you've given us a very ingenious interpretation of the picture, your performance was well within the capacity of any intelligent layman. What I mean is, anyone seeing this photograph for the first time might have made the same remarks. I mean, too, that your exposition in no way proves that this photograph belongs to you. Therefore I must ask you to substantiate your claim to its ownership in a more concrete and definitive manner."

"What you say is true," said SchrummSchrumm. "I'll tell you, then, that the reason I know this picture so well is that its difficulties, intricacies, and symbolism have been explained to me over and over again from my tender boyhood. More specifically—because, when you come right down to it, this is all that concerns you—it's a picture of Allright, Mayor of Mahasky and person of noble lineage, photographed with two of his assistants whose names I don't know, on a rise overlooking that city. I should add that Mahasky is where I was born."

"Mahasky?" mumbled the inspector.

"Allright?" mumbled Director Bushido.

"Just so."

"I am not of the same mind," said the old man after a brief pause.

The inspector immediately tempered his enthusiasm and turned to his colleague with an attentive expression.

"You maintain that this is a photograph of one Allright," continued the old man. "You further maintain that the photograph was taken on a rise overlooking a certain city, namely your native city of Mahasky . . . Well, I maintain that this is our Holy Director in person, photographed on one of his daily strolls through Eden. Likewise with these walls we see on either side of what you've termed 'a rise overlooking Mahasky.' They are incontrovertibly walls, yes, but Eden is also surrounded by walls, and the walls in this photograph are altogether identical with those. See, too, this knoll which is indeed equivalent to what might be called a 'rise.' If one accepted your interpretation—a very big *if*—there would be something rather incongruous, even wildly incongruous, if not outright shocking, about the fact that your Allright and his two companions have scaled this rise overlooking Mahasky for the sole purpose of having their picture taken. I know! You could counter by saying that your Allright did it intentionally, that he meant to inspire the viewer to make a similar effort of his own; an effort that would be the sole means of gaining true insight into the photograph's esoteric meaning. Yet there would still be something in this reasoning that doesn't quite add up. Whereas—follow me closely here—in the middle of Eden there's a knoll, comparable to a rise, which our Holy Director enjoys climbing in the course of his daily walks, and at the summit of which he is very much in the habit of pausing. This is a well-known fact. What's more, I'm sure you'll agree that a rise located next to a city has no great symbolic value. By contrast, a knoll in the middle of Eden intrinsically possesses a precise and undeniable meaning, symbolic in the highest degree, which is inherent in its central position within Eden's walls. This is why our Holy Director enjoys pausing there. Just as he is King of the Quicksands, in which capacity he sits in state at the center of Misunderstanding, he is also Lord of Eden, whose knoll holds a special place in his heart, being its geometric center. One final point to which I'd like to draw your attention, and which I'm sure you'll find conclusive: your interpretation does not account for the identities of the two companions—you've admitted you don't know who they are. Mine *does* account for them, because all of us here know the two companions our Holy Director takes with him on his daily walks: they have the same features and the same colossal stature as the men in this photograph. Furthermore, they have ample reason to feel self-satisfied, as you've so aptly noted, for they are Jules and Jim, our two executioners, the Holy Director's most intimate acquaintances among all his entourage!"

Here the old man stopped; the rapid outpouring of this long explanation had left him slightly winded. As might have been expected, the officer had changed his mind:

"Splendid!" he said. "A truly remarkable analysis, Mr. Director, sir. Especially when one considers that you were tackling interpretations of the most arduous kind." SchrummSchrumm was more than a little put out. Not only did he know perfectly well that the photograph really was of Allright on a rise overlooking Mahasky, not only was it sheer stupidity to claim that a trio composed of the Holy Director of Misunderstanding and two executioners would be out taking daily constitutionals in such a dismal garden, but, most of all, he failed to see what this all-important "test" could have to do with the matter. He was wondering, in short, whether it wasn't all just a lame joke.

It was the officer who, wittingly or unwittingly, elicited further information on this point:

"What score should we award Mr. SchrummSchrumm on the Psychological Aptitude Test?" he asked, darting the excursionist a glance that was not without malice.

"That doesn't depend upon me," said the director. "Besides, all's not yet said and done. I've taken a shine to this young man and have decided to give him one last chance ... Look here," he said, turning to SchrummSchrumm in a friendly manner, "were you paying close attention to my explanation?"

"Very close."

"Good. Now, what can we say with certainty at this juncture? Nothing, save that each of the elements we've cited in support of our respective hypotheses is open to two competing interpretations. To me, they prove that this is the Holy Director photographed on a knoll in Eden; to you, that this is your Allright photographed on a rise near Mahasky ... Do we agree so far? Then here's what I propose. This photograph contains an element neither of us has yet made use of. And this element, rather remarkably, differs from the rest in that it is *not* open to dual interpretations. Find this original element and use it to prove to me, irrefutably, that this is really the Holy Director and not your Allright, as you formerly believed. Find this element for me and I'll give you top marks on your Psychological Aptitude Test #4."

"Hmm," said SchrummSchrumm. "I think I've got it."

"Ah! Have you now?" said the old man, preparing himself to hang on SchrummSchrumm's next words. "Go on, then! I'm listening."

“Would it be the age of the central figure? That’s a piece of evidence all the more worthy of our interest because it effectively refutes the hypothesis of an alternate identity for this person.”

“The age of the central figure!” echoed the old man. “You’ve found it! Bravo! Keep pursuing that train of thought, Mr. SchrummSchrumm, and I’ll award you the maximum score.”

“It’s a question, then, of determining the central figure’s age. Well, he’s undoubtedly a man of great spiritual maturity. He must have a broad tolerance for others, since we see that, despite his rank, he allows his two inferiors not only to be photographed in his company, but to lean familiarly on his shoulders. And his face is more than usually lined. Nevertheless, he’s relatively young. I think we can say he’s over thirty but under forty. There you have it.”

The old man didn’t answer right away. He didn’t seem displeased, per se, but perhaps a little taken aback. The officer gulped, though he was doing his best to hide his astonishment.

“Thirty-five years, or a little more!” said the old man finally, with a laugh—a laugh that rang hollow. “You don’t really think so, do you? Tell me you’re joking!”

“No, I’m not joking,” said SchrummSchrumm.

“Then you’ve made a mistake. Allow me to assist you. I’m not talking about his apparent age, I’m talking about his real age. Careful now! Those are two very different things. To help you onto the right track, I can give you a little hint: the central figure, which is to say our Holy Director, is he thirty-five or is he sixty-five? Does he belong to the same generation as his companions, or is he their senior? Concentrate, this is crucial.”

“The central figure is thirty-five, real age. Though I do admit he might appear older at first viewing,” said SchrummSchrumm in a firm, clear voice.

He had a sense things were about to turn ugly but hadn't been able to prevent himself giving this answer.

"Then according to you, our Holy Director is thirty-five but looks sixty, is that it?" hissed the old man, and when SchrummSchrumm nodded, he said, "Well, I'm telling you he's sixty but looks thirty-five. I administer this oral exam on a regular basis, and this is the first time I've come across an excursionist so stubborn . . . Admit you made a mistake. Understand that your answer could have serious consequences. Lastly, consider this one final hint I'm going to give you: the Holy Director, by design, has himself photographed in such a way that viewers' varying estimates of his age divide the adherents of each interpretation into opposing camps. I mean that people who look at him either think he's their own age, which explains why you put him at thirty and I at sixty, or the age they'd like him to be. And this is the point I want to underline for you: there's some reason—unknown to me, obviously—that's causing you to make this mistake. This is how you can be acting in good faith even while committing the most egregious of errors."

"Yet another brilliant commentary," said SchrummSchrumm. "But I don't think it applies in my case. I insist: the central figure is a young man of thirty who looks sixty."

"Are you implying that I'm deliberately, or—what would be far worse—unintentionally making the Holy Director older than he is?" replied the old man in a tone that had become unendurable. "I will ask you to kindly hold your tongue. It is I who am in the right. And that is because I cannot be wrong."

"Fine," said SchrummSchrumm with bitterness. "I won't say another word. I assume I've definitively flunked the test?"

"Definitively."

"Will my flunking Psychological Aptitude Test #4 have any impact on my departure for the Quicksands?" asked SchrummSchrumm.

But the two men were already shutting the door on him, as if in their eyes he no longer existed.

IV

Announcements were regularly posted on a bulletin board in the main lobby. They were invariably—no doubt on purpose—put up at the busiest times of day, either just before or just after meals. Two sentries who were never seen in any other circumstances stood watch over the sudden mobs these postings incited. There was shouting, shoving, fighting, and a number of excursionists would inevitably have to be rushed to the infirmary after being trampled, wounded, or having their throats slashed, though the culprits could never be identified. For all that, the announcements in question were of little interest: Captain So-and-So was proud father to a seventh baby girl, or the Fellowship for a Greater Understanding of the Gospels was organizing a public talk. There was never any mention of the "symbolism" or "topography" courses promised at their arrival, nor of any upcoming departures for the Quicksands. Everyone was dying of boredom and had nothing to allay their impatience but dreary games of dominos, evenings of charades, and the depressing tales of their amorous adventures. SchrummSchrumm had now been in Misunderstanding for a week.

A small ray of hope entered his life the afternoon Krikri came to ask if he could "enlist the aid of Mr. Excursionist's literary talents" and gave him a few handwritten pages to review. SchrummSchrumm could hardly contain his excitement when he realized that this was one of the daily reports the sergeant was required to file. But disillusionment swiftly set in. The report was an assemblage of the most idiotic drivel imaginable. It detailed the chemical composition and alcohol content of his eau de cologne. It recorded how many yawns and sighs he had been observed to make in a given hour. On such-and-such a night he'd snored. On such-and-such a morning he'd awakened in good spirits, while the day before he'd awakened grumpy ... SchrummSchrumm hotly resented Krikri for inflicting this disappointment on him. The sergeant did not solicit his help again.

It was around this time that SchrummSchrumm decided to stop going downstairs. He kept to his room, lying in bed, hatching schemes so far-fetched that he soon fell asleep. Naturally, having napped all day, he slept badly at night, though he heard no more strange noises. This was how he awoke one morning with a specific idea in mind well before the loudspeaker was due to bray out its daily prayers. He dressed hurriedly, in a fever of anticipation, opened his door without a sound, and congratulated himself on his initiative when he found both the lobby and the area near the hall to the "private wing" empty. Not that this wing was his objective. He meant to go to the end of the seventeen-door hallway and from there explore the part of Misunderstanding as yet unknown to him.

He'd already reached the midpoint of the long, dark corridor when a cough—so discreet it seemed to have been done solely to attract his attention—made his heart nearly burst in his chest. He flattened himself against the wall. But there was the rasp of a cigarette lighter and SchrummSchrumm was stunned to see standing before him the little old man with the yellow beard, the director-cum-archaeologist Bushido.

"Good Lord!" said SchrummSchrumm. "What are you doing here?"

"Waiting for you," he answered with a kindly smile.

"I forgot to mention at our last meeting, sir," began SchrummSchrumm in an unconvincingly conversational tone, "that I'm a fervent admirer of all things archaeological."

"So I noticed," said the old man approvingly. "Which is why I was waiting for you."

"You're no longer angry at me, then?"

"A test is a test," he said flatly. "Speaking of things archaeological, would you like me to show you one of my finest discoveries?"

He paused, as if to give his proposal time to sink in. When SchrummSchrumm made no reply, he pulled him by the sleeve toward one of the last doors in the hall. He walked with an extraordinarily silent and supple step. Taking out a key, he unlocked the door.

"Voilà!" he said, as the door swung back.

The first thing that struck SchrummSchrumm was the stench. He was looking into what appeared to be a cave or grotto, dimly lit by a single lamp. The walls were coated with an indefinable pink substance. The color wasn't paint, though. Stalactites of the same hue, and others that were yellowish, hung from the ceiling. Rising from the floor were clouds of exceptionally fetid steam, so that in addition to its terrible odor, the room was also notable for a degree of heat that put it in sharp contrast with the cool hallway outside. On the far side of the grotto, four steps carved into this revolting pink material led up to a horizontal aperture just large enough for a man to squeeze through, offering a glimpse of a tiny corner of sky.

As he stared around uncomprehendingly, SchrummSchrumm pinched his nose—an ineffectual measure—and willed himself not to vomit. The old man didn't seem the least bit bothered by the smell.

"You're standing in one of the most ancient public urinals on the planet," said the old man gravely. "More precisely, according to my research, I think I can say with confidence that this is the Primordial Pissoir, built by the great Nastarz himself, whose date of construction is lost in the mists of time."

"The Original Pissoir!" said SchrummSchrumm.

"Exactly! I'll tell you how I arrived at this conclusion. Scores of centuries ago, after the great Nastarz had founded Misunderstanding, his successors, naturally enough, erected a number of other edifices, among which was the Factory. The Factory still exists, my dear young man—bear that in mind—and is where we send excursionists who grow bored with life in Misunderstanding: there they engage in metalworking, which keeps them occupied while they await their departure for the Quicksands. But I digress. A brief summary will suffice for you to understand how I determined the whereabouts of our pissoir here. Eden, my dear young man, is before you; one enters it through this opening. The Factory is situated exactly two kilometers behind us, which is to say, at one end of an imaginary line connecting the garden to the Factory. It used to be customary for excursionists, just before reporting to the Factory and again upon leaving, to visit Eden—at least during the first few centuries after Nastarz—to gather fruit and disport themselves, and they used the same opportunity to stop for a piss, and the place where they pissed was this very pissoir in which we now find ourselves. Conclusion? This pissoir does indeed date back to Nastarz's time and was used for many centuries by prehistoric excursionists when they traveled from Eden to the Factory and vice versa."

"Incredible!" said SchrummSchrumm. "But why is it no longer used?"

"An unhappy event intervened, my dear young man. Only a few short centuries after the resurrection and ascension of Nastarz, rumors had already begun to circulate that Eden was bewitched. Its fruits had been poisoned, they said, and its paths hid deadly snares. From that point on, the pissoir rapidly fell into disuse and people went elsewhere to urinate. I am today one of the very few archaeologists familiar with this important landmark. There you have it! You now know as much as I do."

"I'm profoundly grateful to you for having shown me this pissoir, sir," said SchrummSchrumm in what he hoped was a convincing tone. "Of course, I'm not nearly well enough instructed in the arcane symbols of the Excursion to plumb, as you do, the deeper hidden meanings behind all these things. Even so, it's undeniable that these pink deposits and stalactites can be none other than the urinary accretions built up over many centuries of practical use. And I must say, it really makes you think, knowing that thousands upon thousands of excursionists have pissed against these walls, thus leaving behind them irrefutable and indelible evidence of their vocation."

"Bravo!" cried the old man. "You've put your finger on an extremely crucial point. Let me tell you something we, the public officials of Misunderstanding, have seen borne out time and time again: it is in the act of urinating that excursionists rediscover the meaning of true excursionistic enlightenment. That's right! Clearing the seven obstacles that separate them from the Quicksands, flying off to the peaceful heavens of their innocent childhoods, they momentarily escape all the questions, the incomprehension, the impatience, and instead frolic in imagination through the golden fields of a briefly recaptured happiness."

The old man reached an extraordinary pitch of excitement and could no longer contain himself as he spoke these words. He was practically foaming at the mouth, and SchrummSchrumm felt a little frightened by this unexpected burst of lyricism. But it ended as suddenly as it had started.

"Well?" said the man meaningfully, nodding toward the passageway to Eden. "What do you intend to do?"

They had moved closer to the aperture, and SchrummSchrumm felt a delicious draft of fresh air that did him enormous good. He saw trees, flowerbeds, and the sky above.

"It's a garden, nothing more. And there's no one there," said SchrummSchrumm, feigning indifference.

"It'll take only a few minutes to see what you have to see," said the old man with a canny smile.

"Is there something in particular I have to see?"

"Of course there is! You're going to see the Holy Director, young man. Or, to be more exact, a manifestation of the Holy Director. A mirage!"

"What does that mean?" said SchrummSchrumm, concerned.

"We're coming to that, we're coming to that. Excursionists learn in their symbolism courses that no one has ever looked upon a Holy Director's face. The fact is explained in various ways: either he acts through intermediaries, or he's merely a myth, in which case the man people see is just an ordinary actor whose role consists in embodying the powers and virtues traditionally ascribed to the Holy Director. This, of course, is a bold hypothesis, considered blasphemous by many and heretical by a large majority. Support for this interpretation comes from one of the sacred texts of the Gospel of Misunderstanding, in which the Holy Director is described as living somewhere in the city center, omnipotent, yes, but informal, and, above all: anonymous. In any case, myth or no myth, the thing to remember is that it's never the Holy Director you see, only one of his manifestations. Those who think they know the Holy Director because they've seen him in person are committing not only an error but a sin. Thus, even if you do presently enter Eden and meet the Holy Director—as there is every reason to hope you will—you should know how things stand and remind yourself that it's only a manifestation."

SchrummSchrumm found much in this speech to astonish him, but at these last words he could no longer hold back:

"I don't understand. If people never see anything but manifestations of the Holy Director, how can they know him when they encounter him?"

"Oh, excellent point!" said the old man sarcastically. "Didn't I prove to you just last week, through simple deduction and without having ever seen him myself, that there are sure-fire means of recognizing the Holy Director? He smiles, he's sixty-five but looks thirty-five, and he's always accompanied by Jules and Jim, our two executioners."

"My God," said SchrummSchrumm, sweat breaking out on his forehead. "We're not starting this again, are we?"

"We are. This is the highly interesting test you must undergo. Psychological Aptitude Test #5." The old man took out a sheet of paper and handed it to SchrummSchrumm, who didn't even bother to read it. He was disgusted with himself for not having seen where the hypocritical director was going with this. The old man, meanwhile, calmly delivered his final instructions.

"You will now proceed into Eden, my dear Mr. SchrummSchrumm. The place that concerns you, and where you will have every chance of encountering the Holy Director, is easy to recognize: a house on a little island surrounded by swamp, in the middle of a garden ringed by a low wall."

"A garden within Eden, how strange!"

"Strange? On the contrary, I consider it the most natural thing in the world. This place is in fact the first construction built by Nastarz for himself and his people. It is the true heart of Misunderstanding, and we call it Nastarz City. If you think for a moment, you'll see that Nastarz City must be cast in the very image, albeit on a reduced scale, of Misunderstanding and the Quicksands. Nastarz City reproduces the topography of the Misunderstanding-Quicksands complex, though in what I would call an inverse fashion. This is closely bound up with the symbolism of the seven rings of cigarette smoke as explained to you by the Smoke-Blowers, or Wardens of the Forest: just as Misunderstanding has Eden at its center and is surrounded by a Wall, Forests, and Quicksands, so Nastarz City is surrounded by a mini-wall, a modest garden, and has at its center a small portion of the Quicksands, in the midst of which, on a knoll, sits Nastarz's original house. This knoll, and the layout of Nastarz City more broadly speaking, are already far more familiar to you than you'd have us believe, since you possess a photograph of them. A photograph you've entitled 'Allright, flanked by his two assistants, on a rise overlooking Mahasky.' It will, however, be very dark beneath the towering trees, but you'll see well enough to find your way. Be careful: there are sentries lurking in the bushes, steel-jaw traps you might stumble into, and land mines that could go off underfoot at any moment. But let's not get carried away. As I've said before, these are, after all, only rumors. So many legends have grown up around the subject—fantastically ancient legends whose origins are obscure—that the whole of Eden has gradually acquired a sacred, supernatural reputation. Don't be unduly frightened!"

"If that's how it is," said SchrummSchrumm, "why would I go? What will they think back at the hotel? They'll notice my absence and I'll be punished."

The director brushed aside this objection.

"Don't worry about a thing. It's all been arranged."

"It's all been arranged?" said SchrummSchrumm, turning around. But the little old man had already nipped back out into the hallway and was shutting the door behind him. SchrummSchrumm insinuated himself into the aperture, taking care not to rub against the oozing, yellowish deposits. He stepped out into Eden.

V

The fresh air did him good. The winding, overgrown paths intersected each other in unpredictable ways, and the tops of the trees were lost to view far above him. The park was enormous, giving the visitor the horrible impression of wandering in circles. He walked for a while, and when he stopped to get his bearings he could see no sign of any man-made structures in the vicinity. There was no light; the trees formed an imposing rampart. The only indication that people sometimes came here to relax was a wrought-iron table and overturned chairs at the edge of a clearing.

If not for the faint echo of raised voices just then, he would have continued on his way, unsuspecting. Who were these men? Guards? In any case, he looked and immediately recognized the site described by Director Bushido. The strange little dwelling on an island in the middle of a swamp, surrounded by a garden whose wicket gate he had just pushed open, could be none other than Nastarz City.

Its architecture and ornamentation were marvelous to behold. Delicate golden colonnades supported crystal balconies; jade arabesques adorned the walls where statues of pink and black granite were interspersed with sets of ebony shutters. Everything was charmingly diminutive, like a miniature palace. In the garden, a harmonious alternation of rosebushes and rhododendrons with carrots and salad greens attested to the exercise of a highly refined horticultural art. Special care had been taken to showcase one stunted, wizened apple tree. A tiny footbridge led to the island. Like the house itself, it was in a state of advanced dilapidation, but restoration work had been undertaken that had clearly tried to respect its stupendous antiquity. Loose boards had been secured with gold thread, for example, and the whole construction had been given a coat of pink paint.

SchrummSchrumm wasted little time hesitating. He tiptoed through the vegetable garden, crossed the tiny footbridge, and pressed his nose against one of the house's splendid ground-floor windows. As expected, the place was dusty and deserted, the ceiling full of cobwebs: the entire building had been abandoned. He walked along the side of the house. The conversation had been running on in a normal rhythm all this time, and he was almost certain no one had heard him.

When he reached the corner of the house, however, it was all he could do to stifle an exclamation of surprise. The three men leaning against the veranda balustrade engaged in loud discussion were not, in fact, unknown to him. They had an old-fashioned, even slightly ridiculous air about them, an impression that was no doubt due to their outdated and rather shabby clothing. The smallest man, in particular—who stood in the center of the group—was a sight to move any observer to tears, with his top hat, his bow tie knotted around a high, starched collar, and his baggy trousers puddling in folds around his down-at-heel shoes. It was more than a little astonishing to encounter, here on a veranda in Nastarz City, the one and only Allright. His face, of course, wasn't clearly distinguishable, but that gentle, enigmatic smile could belong to no one but Allright, mayor of Mahasky and person of noble lineage. Now the three men stopped talking, and, as if posing for an invisible photographer, the taller two placed their hands familiarly on the central man's shoulders, smiling smug, affected smiles as they did so. What was Allright doing on this veranda, and at such an early hour? Why did the walls of Nastarz City and the lines of this strange little palace so completely resemble the ramparts of Mahasky? What was going on? Was it possible this man wasn't Allright but in fact the Holy Director of Misunderstanding, out for a morning stroll around his Eden, just as the little old man Bushido had declared and proven to him? Was it possible? No! It *wasn't* possible!

"Allright?" called SchrummSchrumm in a soft, gentle voice. "Oh, how happy I am to see you here! I've been searching for you for so long."

Then, as Allright appeared not to have heard him, he spoke up:

"Allright!" he repeated. "It is you, isn't it? Please answer me, I implore you."

"What's that?" said one of the two men flanking Allright. "Who's talking?"

"*We're* talking!" said the other man, apparently baffled by the question.

"Jim," said the first man, "someone's here."

"Let's go get him," they agreed, and seemed to be gearing up to give chase.

SchrummSchrumm didn't wait around to see more. He beat a hasty retreat over the footbridge, which groaned under his weight, bolted out of Nastarz City as fast as his legs could carry him, and hid behind a large tree trunk. There were now several men sitting on the wrought-iron chairs at the edge of the clearing. They'd only just arrived. Clearly they hadn't noticed anything out of the ordinary: they were smoking and chatting in a leisurely manner, their submachine guns resting in the grass at their feet. But when Jules and Jim—for who could these two men be, if not Jules and Jim?—came tearing out of Nastarz City crying "Stop! Stop!" they snatched up their weapons and began running pell-mell in all directions.

"What'd I tell you? There really *is* someone here!" said one of the executioners as the two paused for breath near the garden gate. SchrummSchrumm could see his meaty fingers curled around the grip of his revolver.

"Unbelievable," said the other. "He's going to find out there's a price to be paid for that."

"Where is he?" shouted one of the frantic submachine-gun men.

"Over there!" said the two executioners, gesturing vaguely. "Start beating the bushes."

A few interminable seconds ticked by. There could be no doubt that the guards had the most malevolent of intentions toward him. They were methodically searching every bush and thicket, calling out to one another, "How's it going, pal?" "Going good over here!" "Good here, too!" Nonetheless, SchrummSchrumm was sure they had no idea where he was hidden. He was keeping very still. He was even feeling fairly calm, all things considered. A horn somewhere sounded *toot-toot* and a sickening odor—perhaps from a smokestack at the Factory mentioned by Director Bushido—pervaded the park. Jules, Jim, and the other guards momentarily halted their search. But at that precise moment an event occurred that made SchrummSchrumm lose his wits completely. Suddenly, amid a noisy tumult of snapping branches, three colossal shadows appeared on the far side of the clearing as if they'd come out of nowhere or sprung from the earth like diabolical jack-in-the-boxes. It was three horsemen on spirited chargers. They let out thundering cries of "Avaunt! Avaunt!" as soon as they spotted the guards, who were signaling to them with energetic arm motions. About thirty meters separated the horsemen from their colleagues. They didn't dismount or even rein in their steeds. On the contrary, they maintained their terrifying gallop, shouting something that sounded like "*Viva l'excursion!*" as they barreled full tilt in SchrummSchrumm's direction.

He could see them bearing down on him. They were standing in their stirrups, their eyes flashing, bellowing "Avaunt! Avaunt!" in terrible, irresistible voices. He felt the beasts' hot breath on his face and saw the gleam of buckles and insignias through the clouds of exhalation streaming from their nostrils as these astonishing men, seemingly without noticing him, passed within a hairsbreadth of his hiding place. He fully expected them to crash headlong into the nearest tree, but they either knew these woods like the backs of their hands or were accustomed to this kind of sport, because they vanished as quickly as they'd come, while SchrummSchrumm, throwing caution to the winds, made a desperate, panicked break for it. The sound of feet running behind told him others were in pursuit. The guards were panting and swearing at him, shouting "Faster! Faster!" or "Tallyho!" He was a good thirty meters ahead of them, sprinting for all he was worth, indifferent to the twigs and branches slashing at his face. He must have gone on like this at full gallop for some distance, running at random. At last he came across a villa and, hoping against hope, tried the door. It was unlocked. Inside was a large table laid with place settings as if in preparation for a meal. At the back of the room stood a cupboard and a dusty staircase that probably led up to a mezzanine. Judging that he had no time for the stairs, SchrummSchrumm opted for the cupboard and slipped inside it just as his pursuers reached the villa and halted. He heard them outside, marveling over his sudden disappearance:

"Maybe he's in there," said one breathless voice.

"No, the dining hall's always locked."

There was some further whispering and then footsteps moving away. But just as his hopes were rising again, he heard the door open and someone walked purposefully toward him. "My God!" murmured SchrummSchrumm, sweat trickling down his face. The awful predicament in which he now found himself bore a disconcerting resemblance to the library incident from his second day in Misunderstanding. The man stopped in front of the cupboard.

"I know you're in there, Mr. SchrummSchrumm. Don't be afraid, I'm not going to turn you in."

When SchrummSchrumm didn't respond, the voice went on:

"Allow me to congratulate you on the score you've just earned on Psychological Aptitude Test #6. I'm extremely impressed with your performance."

"Who are you? Are you alone?"

"Yes, quite alone. I'm Jules, Jim's colleague, one of the two executioners."

"So you were in Nastarz City just now?"

The man affirmed that this was the case.

"And you were chasing me?"

"I was. Boy, can you run!"

"Listen," said SchrummSchrumm, opening the door a cautious crack, "if you're Jules and you were chasing me, that means you had orders to catch me. So why aren't you turning me in right now?"

"Simple," said Jules. "We had orders to chase you, but we also had orders *not* to catch you. In other words, we had to make sure everything happened exactly as outlined in Test #6's plan of operation. The plan calls for you to hide in this very cupboard. But I'm the only one in on the plan. Even my colleague Jim doesn't know about it."

"What's going to happen?"

"Nothing. The others are going to turn up in a minute. You'll stay hidden here till all of us are gone. Then you'll calmly go back to your hotel."

SchrummSchrumm didn't doubt the truth of the executioner's words. But this logic—according to which an event could be fully planned in advance even though everyone involved behaved as if none of it were planned—this logic, if it could be called such, utterly confounded him.

"You mean to say," he croaked, "everything went well?"

"Smooth as silk," said the man.

"One thing's certain, at least: they told me Eden was bewitched. That was a lie."

"Oh, Mr. SchrummSchrumm! How can you say such a thing? It all went smoothly, yes, and I'm happy for you, believe me. But it could just as easily have gone very, very badly. Even with us doing all we could to help you, there were still very real dangers for you here in Eden."

"What dangers?"

Jules only winced.

"The others are coming," he said. "We can't finish this now. We'll have to meet up later. Try to attend the execution of a semi-wholesaler in small hardware supplies scheduled in about fifteen days. It's going to be a beautiful ceremony, just wait and see."

"Come on, Jules! The Bavarian-lager delivery guy's here with a shipment. There's a few free bottles in it for us if we help him unload."

"Be right there!" called Jules.

They all went away, leaving the room empty but the lights still on. He eventually found himself back in the narrow rear courtyard that ran behind the seventeen-door hallway. He entered through the library and then, via the deserted hallway, made his way back to the hotel lobby. He was just in the nick of time. As he regained his room, all the loudspeakers in the building came to life at once: "Rise and shine! Rise and shine! . . . Attention! Attention! We shall now recite Prayer Number One together . . ." He dropped to his knees. Would he ever understand this excursion's many absurdities and paradoxes? When the reading from the Gospels was over, Krikri entered as usual.

"Be ready in an hour," he said cheerily. "Assembly in the covered courtyard. You'll be very pleased, Mr. SchrummSchrumm: today's your first training session!"

He shut the door behind him. He hadn't seemed to notice that SchrummSchrumm was fully clothed, his face covered in scratches, and his hands and feet spattered with mud—not to mention his wild, hunted look.

VI

An hour later, the excursionists were assembled under the roof of the deserted inner courtyard. Four ominous-looking Sunday Quicksands Excursion Company tour buses were standing by, two packed with guards, two empty. This was definitely a rule of theirs, which applied in every situation: always have at least as many guards as excursionists. A clerk called roll and the procession directors herded the men into the two empty buses, cracking their whips over the heads of the stragglers. The ponderous leaves of the Great Iron Gate were opened with no ceremony at all, everyone was blindfolded, the metal window shutters were pulled down, and they drove for a considerable time. Then the shutters were raised, the blindfolds removed, and the four vehicles disgorged their passengers.

It was a charming spot. The sun was radiant; the very atmosphere was radiant. Joyful chirpings of birds, gentle bubbling of a brook. The latter, however, was nowhere to be seen. Nor were there any trees. Where, then, was the chirping coming from? SchrummSchrumm noticed, out on the horizon, a forest of poplars swaying lazily in the breeze. But it wouldn't be possible to hear birds as far away as that. Moreover, there was no breeze. And the trees in question, despite their great distance, seemed phenomenally tall. Was this the Enchanted Poplar Forest? SchrummSchrumm shrugged.

They'd been waiting for quite some time—the excursionists contemplating the landscape (peaceful and reassuring in spite of its oddities), the guards standing a little apart and talking among themselves—when three more vehicles pulled up: a small car followed by a luxury tour bus and a flatbed truck loaded with crates. Thirty or so men in black leather trench coats and red leather gloves descended from the bus. SchrummSchrumm heard a whisper run through the group that these men were Accredited Drowners. But what were Accredited Drowners? No one seemed to know. From the car emerged a high-ranking officer and three members of his general staff. The guards who'd ridden on the first two buses saluted the officer as he walked over to take up a position in front of the assembled excursionists. SchrummSchrumm was given to understand that this was Colonel Red-Bartlett.

"Are we going to the Quicksands?" a few people asked.

"No, my friends."

A chorus of protests rose up, but the officer seemed to have anticipated this response: he waited until the grumbling had died down enough that he could make himself heard. Not without a slight motion of his hands expressive of how uncalled-for the preceding outcry had been, he began to address them in a loud, clear voice:

"Excursionists first class, excursionists second class, excursionists, dear children, beloved little lambs: I understand your disappointment. You're all impatient to go to the Quicksands. This is quite natural. Therefore, allow me to explain. The Quicksands Excursion, as you know, is no walk in the park: venturing in unprepared is out of the question; it would be as foolhardy as jumping into the sea without knowing how to swim. We are here for the purpose of putting you through some training exercises that will make you able and competent excursionists. Do you see what we have here? These are the training quicksands. They've been selected because, setting aside the factors of danger and difficulty—since these marshes present markedly less of both—they are an excellent analogue of the real Quicksands. Observe them well!"

A stunned silence followed. One lone voice, piping up from the back row of excursionists, asked respectfully:

"What quicksands? There aren't any quicksands here!"

The colonel hesitated a moment. He blasted the insolent man with a glare like a lightning bolt, then turned his head to see for himself. Shock and disbelief spread over his face.

"Indeed," he said. "Where have the training quicksands gone?"

"They're behind the buses," said one of his general staff.

Red-Bartlett emitted a growl of rage. He ordered the vehicles to be moved aside on the double, and when they were, the excursionists saw that they were standing about twenty meters from a putrid, stagnant pond, dried-out in some places but primarily swampy. It was more or less oval in shape, terminating at one end—the end nearest the assembled excursionists—in a tongue of murky water straddled by a crudely built wooden pier on pilings. The terrible state of repair of this construction, the unreassuring look of the pilings, the absence of railings, and the rotten planks: all these seemed to imply that the pier had been derelict for years. Yet it was painted pink, and the paint looked fairly fresh. There were little pots of flowers—begonias or chrysanthemums—positioned with care at the top of the steps leading up to the pier deck. "Strange birds, strange poplars, strange sands, strange pier!" thought SchrummSchrumm as he gazed at the slick mud glistening around the base of the pilings. The group descended the bank and stopped at the water's edge. Once again the colonel called for everyone's attention.

"Here is your training ground, my friends," he said, indicating the whole sorry structure with a sweeping, lyrical gesture. "Oh, I know! Some of you are already thinking: 'That's just a duck pond with a few two-bit patches of wet sand!' And you're absolutely right. Nothing you see here compares with the challenges you'll have to face on Excursion Day. But that doesn't mean this isn't a valuable training exercise all the same. It will provide you with both an introduction to the Quicksands and first-hand experience you can draw upon during your Excursion. So let's get down to business. Our objectives in putting you through this exercise are threefold. We want to improve your balance, firstly, which is the primary skill you'll need in order to take part in the expedition. This pier is pretty standard fare, except that it's extremely narrow and the planks are in bad condition. You'll have to demonstrate your balance and coordination by getting to the end and back without falling. Look sharp, because it's no cakewalk. Far from it. If you do manage to get all the way across and back safe and sound, count yourself lucky! You'll be spared, at least for today, the singularly novelistic anxiety of getting stuck and sinking. Which leads us to objective number two: we want to bring home to you—in the most concrete, visceral terms—that if you personally have never fallen victim to an accident, you might *think* you know what it's like, but you really don't know the first thing about it. This exercise will enable you to experience, in the most intensely realistic way possible, those indescribable moments just before you begin to go under, and those even more indescribable moments when you feel yourself being sucked downward by the treacherous mire. Believe you me, once you've lived through those unforgettable minutes a few times, you'll have a good, healthy fear of the Quicksands, which is the cornerstone of prudent behavior. This brings us to the final objective, namely teaching you what and what not to do when an accident strikes. Here again, I'm sure some of you will be saying, 'But we already know what to do!' Don't kid yourselves. A feature peculiar to the Quicksands is that any poor soul who gets caught in them on his own is lost. That's why we never venture into the danger zones except in relatively large groups. The question most relevant to today's training is, What moves do you need to make in order to save yourself? Well?" He glanced around the group. "Who can tell me?"

A few reasonably intelligent guesses were thrown out. Find a foothold or something to grab onto. And if there isn't anything? Try crawling toward the nearest bank. Preposterous! The impossibility of such an operation was conclusively proved to them. They were out of ideas.

"Now you understand," said the colonel. "You mustn't move at all, because any movement, no matter how slight, can only hasten your end. Do you imagine, perhaps, that it would be helpful to scream and holler and wave your arms in the air? With the muscular tension and psychological disturbance this would entail? Of course not! It should come as no surprise when I tell you that if you fall in—as some of you inevitably will today—all that's required of you is courage, determination, and presence of mind. Listen carefully. You calmly allow yourself to sink. You keep a cool head. You quickly take your pulse to make sure your heart rate's not too high. You stay in the present moment—immerse yourself in it, so to speak—that moment unlike any other, when a slow death by drowning is potentially overtaking you. And you do these things, above all, without making a peep! Good! Then, but only when you're actually in the process of being sucked under by the devouring sands, you call for help, once—only once!—and, if at all possible, you do so in a distinctive and original manner (for example: 'Save me! Tra-la-la-la!'). Next? Next you wait for the Accredited Drowners, who will spring into action. In the unlikely event that they're slightly delayed, you mustn't lose your nerve. It will be a good exercise in self-control. You might take the opportunity to compose a quatrain in praise of the Holy Director (as I myself did the first time I became stuck) ... But there's no need to dwell on this improbable eventuality. We were speaking of the moment when the Accredited Drowners rush to your aid. Firmly planted on their strong, muscular legs, they'll toss you a lasso. If your hands are free, you'll get a firm grip on it and hang on for dear life. They'll soon have you out. If you're already in up to your neck, they'll adroitly loop the lasso around your head, they'll pull—gently, so as not to strangle you—and in five minutes' time, Bob's your uncle! The important thing is not to interfere with the Accredited Drowners' work in any way, because they represent your salvation, and all it would take is one sudden move from you at the wrong moment to find yourself strangled after all, despite their best efforts ... By the way, let me take a quick sidebar here to tell you a little more about the extraordinary men who make up the Accredited Drowners. I've hand-picked each and every one of them for size and strength. These are genuine athletes in whom you can place your absolute trust. They've passed very tough exams to earn their diplomas. To put a human face on these invaluable assistants, I'll to introduce you to their chief, Warrant Officer Bubu. Bubu! Come on up here a minute so our friends can get a look at you and admire your magnificent physique!"

The crowd parted to let Bubu through. He peeled off his black leather trench coat and red gloves. Underneath he was wearing black silk tights with a crimson death's-head design. He pulled a black ski mask over his head. Having covered his face, he struck a bodybuilding pose and held it, changing his position at intervals so the group could admire him properly. After two or three minutes of this exhibition, he left the way he'd come and resumed his place among the others. Red-Bartlett was about to continue his lecture when a member of his staff came running up, trying to get his attention. Whatever the message, he didn't want to say it out loud in front of the excursionists, so he just pointed toward the truck where the last of the crates were being unloaded. SchrummSchrumm saw that the Accredited Drowners had already opened several of them and taken out lassos, which they were twirling above their heads.

"Well, Fasola?" said the colonel impatiently. "What is it now? Speak up, man!"

"There are no gaffs!" blurted Fasola. "We left them in Misunderstanding."

For a few moments, Red-Bartlett seemed completely floored by this news.

"No gaffs . . ." he repeated in a small, lost voice.

But after staring into the distance for a second or two, he seemed struck by sudden inspiration. He beckoned to Fasola and whispered something in his ear.

"Excellent idea, Colonel!" said Fasola, and trotted back over to his colleagues, with whom he exchanged a few excited words. Some twenty guards set off in the direction of the Poplar Forest. The colonel raised his voice to address the excursionists once more:

"In conclusion, dear children, I appeal to your good sense as well as to your goodwill. Throw yourselves wholeheartedly into this training, even if our methods seem a little rough-and-ready at first, and even if you don't understand all the reasons behind them. Later you'll come to see how right we were to act as we did, and you'll be glad you trusted me and the Accredited Drowners. Ultimately, in return for our devoted service, we ask nothing but your love. Because we love you, gentle friends. We do! Love us back! I'll leave you with this: Chin up! And may the best man win!"

These closing words, delivered with such conviction—the colonel had placed one hand on his heart, and with the other had unashamedly wiped away a tear—won over the excursionists, and they cheered lustily, "Viva Colonel Red-Bartlett! Viva the Quicksands!" Sustained applause followed, and when silence finally returned, the guards had returned, too. They brought with them gaffs cut from the trunks of poplar saplings: smooth, straight, and solid. "Pretty puny trunks for poplars that are supposed to be so tall," thought SchrummSchrumm. Fasola and Bubu presented themselves before the colonel.

"Well, is everything ready now?" he asked.

"Everything's ready," said Fasola. "Best gaffs we've ever had."

"Still, it would've been much better if the other gaffs hadn't been left behind in Misunderstanding," said Bubu, affecting to speak only to the colonel. There was clearly a simmering rivalry between him and Fasola.

"Come now, gentlemen! Let's not snipe at each other on such a beautiful day," said Red-Bartlett.

Fasola and Bubu hung their heads. SchrummSchrumm noticed that the Accredited Drowners, without waiting for their leader, had taken up positions atop large cement blocks that must have been resting directly on the bed of the pond, which wasn't especially deep at this point. They were arranged in rows on either side of the pier as well as beneath it, each man with a lasso in one hand and a gaff in the other. He regretted having given his attention to the conversation between the colonel, Bubu, and Fasola instead of watching to see how the Accredited Drowners had reached their places. Now it was too late. A whistle sounded, and the guards separated the excursionists into three squads of ten, lined up single file in front of the pier steps. SchrummSchrumm was in squad three.

"Are you ready, entirely ready, absolutely ready?" Red-Bartlett inquired.

From all sides, the guards and Accredited Drowners responded in unison:

"We are perfectly ready!"

"That's the spirit!" cried Red-Bartlett. "Let the games begin, men!"

"Hooray!"

Squad one—surrounded and encouraged by the guards—hustled energetically up the steps. As soon as they were on the pier, however, their enthusiasm flagged; they hung back, fearing—with good reason—that they might fall into the sludge. This didn't faze the guards, who knew their job. They stopped offering vocal encouragement to the men at the front of the line and began pushing vigorously on those at the rear. Soon enough, what had to happen did happen. As the pier was too narrow to accommodate two excursionists walking abreast, the men being shoved fell awkwardly on those ahead of them, who tried to brace themselves against the backs of those further ahead. Like a house of cards, the entire squad eventually lost its balance and toppled comically off the pier, some to the right and others to the left. The last men in line hadn't advanced very far onto the deck and were the only ones able to extricate themselves unaided. Those in front had fallen from the middle of the pier, right where the muck looked deepest.

"Help! We're dying!" they howled, forgetting all Red-Bartlett's instructions about staying calm.

Their heads alone were above the slime. SchrummSchrumm was afraid they were about to go under, but the Accredited Drowners, either by slipping lassos around their necks or by supporting them with gaffs, maneuvered them gradually toward the pilings where they were hauled up one by one, trembling, dripping, and in shock.

"Squad two, your turn!" ordered Red-Bartlett.

The next ten men advanced to the pier. It was obvious that the guards were going to have a tougher time of it with this group, since the excursionists had been observing their methods and had seen them push their unfortunate colleagues. Once at the top of the stairs, they refused to go any further. The guards were forced to grab them and carry them bodily onto the deck. This would have been a fine idea if not that the guards themselves, by this very act, were now prevented from retreating back down the stairs, because the next excursionist in line was also being carried up by a guard. They had no choice but to make the precarious crossing along with their victims. They did well for the first two-thirds of the pier, with a guard between every two squad members, but then one excursionist started teetering dangerously and things happened exactly as before, with the entire line losing its balance, only this time there were as many guards in the mud as excursionists. The Accredited Drowners manifested an appalling partiality in their rescue efforts, fishing out their colleagues first while ignoring excursionists begging for help.

The colonel was infuriated at the sight of his subordinates tumbling into the mud in such an undignified manner.

"No! No! No! No!" he screamed like a man deranged. Pulling aside the guard in charge of squad three, he declared he would lead the exercise himself. It was SchrummSchrumm's turn on the pier.

"I'll show all of you what I'm made of! Let's go!" said Red-Bartlett.

They reached the steps just as the Accredited Drowners were pulling out the last survivors. They were in bad shape; some of them had spent so long in the sludge they could hardly breathe. The colonel waited until the Accredited Drowners were back in starting position. Then, boldly taking his place at the head of the column, he gave the order: "Forward, men!" The superseded squad leader, not to be outdone by his commanding officer, was right behind him. Last came the excursionists. SchrummSchrumm was fourth in line.

The colonel hadn't been lying about his experience. He progressed cautiously but rapidly, testing the planks two or three times before each step. The men coming after him had only to imitate his movements as precisely as possible. But fate seemed to have ordained that nothing would go right that day. All was well until one of the planks—which had supported the weight of several previous excursionists without incident—unexpectedly snapped. Other planks immediately gave way as well, and, as if a trap door had opened beneath their feet, the colonel, the squad leader, and all the excursionists dropped into the pond.

SchrummSchrumm had time to cry out once before mud filled his mouth, flooded his nostrils, and stung his eyes. He soon realized, however, that the marsh was barely more than shoulder deep. In any case, it couldn't be quicksand because he hadn't been pulled straight in; it was just very dirty water, which, contrary to the colonel's assertions, allowed for some freedom of movement. Around him, chaos was erupting. There was screaming and moaning; lassos whistled through the air and gaffs were being jabbed into the muck from all sides. Amid the uproar, one particular theme predominated: "Where's the colonel?" "Save the colonel!" "Colonel, where are you?" SchrummSchrumm heard a feeble "I'm here." It was too faint for the rescuers to have heard. The voice had come from behind one of the wooden pilings, and SchrummSchrumm finally spotted Red-Bartlett, who was making a heroic effort not to call out for help. He was in dire straits: he couldn't touch bottom, and though clinging to a piling, he was slipping inexorably further and further down. SchrummSchrumm managed to reach him and saw three lassos and two gaffs converge nearby. He secured the nearly unconscious colonel and, taking hold of a gaff, succeeded in pulling the officer free of the muck before being helped onto the bank himself.

Red-Bartlett came to fairly quickly; he'd sustained only a minor bump from his collision with the piling. As they were getting him out of his clothes, drying him off, and rubbing him down with eau de cologne, they told him how SchrummSchrumm had called for assistance and helped him out of the mud. He asked for this intrepid excursionist to be brought to him, and as soon as SchrummSchrumm stepped forward, the colonel embraced him warmly, calling him "my savior," and "my brave hero."

These expressions of friendship and gratitude were short-lived. ". . . Farewell, dear son," said the colonel, dismissing him. Fasola took down the hero's name in a little notebook, along with his identification number and the circumstances surrounding his heroic feat. Then SchrummSchrumm, somewhat disappointed, rejoined his companions in misfortune who, damp and shivering, were drying themselves in the sun. They'd spread their clothes on the ground and he did the same. Red-Bartlett was now talking to Bubu and Fasola, who seemed to be in agreement with whatever he was telling them. It was the latter who took it upon himself to break the unpleasant news to the group:

"You see now that it wasn't as bad as you thought! Nevertheless, Colonel Red-Bartlett is justly dissatisfied with your results and has decided that you will not be returning to Misunderstanding in the buses but will instead make the journey on foot. Anyway, a long walk will do you a world of good after the dunking you've just had . . ."

Everyone watched as Bubu, Fasola, and Red-Bartlett drove off in their car. The Accredited Drowners, after loading their gaffs and lassos onto the truck, climbed back aboard their luxury tour bus and departed, too. The other buses were driven away empty, leaving the guards stranded along with the excursionists. They were thus given the opportunity to share, albeit involuntarily, in the alleged benefits of the walk. The guards were too discouraged to maintain strict discipline and the troop straggled along in disarray. Some of the excursionists were still practically naked, others were just pulling on the last of their clothes, and those lagging behind were urged on with whips.

"Young man," said one excursionist, clutching SchrummSchrumm's sleeve, "I had the distinct impression that instead of helping me with their gaffs, the Accredited Drowners were pushing down on my head and shoulders. If I hadn't managed to shake them off, they would've drowned me for sure! Young man, what do you think of that?"

"How did you get out of the mud?" asked SchrummSchrumm, unhooking the man's fingers from his jacket.

The man said he'd been pulled out by a giant who'd simply lifted him up by the back of his collar and plopped him down on dry land like a sack of potatoes.

"There you are, then!" said SchrummSchrumm with a shrug and a furtive glance at the guard walking beside them. But this guard seemed a good-tempered sort: he was sweating profusely and paying no attention to the talk around him. They walked on. Though the Poplar Forest was no longer visible, they were now within sight of the wall. Evidently they'd taken a shortcut, and when they emerged onto the road to Misunderstanding, SchrummSchrumm felt sure that the barbed-wire entanglement couldn't be far off.

He was wrong.

At a certain point along this dreary road, and turning its back, so to speak, on the dreary wall, stood a delightful-looking building of pink stucco. The blue shutters, the two little white turrets, the red tile roof, and even the laundry hanging out the windows to dry, all contributed to the gaiety of the place. A luxuriant garden surrounded the property, and the identity of its lucky owner was not left to conjecture: the information was given in two-meter-high letters on a large banner above a gigantic portrait, both of which were suspended from a kind of gantry: "His Excellency the Holy Director's Hacienda." This portrait startled SchrummSchrumm, since the features of the mustachioed man it depicted were clearly distinguishable. This thin, sickly face with its low and somewhat bulbous forehead, its sunken cheeks, and its incipient jowls made all the more evident by unflattering sideburns—in short, this stupid-looking man who seemed to regard the excursionists with a simpering smile—could this really be the face of the Holy Director? If so, the man SchrummSchrumm had seen that morning in Nastarz City was *not* the Holy Director but Allright. But what would Allright be doing with Jules and Jim? Which was Allright's true face, and which the Holy Director's?

To top off this series of conflicting impressions, a young couple presently appeared in rather extraordinary outfits. The lady wore a blue dress with black flounces. Her slippers and parasol were of the same material, and she had a rose tucked into her blonde hair. The man was decked out in an elegant hunting costume of green velvet and a little Tyrolean hat with two red feathers. He was assisting the lady as she walked across the colored pebbles of the front lawn.

"Who's that?" someone asked in a reverential tone.

"That's Miss Adelaide, the Holy Director's only daughter. The man she's with is her fiancé, Colonel Negas of the Elite Company . . ."

By now everyone had noticed the couple and the guards had finally realized what a stir of emotion their appearance, and that of the Hacienda, was causing among the excursionists. They shouted at them to fall in line and, reverting to the bullying role they'd abandoned during the first part of their journey, ordered them into a double-time march. But it was too late. Impervious to the blows raining down upon them, SchrummSchrumm and his fellows gazed mesmerized at the couple. Most had seated themselves on the ground. Many were remembering their own sweethearts or children back home and were fishing out photographs from their pockets to show, somewhat pathetically, to the men around them. Many others were surreptitiously wiping their eyes. "How many kilometers have I traveled since my first excursion?" wondered SchrummSchrumm. "How many oceans have I crossed? How many peaks have I scaled? When will I give it a rest?" Seeing that everyone was lost in his own thoughts, the guard in command decided to go have a word with the young couple. They, utterly absorbed in one another, had as yet noticed nothing. The young man had gone down on one knee and was passionately kissing the young lady's hand, which she proffered with charming coquettishness. It was an unfortunate moment for the officer to interrupt, and he cleared his throat discreetly to make his presence known. Young Colonel Negas sprang up instantly, seeing first the officer standing beside him and then the group of curious onlookers several meters off.

"Good God! Who are these men?" cried the lady in a terrified voice.

"Good God! Who are these men indeed, officer?" said the young man rather stupidly.

"Excursionists on their way back from training, Your Excellencies!" said the chief guard, with a movement in the young lady's direction that was probably meant as a deferential bow, but which was so clumsily executed that both she and the colonel burst into laughter.

"Take care, Excellencies," he went on, swallowing his shame, "they've fallen into a pond and smell very bad. They're also tired and surly."

"Oh my!" said Adelaide, frightened. She took out a finely embroidered chambray handkerchief and waved it in front of her nose. "It's true, they do smell awful!" She made a pouty face.

"What do you intend to do with them?" said Colonel Negas.

The guard replied that he was going to march them straight to the wash house. The young man applauded his initiative.

"Be sure to have them ready for next week's ceremony," he added, raising an admonitory finger.

"Have no fear, Colonel," said the guard. "In any case, you can see for yourself that they'll lack for nothing!" This last sentence was spoken with a gesture toward the windows where the wet laundry hung.

Colonel Negas chuckled and gave a nod to the guard's military salute. Princess Adelaide made the same type of bow the guard had attempted with such ridiculous results, only she pulled it off with incomparable grace. Then she folded her parasol, put her arm through her fiancé's, and the two of them strolled away from the disgusting men.

The guard was seething with rage and took it out on the excursionists. Worried that they would sully the fancy gravel of the garden path, he made them walk on either side of it, in the beds of flowers embalming the air. They did in fact leave nauseating traces of their passage in their wake, and the roses were the dirtier for it. SchrummSchrumm, deaf to the excited chatter around him on the meaning of the mysterious ceremony just mentioned, was daydreaming over the enchanting figure of the young lady. The group skirted the gardens and circled around the buildings, reached the iron gate, and from there proceeded to the inner courtyard. A short time later they were back in their rooms, where they could wash up and change into clean clothes.

Lunch that day was more substantial than usual, perhaps to restore them after the morning's ordeal. The guards—not to mention SchrummSchrumm's companions—had a lot to say about his recent feat. They drank toasts in his honor and there was talk of awarding him a medal or giving him some sort of public commendation. Little of interest, however, was said about the practical results of the outing. SchrummSchrumm decided to get as much information as he could out of Krikri as soon as he came on duty in the lobby, but the sergeant refused to enlighten him. By the end of the day, no one was any the wiser. There was, however, one development: a messenger brought SchrummSchrumm a note. He'd been summoned next morning to the office of Mr. Burns, Deputy Director of Misunderstanding and Chief of the Secret Police. To whom did he owe this dubious honor? Had Krikri turned in an unfavorable report? Had Leopold denounced him? With these troubling thoughts in mind, he spent a very anxious night and did not sleep well.

VII

A guard came in person to collect him. Krikri did not appear and therefore seemingly had nothing to do with the summons. SchrummSchrumm was first escorted into an elevator, then ushered aboard a little electric train that was luxuriously appointed with leather cushions, pornographic etchings above the seats, ambient music, and bottles of various liquors within easy reach. Their route took them through poorly lit tunnels at a prodigious speed. They stopped at a sort of underground station, took another elevator, and, after ascending a staircase, eventually reached the office of Mr. Burns, Deputy Director of Misunderstanding and Chief of the Secret Police. The guard hadn't said a word throughout the entire journey. He now turned and left.

The only thing for it was to put on a brave face. The office walls were covered in sumptuous black silk. There were many windows, all with their red curtains drawn except one, through which SchrummSchrumm thought he could glimpse a vaguely familiar garden. The room was dimly lit; so dimly that at first he could see only the Chief of the Secret Police—or at least the man he took to be the Chief of the Secret Police—sitting behind the room's sole article of furniture. But he soon perceived that there were two other people in the room, a man and a woman. The man was soberly dressed, just like the man at the desk. He sat astride a wooden rocking horse mounted on two caskets—child-size caskets—and had worked up quite a sweat, going at his strange diversion with great ardor. It was the sound of the caskets that had attracted SchrummSchrumm's attention to his corner of the room—the darkest corner by far. The woman was nearer to Mr. Burns, seated on a golden swing suspended from a beam inlaid with precious stones. She was very beautiful, though she must have been nearly forty, and wore an indecently skimpy lace negligee. She'd thrown a mantilla over her bare arms. Two enormous black dogs sat on their haunches and regarded her placidly. In contrast to the frenetic agitation of the man on the rocking horse, the woman's movements were slow and languorous. Neither showed the slightest interest in SchrummSchrumm. The man at the desk must have given some signal to the rocking-horse man, because he dismounted with a look of regret and came over to sit in an armchair. SchrummSchrumm was motioned into another armchair beside him. He now became the subject of attentive scrutiny.

"Good morning, Mr. Excursionist," said the man behind the desk. "My name is Burns. I'm the Deputy Director and Chief of the Misunderstanding Secret Police. This is the President of the Inquisitorial Investigating Committee," he said, indicating the other man. He didn't introduce the woman on the swing, which was just as well, because it didn't seem likely anything would snap her out of her trance. SchrummSchrumm nodded politely.

"Let's get down to business," continued the Deputy Director. "It isn't often an excursionist is summoned here: the reason you're in this office today is quite simple. The President of the Inquisitorial Investigating Committee and his team would like to put you through an examination. But these gentlemen's methods don't have my full approval, which is why I decided to be present at the meeting."

The president chose not to acknowledge this remark about his methods. With a bland smile, he said:

"Mr. Burns, our administrative differences need not be thrashed out before members of the public, but I must emphasize once again, for the record, that this arrangement of yours is extremely problematic. The General Regulations explicitly prohibit the interrogations of any Investigating Committee from being conducted in the presence of an uninitiated third party, even if that third party is the Deputy Director's wife"—he said this with a leer at the woman on the swing. "Obviously, I have no choice but to submit to this incomprehensible demand of yours, but it is the authority of the Grand Inquisitor himself that's being trampled on here. I do hope you've carefully considered the consequences such an intolerable transgression is liable to entail for you. In any case, I'll be detailing your little machinations in my report."

"May we begin now?" was the Deputy Director's only reply. When the president had given his consent, he pressed a button and the room was at once agreeably lit. It was larger than SchrummSchrumm had thought. There was a wet bar at the back and an interior wooden stairway giving access to the private apartments of the Deputy Director and his wife. Against the wall opposite the red-curtained windows was a row of chairs. He had no time to examine the room further, because just then the Investigating Committee made its rather noisy entrance.

There were seven of them, and they were in the thick of a discussion: seven gentlemen dressed entirely in yellow, with shoes, gloves, and hats to match. The cords around their waists were gold interwoven with a few black threads. SchrummSchrumm saw that they also had a curious coat of arms emblazoned on their chests, presumably that of the Grand Inquisitoriat, depicting a platter of crimson sauerkraut surmounted by a green swastika. The committee president, he noticed, wore the same emblem. Despite these rather troubling symbols of their power, they showed marked deference toward the Deputy Director. Only SchrummSchrumm was intimidated by these self-important men, who for all their absurd yellow getups and ridiculous emblems, were nonetheless here to subject him to an interrogation of which he knew nothing except that the Deputy Director had reservations about its "methods."

They stopped at the threshold. SchrummSchrumm and the president rose from their chairs; Mr. Burns remained seated. One of the seven stepped forward holding a typewritten paper. He bowed from the waist and intoned:

"We are the seven experts of the Inquisitorial Investigating Committee. Ave! Ave!"

"Ave! Ave!" repeated SchrummSchrumm.

The whole of the little company stamped their feet on the floor as if they were cold and trying to warm themselves. This went on for some time.

"Are you going to tell me what this is all about?" asked SchrummSchrumm, whose nerves were at the breaking point.

"Naturally!" said the president. "We may begin," he told his team.

The experts didn't need to be asked twice. They surrounded SchrummSchrumm and commenced a series of scientific tests. One of the fools rolled up SchrummSchrumm's pant-leg, a second bent down, and a third said, "Look at me, please!" When SchrummSchrumm looked, the first and second experts, who together had been holding his leg, bit as hard as they could into the fleshiest part of his calf. "Ouch!" cried SchrummSchrumm. This was precisely the reaction they'd anticipated. Indeed, a fourth expert was standing by with a stopwatch to measure the time elapsed between the moment his colleagues planted their teeth in his leg and the moment he hollered. "Nine-tenths of a second," he announced. "Excellent!" said the president, who was closely following the progress of the test. SchrummSchrumm was wondering what it all meant and tried to catch the Deputy Director's eye, but the latter was apparently satisfied; all he did was give him a friendly wink. "Let us proceed," said the president. It was now the sixth and seventh experts' turn. These two had done nothing up till now, and all eyes were on them. They took a few halting steps toward SchrummSchrumm, paused, changed their minds, and went back to hold a whispered conference with the president and their fellow experts.

"Reflexes slightly impaired. And he's suffering from fatigue," said one.

"We'll see about that," retorted the president.

"Ave!" said SchrummSchrumm, sticking out his tongue. "I'm an excursionist first class. Ave! Ave!"

They looked at him without surprise, as if no one had expected him to act any differently, but their dithering intensified and a growing indecision was written on their faces. He heard odd snatches of their whispers: "Let him be! We have all the time in the world." Then, more distinctly, as they gave him a long stare: "He must be made to vomit, you know that perfectly well!" He was now starting to worry. The Deputy Director, too, seemed to sense that there could be no good in a conversation from which he was being repeatedly excluded by everyone turning their backs on him whenever he tried to join the huddle. The huddle, however, soon broke apart. The president had taken out a packet of bonbons and was courteously offering them around. When SchrummSchrumm's turn came, he accepted one. His guard being thus relaxed, someone used the opportunity to sneak up behind him. His arm was twisted and wrenched backward, forcing him to double over, and a noose was slipped over his neck. It was drawn tight and they began strangling him purposefully.

"Let him go!" shouted the Deputy Director, leaping into the fray.

But no one listened. The noose was pulled even tighter, a red fog filled SchrummSchrumm's vision, and he felt he was dying. Then they released him.

"There you have it!" said a voice that seemed to come from miles away. "Easy as pie! The method works like a well-oiled machine."

It was the president's voice. The red fog quickly dispersed. SchrummSchrumm realized he was on his knees and had vomited. He was afraid he might have ruined his clothes, but they'd knotted a towel around his neck: they were evidently practiced hands at this. He wiped his mouth and, supporting himself with his right hand, tried to rise. Someone came over to help him up. As he was getting to his feet, he saw the clerk put away his typewritten paper. The Deputy Director looked very cross.

"Better?" said the president.

SchrummSchrumm nodded.

"Perfect! In that case, our work here is done. You've seen for yourself that our methods aren't so terrible after all. We know what we're doing!"

For no apparent reason, the members of the Investigating Committee burst into applause at this last sentence. A few made their way to the door and left. Others were about to follow but decided to wait for their president who, having picked up his hat, was speaking icily to the Deputy Director:

"Mr. Burns, our task has not been an easy one. Though we've assembled myriad reports and conducted a staggering number of interrogations, the results have been disappointing. Most disappointing. We could without a doubt have reconstructed, if not the entirety of the facts, at least their mysterious outlines. In any case, we could have filled in many, many blanks. But in order to do this, we would have needed the benefit of your cooperation. It pains me to note that, once again, and in spite of your assertions to the contrary, you've done everything in your power to thwart my investigation ... An Inquisitorial Investigating Committee is endowed with far-reaching powers, Mr. Excursionist," he went on, addressing SchrummSchrumm, "yet these powers are effectively nullified within a Holy Director's sphere of governance. It is one of the paradoxes of the 'Splendid Hierarchy' that our Committee members—who are by definition a grade above Mr. Burns—must obey him in this. I'm sure he'll be delighted to explain to you how complex, and at the same time how amusing, the situation is."

"The majority of public officials are on our side," Burns replied calmly. "The Holy Director himself supports us."

The president lowered his eyes thoughtfully for a moment, then concluded, making a point of speaking only to SchrummSchrumm:

"The Chief of Police alludes to a reform that was indeed initiated by the Holy Director of Misunderstanding. Other sectors were won over to this revolutionary movement ... At the Grand Inquisitoriat, we don't see things in the same light: we favor the old methods. Goodbye, Mr. SchrummSchrumm. On behalf of the Committee, I wish you luck."

SchrummSchrumm smiled weakly. The Committee members who had stayed behind broke out into fresh applause and headed toward the door, where two guards were waiting for them. "Ave!" they said. Burns, SchrummSchrumm, and the woman were left alone. The woman had remained on her swing through the entire meeting, and SchrummSchrumm hadn't thought to watch her reactions. He'd noted nonetheless that all the Committee members had acted as if she didn't exist.

"Well," said Burns almost cheerfully, "gone at last! That wasn't too hard on you, I hope?"

"I owe you a debt of gratitude, Mr. Deputy Director," said SchrummSchrumm.

"Please, don't mention it. I always stick up for the excursionists. It's my job."

"Where do those people come from? Who is this Grand Inquisitor? I've never heard of him before today."

"Even we ourselves don't know, my dear Mr. Schrumm-Schrumm. But maybe I can give you some idea of what the Grand Inquisitor is by telling you that I am to him what you are to me, relatively speaking, which is to say, technically nothing at all . . . But that's not what's important here. Tell me instead your own thoughts on what just happened."

This time, SchrummSchrumm blinked. The Deputy Director must have noticed, because after a glance at his wife, he continued:

"Look here, Mr. Excursionist, what divides us, meaning us and the Grand Inquisitoriat, are our divergent views on the sacred texts. One of the Grand Inquisitoriat's guiding principles is respect for the literal meaning of these texts. An understandable approach, given that the Grand Inquisitor's mission is to suppress error, to tear it out root and branch; put another way, it's to take moral inquiry to its most extreme limits, based on a strict interpretation of the sacred texts. But here in Misunderstanding, such an approach is indefensible: our job being primarily to organize excursions to the Quicksands, we're naturally inclined to break away from the texts and address things from a practical standpoint. Besides, even supposing we were in the wrong and the attitude of the Grand Inquisitor's collaborators was dogmatically correct, we'd still have good grounds for acting as we do, namely that it's impossible—short of looking at everything through an exclusively moral lens, as the Grand Inquisitoriat does—it's impossible, I say, in our day and age, to apply literally texts that were written, some in eras extremely different from our own, others in epochs so remote that we can't even fix a precise date for their composition, the truth being that this date is lost in the mists of time."

"You're referring to the Gospel of Misunderstanding?" said SchrummSchrumm, who was more than a little bored by such considerations.

"Precisely! But let's set aside the Gospel for the moment, because that's not the text on whose interpretation we and the Grand Inquisitoriat disagree, but rather the Commentaries. What are the Commentaries, really, if not the collected writings of Nastarz's principal successors? You can easily understand how radically these commentaries might differ from one another, depending on whether they were written in distant or more recent periods. Take, for example, the one-hundred-and-eleventh successor of Nastarz, who lived, so they say, some eighty centuries ago. He was unquestionably a great Holy Director. But he was very much of his time. A blessed time, Mr. Excursionist: men were in what you might call a natural state of beatitude. False conceptions of the excursionary symbols were almost unheard of. Accredited Drowners and excursionists joined voices in song during Quicksands Excursions. It was the time of holidays, of venerable saints. A golden age, for all intents and purposes: no need for submachine guns atop the walls of Misunderstanding, nor for barbed wire around them; no need, either, for executioners . . . Is such a state of affairs even imaginable in our day? Obviously not! Now let's consider the opposite end of the spectrum: the one-thousand-and-thirty-fourth successor of Nastarz, who lived a mere two hundred years ago. He, too, was a great man. It was he who was dubbed the 'Warrior Holy Director.' A sad era, in comparison with the preceding one. He had to lead a holy war against the heretics massed by the millions in a few regions on the wild outskirts of the Enchanted Poplar Forest. After multiple crusades, he succeeded in exterminating them. He executed their priests, who'd been organizing sham Sunday excursions in mockery of the true ones, and converted the remainder of the wretches by either persuasion or threats. He was a very great Holy Director indeed. But he, too, was of his time. His commentaries, which make perfect sense when viewed in their original context, are anachronistic today. To be sure, they're still invaluable as far as symbolic, metaphorical meaning goes. But to take them literally is patently absurd."

"Undoubtedly," said SchrummSchrumm, now deeply impressed. "I don't know the Gospel very well, let alone the Commentaries, but I must admit I'd never have thought to consider the problem of the excursionary symbols in that light."

"I'm glad to hear you say so, my dear Mr. SchrummSchrumm," said the Deputy Director, visibly pleased. "I'll give you a brief overview of the goals our reform movement has set for itself. I take it you earned your deportment certificate as part of becoming an excursionist first class? So you're aware of the proper course of action, according to ancient tradition, if you ever by some unlikely twist of fate find yourself in the presence of a manifestation of the Holy Director."

"I should prostrate myself before him and take care to avert my gaze from his Holy Form," SchrummSchrumm said.

"Your answer is correct. And yet, if you did—by some unlikely twist of fate—find yourself before our Holy Director, he'd be extremely annoyed if you prostrated yourself before him."

"It's the done thing everywhere," said SchrummSchrumm. "I know from personal experience that prostration is obligatory before Her Highness the Princess Hicciné, the Right Reverend High Priest of the Chameleon, and the King of Synonym City. Shouldn't the ritual require at least this much?"

"Our Holy Director has rescinded that article of the Protocol. In the face of fierce opposition, and even though the innovation was the cause of our rift with the Grand Inquisitoriat, we no longer prostrate ourselves in Misunderstanding."

"I see," said SchrummSchrumm. "The reform does credit to Misunderstanding, and it's moving with the tide of history. It's historically inevitable."

"No, Mr. Excursionist, you don't understand at all!" replied Burns with a quaver in his voice. "Not that I hold it against you. Even among Misunderstanding's public officials, who aid and support us, very few realize how much our Holy Director is to be admired for his wisdom and firmness of purpose. If I told you how hard-won this first, small victory was, you'd scarcely believe me. The Grand Inquisitor's inner circle immediately branded it 'blasphemous and demagogic.' They refused to concede the obvious. They tried to explain this alteration of a centuries-old Protocol—instituted by Nastarz himself—in a way more comforting to their own ideas. In a word, they decided there could be only one explanation: the Holy Director of Misunderstanding was publicly manifesting his displeasure with the manner in which people were prostrating themselves before him, these prostrations having doubtless devolved, through long custom, into little more than low bows. It was a skillful interpretation because it legitimated the supposed directorial wrath and justified such an extreme measure. They declared in an official statement that the Holy Director of Misunderstanding, King of the Quicksands and Lord of the Ultimate Excursion, 'had preferred to ban the obligatory prostrations before his Holy Form rather than countenance those who prostrate themselves to him without grasping the profound, esoteric meaning behind the act . . .' Then they sent specially appointed 'choreographo-prostrators' to Misunderstanding with the task of instructing our public officials, and any excursionists visiting the Capital, in the proper, traditional mode of prostration before the Holy Director, that is to say the mode imbued with the highest degree of respect and veneration imaginable . . . And what do you think happened next, dear Mr. SchrummSchrumm? Well, it was simply sublime! Not only were the choreographo-prostrators sent packing, but three days later our Holy Director dispatched a petition to the Grand Inquisitor that was simply incredible.

"Let me say in passing that my venerated superior has absolutely no talent as a writer, and it's said the Grand Inquisitor found his message so incoherent and disturbing that he refused to send it on to his Chapel for public reading, instead locking it away in his secret safe so no one would ever learn of it . . . But I digress. Here's what was in the directorial petition: I read it because I was the one who sent it by special post.

"A young king lives in a fantastically lavish palace and is surrounded by an opulent court. Tour buses packed with excursionists travel hither and yon across his vast kingdom. Of course, there are submachine guns tucked into every crenellation of the city walls and legions of guards and soldiers ruling over the populace with an iron fist, but he knows nothing of these things, cloistered as he is within his palace of a thousand gardens. He lives in ignorance. He ought therefore to be happy. But happiness eludes him. And so it is that one morning, the king awakes and his servants, eunuchs, wives, and courtiers gather round him as usual to wish him a joyous day. They sing hymns together in his honor—to an irritating, monotone melody—and throw themselves on the ground as they hail him: 'Our King! Our fair King!' On this particular day, however, he feels he needs words of love and friendship rather than songs. He wants to clasp one or the other of them to his bosom. They flee from him, horrified. The young king persists. With a willingness that would touch your heart, he goes so far as to clothe himself in rumpled old royal robes and put his crown away in a cupboard so as not to frighten people with the signs of his royalty. It's no use: still he gets the same hymns of veneration, in the same irritating monotone, instead of the words of love and friendship he desires. He dismisses everyone. Then he slips out of his palace through a secret passage and sees, for the first time, what's really taking place in his kingdom.

"He passes spies sneaking in and out of covered porticos—spies whose mission is to invert the meaning of symbols and to corrupt beliefs. He passes those who send nightmares and illusions. He passes thieves, those who steal the Golden Apple from the Eternal Apple Tree, those who trespass in the Forbidden Garden, Nastarz's Orchard, Eden, to steal the Golden Apple. He passes watchers peering out of guard towers. He passes all these people, and an immense sadness begins to weigh upon him.

"Next he comes upon two executioners with a great crowd gathered around them. They're about to execute the semi-wholesaler in small hardware supplies. They slit open his belly and chest with a knife; they remove his heart and toss it to a pair of huge, black dogs with placid eyes; they pull out his steaming entrails and divide them into seven small piles, placing on top of each a pink ribbon called 'inviolable.' The king wants to intervene, but the crowd doesn't recognize him, doesn't know him, doesn't listen to him.

"Finally, he meets two elderly people. He sees them on the opposite bank of a dismal pond, not far from a tumbledown wooden house, which in turn is not far from the barbed-wire entanglement. He takes them for a harmless old couple. The man is carrying a suitcase; the woman is pushing a little covered handcart. She has green hair tied up in a black scarf; she has red eyes and black teeth. Who are these two old people? Where did they come from? A plump, rosy toddler plays beside them. The king calls out to them: 'Hello! Come here! Who are you?' 'Be right there!' they reply. They begin to run. They round the pond at such a clip that the king fears the handcart will overturn and spill its contents. When they reach him, he sees that the cart contains a cradle. The old woman keeps a firm grip on it with both hands. Her hands are green, her nails red, her veins black. How strange this cradle is, and how dreadful the baby laid inside! It is dead. Its little body is rotting, its skull is oozing all over the pillow's fine embroidery.

"'What's that?' asks the king, pointing to the cadaver.

"'That's my darling baby boy,' replies the old woman. 'My youngest, the apple of my eye. Him,' she says, indicating the plump, rosy toddler, 'he's the firstborn.'

"'He's *my* favorite,' says the old man.

"During this exchange, the old woman has bent down and pulled back the baby's blanket; the stench is horrible. She tenderly lifts out the little decomposed corpse.

"'Feeding time,' she says. 'Come, my handsome little man, drink up!'

"She gives the corpse her breast and sings it a lullaby, closing her eyes. The plump, rosy toddler looks on; he doesn't understand. The king recoils and says, aghast:

"'Who are you? Where did you come from?'

"They don't reply. The old woman has laid her favorite cadaver back in its cradle and is tucking it in. Then she starts stripping off her clothes. When she's completely naked, she says, 'This is the dance of Salome.' She jiggles her limp, pendulous breasts, shakes her sagging buttocks, and works her hips and varicose-veined thighs. The old man watches her, licking his lips and showing every sign of the most ardent lechery as her wriggling becomes ever more obscene.

"'Oh, my beauty! My beloved!' he cries out at last. 'What is your demand?'

"'I want the head of your firstborn!' she answers. In her excitement, she tears the last remaining tufts of greenish hair from her scalp.

"It is no sooner said than done. In a twinkling, the old man whips out an engraved silver platter and an ax from his suitcase. The old woman seizes the child and holds him still. The child says nothing. 'Wait! Stop!' cries the king. In vain. 'Swish!' goes the ax and 'chock!' the neck is severed. The old man sets the head on the platter and presents it to his beloved . . . The king runs away screaming. He throws himself on the ground, he sobs, he pleads.

"It is then that the sound of galloping reaches his ears. He lifts his head. A voice booms: 'How's it going, pals?' Other voices answer: 'Going good over here!' 'Good here, too!' The galloping sound increases. The horizon grows pale, a cloud of multicolored sand slowly rises, and three magnificent horsemen appear. The king believes he recognizes them. 'These are the horsemen of Eden, the mad horsemen of the Enchanted Garden,' he says to himself. But these horsemen who approach are wheeling and prancing in midair. Awe-inspiring are they, they and their mounts, with their rippling golden manes and ringing emerald hoofs. The riders raise gleaming trumpets to their lips. Thrice the trumpets blare, and thrice a call resounds, a call so strange that the king is wonderstruck. He wants to call out to them, but a voice says to him, 'King, fair King, you have a kingdom and you know it not; you have subjects and they know you not. Unknown to all, without family, without friends, without a name, without prayers, without excuses, King and yet powerless, you are a king and yet you are not. Such is your fate, King, fair King.'

"The story ends with the king returning to his palace and attempting to flee disguised as an excursionist. But he's recognized and caught. He's firmly secured to his throne, where he utters horrible screams of agony—hardly in accord with his royal dignity—as the assembled inhabitants of the palace—courtiers, wives, eunuchs, and servants—sing an even more irritating hymn in his honor . . .

". . . Since then, my dear Mr. SchrummSchrumm, the whole business seems to have been settled. But, as you now understand, we've set our sights higher. We aim at nothing less than a radical reform that will effect a paradigm shift both in the interpretation of excursionary symbolism and, at the same time, in our relations with excursionists as we help them grasp these symbols. In other words, we want a comprehensive reform. A reform to which, fortunately, whatever you may say, not all Holy Directors are as opposed as the Princess Hicciné, the High Priest of the Chameleon, and the King of Synonym City."

Now SchrummSchrumm was fully won over. What a broad-minded program! What a broad-minded enterprise! Alas, in the middle of this engrossing discussion, they were interrupted by a dirty, hairy man of about sixty who bumped into SchrummSchrumm as he passed, then stopped in front of the Deputy Director. The latter smiled, recognizing his visitor.

"So it's you, you old rascal!" he said affectionately. "What do you want?"

"Cross my heart and hope to die, stick a needle in my eye," said the old man. "I bring bad news!" he added, glancing at SchrummSchrumm and the woman in turn. Finally he leaned forward and whispered something to the Deputy Director.

". . . Not that they need them today," he finished in a louder voice, "but they must get them back: it might cause trouble down the line."

Mr. Burns emitted a long hiss of irritation.

"Fine," he said. "I'll take care of it."

"Good!"

This incomprehensible dialogue over, the funny little man nodded and went back the way he'd come, again bumping into SchrummSchrumm. There was a moment's silence. At last, the Deputy Director broke it by turning toward the woman and saying, "Martha!"

". . . Martha's my wife," he explained to SchrummSchrumm. "She likes to stay here. She doesn't say a word. She always behaves herself . . . Martha!" he repeated.

The woman slowly descended from the swing as if emerging from a dream. She was quite tall. Her face was shining and her eyes had a strange glitter. The moment her bare feet touched the floor, the two dogs, who had been watching her placidly the entire time, stood and came over to rub themselves affectionately against her legs. They were black and enormous. They nearly knocked over the Deputy Director, and she gave them a little kick to shoo them away.

"Martha," said Burns, indicating the dogs with a clumsy gesture, "these animals don't belong to you."

"Pish!" she said. "They do so belong to me. They do, I tell you."

"Listen to me, Martha, these beasts may seem loyal and loving, so I understand why you've let yourself get attached to them, but they don't belong to you, I promise you they don't. You need to return them to their rightful owners: these are working animals."

The woman looked at her husband with an air of innocent surprise.

"Really, my friend, I don't understand you," she said carelessly. "It was you yourself who made me take these dogs, just the day before yesterday. Don't you recall?"

"Please, Martha!" Burns broke in, sounding miserable.

"Very well," she said with a sigh. "I'll stop lying. Anyway, I can get the dogs out of your hair right now, if it's so important to you. They're very good about obeying me, you know."

"Yes, make them go away."

Martha sent the dogs away by saying, "Tobias! Tobias!" in a voice so soft and sweet it left SchrummSchrumm speechless. The dogs immediately left the room, but whining and with their tails between their legs. The woman followed her dogs up the stairs, just like in a stage play. SchrummSchrumm gathered that the interview was over. And indeed, Burns rang for someone and SchrummSchrumm was taken back by the same train, where he lounged comfortably on the leather cushions and contemplated the pornographic etchings while sipping a glass of whiskey.

VIII

Something new was going on at the Bushido. During his absence, a large wire-grille barrier with a teller window in the middle had been erected in the main lobby, partitioning off half the room. Excursionists were waiting in line at this window. On the opposite side of the grille stood a group of petty officials, apparently charged with carrying out some sort of administrative formality. SchrummSchrumm learned that an official memorandum had been read aloud earlier. The majority of the hotel guests had been put on one list, the "blue" list, while a very few—only five in total, SchrummSchrumm among them—had been put on a second, the "green" list. Every excursionist, depending on his assigned list, had to sew either a blue or a green disk onto the fronts and backs of all his clothing. The cloth disks were being distributed at the window where everyone was waiting. Krikri greeted SchrummSchrumm and told him to join his comrades in the distribution line. Nearby, in the cafeteria, those lucky enough to have been served already were eating and chatting. The clinking of forks could be heard. An appetizing aroma wafted in on the air. SchrummSchrumm largely ignored it; he was tipsy, having drunk a fair amount on the train ride back. He went to calmly await his turn. His neighbors in line were discussing the news: a warning had been issued that, starting tomorrow, any excursionist caught without his disks would be subject to punishment. Word had also spread that the "blues" and "greens" were to be segregated in the coming days. Belonging to the privileged green group came with a number of advantages. Greens were excused from further training at the pond and were entitled to "upgraded" meals and more comfortable living quarters. Finally, and most importantly, their departure for the Quicksands would be moved forward . . . SchrummSchrumm listened eagerly to the talk. Nevertheless, the wait time soon began to seem abnormally long. Stepping to one side, he saw that the employees had gone away and the window was closed. And yet, peering a little harder through the grille, he realized the employees hadn't left after all: they were having a leisurely conversation at a little table on which were three full coffee cups and a steaming coffeepot. A sign had been hung at the teller window where all could see: "Closed. Please wait patiently with no grumbling."

A long interval passed. Occasionally the window would open and two or three men would receive their fabric disks. But soon enough the employees would close it again, hang out their sign, and sip their coffee while making disparaging remarks about those still waiting. Another long interval. Then there was a stir in the line, a murmur ran through the crowd, and SchrummSchrumm saw that the gate portion below the window had been opened like the lower half of a Dutch door. One of the employees stepped through. His uniform had most definitely been borrowed for the occasion: he was sporting a white jacket with handsome insignia and carrying a gold riding crop. Nevertheless, after the vague rumblings of a moment ago, a heavy and almost respectful hush descended on the group as this pompous official began his formal inspection. SchrummSchrumm noticed his neighbors were standing at attention. Though privately laughing to himself, he did likewise.

"You," said the official.

"Me?"

"Yes, you! Through here!"

SchrummSchrumm didn't budge, afraid there had been some mistake. But the man repeated his order. He pointed to the opening below the window. SchrummSchrumm obeyed, having no idea what was happening, and endured the outraged stares of the other excursionists. He was pushed through the gate and found himself on the other side of the grille, the good side, the employee side. There were four of them, including the man who'd just come out and who was now regretfully relinquishing his beautiful borrowed jacket and gold riding crop. A fifth cup was quickly produced. SchrummSchrumm was invited to have some coffee.

"Oh, I couldn't! The others are waiting!" he protested, indicating his companions, who were sighing and muttering restively.

The employee who'd come to fetch him stared at SchrummSchrumm for a second, uncomprehending. Then his face lit up and he nudged one of his colleagues in the ribs:

"Did you hear that? 'The others are waiting!' Mr. SchrummSchrumm is a rare bird. He has a sense of humor you don't often find in excursionists."

"You know my name?"

"Bah!" said the man.

SchrummSchrumm spoke again:

"Tell me, why are you making them wait so long? Is this how it's always done?"

"Yes, always," they answered. "And to explain why it has to be done this way, understand that one of two situations must apply: either those waiting at the window are true excursionists, in which case they're fully capable of waiting all day or even longer, or they're not excursionists worthy of the name, in which case there's no reason to trouble ourselves over them. In fact, we're teaching them a valuable lesson by making them wait so long!"

SchrummSchrumm, who had always been dumbfounded by this kind of logic, could think of nothing to say. The employees took advantage of his silence to steer him onto a chair and set a piping-hot cup of coffee before him, at the sight of which those on the other side of the partition licked their lips.

"Don't people ever complain to your superiors?" asked SchrummSchrumm after a moment's consideration.

"Of course they do!" chuckled the others. "There's no end of complaints! But complaining gets them nowhere. Apart from the fact that our official duties at the window—however trivial—have won us friends in high places, we're acting in accordance with the precise instructions we were given."

"This time," said SchrummSchrumm, sipping his coffee, "I refuse to believe you! You must be pulling my leg."

"We'd never take such liberties with you, Mr. Excursionist, sir," objected the employee who'd ushered him in. And, without further explanation, he waved a form in front of him. "See for yourself," he said encouragingly, while his colleagues made disapproving gestures. But he snapped "Enough!" and they bowed their heads.

The paper was much like those that issued testing orders. SchrummSchrumm read. Incredible as it seemed, employees really were instructed to subject the excursionists to as much waiting around as possible. "Err on the side of longer waits rather than shorter," explained the memo, which suggested, as the "surest means of exhausting the morons' patience," that employees close their windows every half hour and sit around indolently drinking coffee right under the excursionists' noses, all while making humiliating wisecracks at their expense.

SchrummSchrumm handed back the paper and looked at his fellow excursionists. He hated to admit it, but now that things had been explained to him, he realized that being on the good side of the grille had a considerable effect on one's state of mind. One felt at ease here. One had a sense of power and security. In short, one became another man. And so he accepted a second and then a third cup of coffee, while his eyelids drooped and he let himself slump onto the tabletop. He must have even dozed off for a minute, because the head employee jerked him out of his slumber with a strong yet respectful shake and informed him it was time to go back.

"Here are the disks you'll wear from now on," he said, setting a pile of circular green cloths before him.

SchrummSchrumm thanked him kindly. He shook all the employees' hands and, without further ado, ducked back out under the ticket window. The others booed and hissed as he appeared. But he was unashamed.

The cafeteria was now empty, food was no longer being served, and the kitchen smells had vanished. This was enough to set his conscience at rest. Though he'd unquestionably been given preferential treatment—albeit for reasons that remained mysterious—he'd been deprived of his meal the same as everybody else. As he made his way back up to his room, he glanced down at the officials. From the fourth-floor landing, they looked like overgrown insects. They'd chosen a new clown for themselves in the person of an elderly excursionist and were making him hop around the room as they shouted: "Giddyap! Good doggie!" SchrummSchrumm was suddenly weary. And it wasn't the same fatigue he'd felt the last few days. He was making too much of these trivial incidents, that was the truth of the matter. Still, despite his repeated admonitions to himself, this bad feeling stayed with him for the rest of the afternoon, which he devoted to sewing green disks onto all his clothes.

Near the end of the day, his window being open, he heard shouts coming from outside:

"Make way! Make way for the noble Basil!"

This was the first time SchrummSchrumm had seen anyone pass through the desolate vacant lot, which looked like the end of the earth. An intense curiosity drew him to the window. Two black men with gold rings in their ears were carrying a palanquin on which an excursionist lay reclined. The man bore a striking resemblance to the Basil he'd met on the bus. This Basil was richly attired in Oriental garb, wore a turban held in place with a large emerald, and was casting proud, scornful glances left and right. Walking beside him was the spitting image of Broadway, Basil's personal secretary, whom he'd also met on the bus.

"Hey there! Basil! Broadway!" he called.

The two men raised their heads, looked at him appraisingly, then turned away. They disappeared from view as the black men shouted again:

"Make way! Make way for the noble Basil!"

SchrummSchrumm was left wondering whether he really had seen the same two excursionists he'd met before. To all appearances he had. On the other hand, it was hardly likely. In any event, he saw them a few minutes later in the lobby, though he didn't dare go up to say hello. The new rules were already in force, and virtually all talk between blues and greens had ceased. The four other greens were men a little older than himself. He'd hardly noticed them before today, and he managed to put on a friendly face for them. Shortly thereafter, as everyone was heading in to dinner, another news bulletin was posted: a celebration had been planned which would include a banquet and various festivities. In particular, His Excellency the Holy Director would be appearing in several paradoxical forms and would give a stirring keynote speech. The guests were encouraged to wear their best attire.

What was this celebration in honor of?

The guards tried to evade the question, repeating over and over that it would be a spectacular ceremony and extolling the Holy Director's incomparable oratorical skills. But, pressed for an answer, they finally admitted that the celebration coincided with what was, technically speaking, the end of the training period, meaning that afterward the blues and greens would part company for good.

IX

The room in which the festivities were being held was at the end of a hallway that could only be accessed via a small courtyard, which was itself at the end of a second hallway accessed via a second courtyard, preceded in turn by other hallways and other courtyards. The excursionists were well rested and all were smartly dressed. The guards had donned their regulation sergeant-first-class uniforms. They were stamping around proudly in their boots, each gripping a heavy carbine rifle. All of them, guards and excursionists alike, paused on the threshold to take in the sumptuous decor.

The room was about fifty meters long and thirty wide. A dais had been set up at the back, on which there was an unoccupied table, apparently reserved for the Holy Director and his high-ranking guests, as its seats included two glittering thrones, one gold and one silver. In front of and below the head table were other, smaller tables laid with food. These tables were divided by an aisle running down the middle of the room. On the walls hung tapestries bearing the Excursion's coat of arms: barbed wire *gules* and a carbine *or* on a field *vert*. Gigantic incense burners perfumed the air, and a large crowd of unknown excursionists was already gathered.

As SchrummSchrumm was contemplating this splendor, cries of joy went up from the room. Some women and children—the first he'd seen in Misunderstanding—had just entered. Family members, separated for weeks, fell into each other's arms with the guards' encouragement. SchrummSchrumm spotted Basil and Broadway waving to him, but Krikri wouldn't let him join his former companions. The greens were at a table apart from the rest, where they were stuffing their faces just as greedily as their blue comrades. All this commotion was at its height when an impeccable voice rang out:

"Are you ready, absolutely and entirely ready?" it inquired.

"Yes," answered the crowd.

"We shall now recite Prayer Number One together."

The assembly, which SchrummSchrumm estimated to number about five hundred, launched into the ludicrous verses:

"To the Excursion Director, we give thanks.
"For obscurity dispelled,
"For the tempest that is quelled,
"For the wall whose height is unexcelled, we give thanks.
"For the madness subjugated,
"For despair and pain abated,
"For the loveliest Sands eye e'er beheld, we give thanks."

"The procession arrives!" concluded the voice. "Attention! Attention! For without attention, there is no true procession."

There were, in fact, five little boys and five little girls walking into the room, all dressed as angels and singing "Hosanna! Hosanna!" with heartfelt conviction. They had wings affixed to their backs and were scattering rose petals from baskets hung around their necks. Next came twenty guards, selected from among the tallest and brawniest of their class, carrying twenty monumental torches and rolling their terrible eyes. They were followed by a flotilla of courtiers and petty officials, among which

SchrummSchrumm spotted good old Bushido, easily recognizable by his long yellow beard. These men, at least, comported themselves with dignity. They had gold cords around their waists and the Misunderstanding coat of arms repeated two, three, four, five, or even six times down their shoulders. They lined up before the table of honor, the torchbearers behind them, the petal-strewing children sitting at their feet.

Then the Holy Director made his appearance, trembling with emotion and giving little grunts of satisfaction. A golden tiara encircled his brow and his body was draped in a purple tunic immodestly displaying his scrawny chest, thin arms, and potbelly. He was in a four-horse chariot drawn by four unlucky wretches in dunce caps adorned with ass's ears, who emitted pathetic cries of "Hee haw!" as they pulled. As if the crowd thrilled and at the same time frightened him, the Director was hiding his face behind the hand unoccupied with his reins, though he couldn't help stealing eager peeks at the audience from between his first two fingers, both adorned with gargantuan diamonds. There was something unreal about this manifestation, and SchrummSchrumm examined the eminent and yet pitiable personage with a feeling approaching horror. This wasn't Allright, thank God. Nor was it the man he'd glimpsed in Nastarz City. Nor the man depicted in the giant portrait outside the hacienda. So what sacred form of the Holy Director was this?

There were further surprises in store. Behind the Holy Director came the Deputy Director, imitating his superior in everything from dress to bearing to facial expressions, but in each case with an extra dash of absurdity: their difference in rank still had to be marked. The deputy, too, wore a kind of toga, but in pink. His tiara was of silver, and the wretches pulling his chariot had been reduced to a single pair. One behind the other, the two supreme leaders of Misunderstanding received the crowd's cheers of acclamation. The excursionists were enthralled. The guards, in their usual martial attitude—left fists against their chests, carbines raised—formed a guard of honor. The little boys and girls tossed their rose petals with renewed energy. Only the courtiers and officials seemed impatient to eat. As soon as the two men descended from their chariots and took their places on the thrones, there was a mad rush on the food. When everyone had refreshed themselves, the herald announced:

"The Holy Director will now deliver his speech. Silence! Silence! For without great silence, there is no true declamation."

The announcement was hardly necessary, as the preparatory activities being undertaken around the buffoonish chief executive were sufficient in themselves to alert everyone that he was about to speak. Two footmen had taken hold of his august person. One propped open his jaw alarmingly wide while the other crammed in a sort of rubber pear. Rhythmic pressure was applied, a liquid whose purpose was in all probability to fortify his vocal organs spurted out, and the Holy Director was heard to remark *whaalalooglugiug* as an expression of divine bliss washed over his features. Finally he rose, closed his eyes, and flung out his arms in a dramatic gesture—in short, he tried by every means at his disposal to present the illusion of sudden inspiration, though the speech had obviously been minutely choreographed—and began:

"My dear, beloved children who, in quest of Our Holy Excursion, have abandoned hearth and home, wives and children to come to Misunderstanding, today is a day of rejoicing. True, as blues and greens you must soon be divided from one another, but though disunited and henceforth traveling separate paths, you shall

all end your journey at the Quicksands. Therefore, may peace be in your hearts and joy shine in your faces.

"Ah, excursionists, women, men, and children! What a dream life you lead! Now here, now there, wandering hither and thither so agreeably and instructively. And what satisfactions unknown to the vulgar masses are yours! Indeed, only those who practice excursioning are given to discover certain refined delights, such as strolling through a cheerful pastoral countryside with a tractable young lass. A skiff has been rented for rowing on a nearby pond: what could be more natural? The weather is mild, it is a fine summer's afternoon. Soon, lulled by the hypocritical motion of the oars, the lass falls asleep in the skiff. Yes, I know all about such things, I am familiar with those delicious excursionistic sensations, my brothers, or at least I *was* familiar with them, years ago, when ablaze with the vocational fire. I will therefore say no more of these lawful and legitimate pleasures; they are woven into the very fabric of the excursionist's profession, and their notoriety is already widespread. The excursionist, in his heart of hearts, silently assimilates and, dare I say, draws nourishment from them. Instead I will outline, for the benefit of the children within the sound of my voice, those traits inherent to the conscientious excursionist. Oh, let those young ones, those dear little beings already consumed by the all-consuming flames of the vocation, hesitate no longer, but make haste to join the Excursionist Youth Organization as soon as they are able. They will find, in the bosom of that group, all the warmth their elite souls deserve.

"The first of these traits is confidence, my darling children. A confidence most often grounded in facts sufficiently prognostic to be taken as conclusive. Your elders who number among our ranks can recall certain telltale incidents from their childhoods and construe them as proof that their calling was genuine and their vocation written in the stars. For example, while still an infant, every future excursionist displays a remarkable flair for scaling the sides of his crib. He pulls vigorously on his nurse's or mother's teats, and, getting a firm grip on her hair, climbs up onto her shoulders. These are unmistakable signs!

"The second trait of the excursionist is imagination. And this imagination, too, is so precocious that one can immediately identify the future excursionist in any group of children. He is the one sitting in the back of the class, picking his nose and dreaming of grand and perilous expeditions. To give an example from my own life, I can clearly remember, at the age of thirteen, winning the annual poetry prize awarded by the esteemed Junior Excursionist Poets Society through my precise observations of a schoolfellow (who surely became an excursionist himself!) extracting yellowish boogers from his pimpled nose and eating them with a marvelously satisfied air, having first studied them at length from every angle. I drew the main inspiration for my sonnet from these observations. Will you permit me to read it to you?"

The question was met with a ripple of murmured consent. Many of the courtiers begged to be allowed to hear the "divine poem," and no sooner had they done so than the Director, like a ham actor, unfolded a piece of paper and began to recite with feeling:

"Ye who, denied ideals and joys complete,
"Do pick your noses with dispassion
"And, seated at the back of classrooms dark,

"Dream of sublime excursionistic feats,

"O childlike natures, hark!
"'Tis ye who, scorning every danger, fashion
"Misunderstanding from utopian ore.

"And yet the day will come, how well I know,
"When, boarded on the train of Adven-*tyoor*
"Ye all shall to the shining Quicksands go."

These atrocious verses garnered thunderous applause from the courtiers. The excursionists maintained a prudent silence, but a few guards must have been planted among them, because belated chants of "Bravo!" were sent up from that quarter as well. The Holy Director seemed to bask in his success. He thanked the audience with a bow and, calling once again for quiet, continued his speech:

"By dint of these essential traits that you, dear children, are cultivating in yourselves, the United Excursions may one day—who's to say?—regain their former glory, now temporarily in eclipse. Ah, if only you could have seen Misunderstanding in the time of the Great Influx, my friends! The ramparts of the Holy Excursion were encrusted with gems and glittered across the six continents, striking fear and respect into every pagan breast. Misunderstanding, the Heart of the World, was truly resplendent! And yet, take note: the excursionists of those times did not enjoy the benefit, as you do, of all the conveniences attendant on the advance of civilization. They sometimes had to march for days on end to reach an excursion site. Even so, the sevenfold holy name of the Ultimate Excursion was no less well known among the far-flung savages. The Monument to Fallen Excursionists, erected not far from here, attests to the fact. It commemorates those heroes who have disappeared on excursions past . . ."

Having pronounced these last words, the speaker fell silent, and everyone initially assumed he was marking his respect for the dead men. But then a series of events occurred leading them to believe he'd stopped for entirely different reasons.

First the audience noticed he was muttering unintelligible phrases to himself, among which, every so often, they could hear: "Ah! Wasn't it grand! Ah! Wasn't it fine!" Then his face reddened, the veins at his temples began to bulge as if he were choking, and a scrap of paper fell from his hand: the poem. He let loose something like a loud, powerful belch. At the same time, raising one arm in a gesture both ridiculous and admirable (because it must have cost him a considerable effort), he squeaked out: "*Adios, amigos*! I shall return!" Lastly, his head lolled to the side and he fainted into the arms of his colleague, the Deputy Director.

The deputy, sobbing with emotion, turned to the crowd:

"It's an accident, friends. A most deplorable accident!"

A group of four guards was already trotting over. They seized the Holy Director by his arms and legs, hoisted him onto a stretcher, and lifted him. As they were carrying him away, one final incident added to the ludicrous tone of the whole event. The Deputy Director, very tenderly, attempted to smooth his superior's hair. Unfortunately, he was rather clumsy about it, and the whole room saw the toupee that had been covering the directorial bald spot tumble to the floor. It fell near the deputy, who, after a few seconds' indecision, picked it up delicately between his thumb and forefinger, eliciting giggles from the children in the front row. Of course he immediately dropped it again and, wiping the sweat from his brow, said weakly: "The celebration shall continue!" His heart wasn't in it, though, and it was amid this cheapened, funfair atmosphere that the herald announced:

"Ladies and gentlemen, dear excursionists and darling children, despite the regrettable fainting fit that has come over our Holy Director, the celebration shall continue. Here, for your entertainment and instruction, is a mimogram entitled 'Appearance of the Solemn Form of the Excursion's Holy Director.'"

There was a loud rumble. The red curtain emblazoned with the Misunderstanding coat of arms was drawn aside to reveal a large panel sliding in the opposite direction. When both panel and curtain were out of the way, the room was open to the elements and, at the end of a short cul-de-sac, the scene before them was framed as in a theater. A cloud of multicolored sand began whirling closer as the sound of furious galloping was heard, in addition to the following dialogue:

"How's it going, pals?"

"Going good over here!"

"Good here, too!"

SchrummSchrumm was on the edge of his seat. Had the mounted guards of Eden been brought in for this mimogram? But no, these weren't the mounted guards of Eden, anyone could see that: the approaching horsemen were wheeling and prancing in midair. Awe-inspiring were they, they and their mounts, of platinum and bronze, respectively. Rippling were their leaden manes; ringing were their iron hoofs. The enchanted riders raised golden trumpets to their lips and thrice the trumpets blared. At the first blast, all the spectators fell to their knees. At the second, the cloud of sand transformed into a dizzyingly tall palace whose steep stairs the Holy Director himself was ascending with dignified mien. (The face and body of this extraordinary man were now wreathed in flame, and he held in one hand a shining globe depicting the symbolic routes of all the Sunday excursions. What's more, hosts of angels and archangels were singing his praises. The onlookers saw with miraculous clarity how wise they had been to consecrate their lives to excursioning.) At the third and final blast, the enchanted palace, the solemn form of the Holy Director, and the metallic horses and riders vanished simultaneously. It was all over. Everyone around SchrummSchrumm—officials, guards, and excursionists alike—staggered unsteadily to their feet.

The herald announced crisply:

"You have just beheld the fifty-seventh manifestation of the reign of our Holy Director, King of the Quicksands and Prince of Misunderstanding. On the subject of which, I have terrible news. Our Holy Director, already seriously weakened by the fainting fit that prevented him from finishing his speech, did not survive the enormous exertions demanded by his role in producing the extraordinary phenomenon to which you have just borne witness. Our Holy Director, in his fifty-seventh form, is therefore dead. Long live the Holy Director! As a sign of mourning, the celebration will be terminated. Return to your rooms and reflect upon what you've seen!"

X

Nothing more was said about this death, whether symbolic or otherwise. There was no official news bulletin and no one was invited to attend the interment, if indeed there had been one. This would have seemed remarkable in any other circumstances, but the excursionists had passed the point where anything could astonish them . . . The first truly important change came the day after this morbid and incomprehensible farce. When he awoke, SchrummSchrumm was intrigued by the sound of an unusual commotion in the building. Krikri popped in as if by chance—very opportunely, in any case—to inform him that this was due to the relocation efforts now underway, which would make the new division of excursionists into blues and greens official. "Come and see!" he said. Downstairs, trunks and suitcases were being hauled away, orders were being given, and kicks were being dealt out to those blues not moving fast enough. But on SchrummSchrumm's floor, everything was calm. The sergeant opened the doors of neighboring rooms that had been occupied only yesterday: all were vacant. "From now on, the fourth floor will be the exclusive domain of our green excursionists, the only ones worthy of the name!" he said as he left. SchrummSchrumm found his four unlucky companions. All took a gloomy view of the situation. Not even the most pessimistic, however, predicted the discovery that awaited them a few hours later: the staircase had been bricked up. The work must have been carried out with superhuman speed and secrecy, because not a sound had reached them. Krikri, when summoned, explained that "things being what they were, they were not otherwise." In concrete terms, the only thing left for them was to bide their time until their departure for the Quicksands, a departure they could now count on as a certainty and which would be fast-tracked to the maximum allowable degree, given that they'd attained the exceptional honor of the green disk. As far as their floor was concerned, though one end had been walled off, a second egress remained: a door Krikri showed them but which he said would be kept locked.

This marked the beginning of a very dull, very monotonous period of their lives, despite the fabulous amenities suddenly placed at their disposal. Using their golden telephones, they could order the most lavish meals imaginable at any hour of the day or night: the dishes would be brought up promptly. It was always Krikri or one of the other four guards who provided this room service, however. Lucette and Lulu no longer appeared. They could also order women, children, and men. But though admirably trained from a sexual standpoint, all were invariably deaf-mutes who could anticipate the slightest erotic whim but were utter morons in every other respect. In short, after amusing themselves for a while with unspeakable orgies, the excursionists grew bored even of these excesses.

Thus a long week dragged by. They had no news at all of their former companions. Every time he saw Krikri, SchrummSchrumm would ask:

"Have you gotten an answer yet? The answer I've been anxiously waiting for?"

"An answer to what?"

"To the letter I sent the Holy Director."

SchrummSchrumm hoped Krikri would ask him when and how he'd sent this letter—which of course didn't exist—or tell him the Holy Director was dead, or something along those lines. But Krikri had changed a great deal and now deftly avoided such traps as if they were child's play. He was never absent, keeping a close watch over all of them with exasperating patience.

At last, one day—it was pouring down rain, and from the safety of his window SchrummSchrumm had been watching the mists slowly envelop Misunderstanding's dismal horizons—there was a knock at his door and a voice asked permission to enter. It wasn't Krikri, nor could it have been any of the other four greens or their guards: they'd long since abandoned such formalities with one another. SchrummSchrumm went to answer it and was confronted with one of those horrible creatures called "little obese nudies." This one strongly resembled the specimen he'd seen with Lieutenant Medullus the day of his arrival, the only difference being that it was stark naked. This sexless being was disgustingly fat, the transparency of its skin was at once marvelous and repulsive, and its limbs were mere stumps. As a crowning obscenity, its bloated face had been carefully made up: rice powder on the cheeks, black eyeliner, red lipstick.

After rubbing his eyes to be sure that this was not, through some freak, simply a bad dream, SchrummSchrumm dodged to one side and tried to slam the door in its face. This was exactly the wrong reaction. The monster, until then perfectly motionless, sprang onto his shoulders with remarkable agility and pulled SchrummSchrumm's ear until he howled in pain and rage. Having given this proof of its corporeal existence, the little obese nudie let go of SchrummSchrumm's ear, dismounted, and landed on its hind stumps, immobile once again as if nothing had happened. No longer able to deny the phenomenon's reality, SchrummSchrumm faced up to it bravely:

"Who're you?" he asked, on his guard for a second assault.

"I am Alfred," replied the monster in a grating, curiously metallic voice, rattling off the words in an odd cadence.

"Fine, but what are you here for?"

"I have come to inform you that you are summoned with the utmost urgency to the office of Colonel Red-Bartlett, my beloved and revered master, who has sent me to you as his messenger."

"That's more like it," said SchrummSchrumm. "Now we know where we stand. Please inform the colonel that I will attend the meeting as soon as Krikri, my guard, grants me authorization to leave the hotel."

The momentary sound of motors whirring inside Alfred's head betrayed the struggle he was undergoing as he grappled with this problem. He finally managed to resolve it, however, in his own way. He repeated:

"You are summoned to the colonel's office. You must come."

"No," insisted SchrummSchrumm, "I can't leave without Krikri's permission. He'd flog us both."

"You must come," repeated Alfred.

"No!"

This might have gone on for a long time had not Krikri appeared at that moment. He glanced at Alfred without batting an eye.

"I heard noises. Has this dreadful little creature been pulling your ear?"

SchrummSchrumm said that he had. Alfred was hanging on their every word with exaggerated attention.

"Oho! He pulled your ear, did he? Well then, we're going to have to punish him."

SchrummSchrumm furrowed his brow, annoyed that he had no idea what was going on.

"Isn't it right that he should be punished for being so rude to you?" continued Krikri in a state of gleeful anticipation. "Anyway, if he pulled your ear, it means his mission is complete. And when a little obese nudie's mission is complete ... Watch this!" He took out a leather case and drew from it a long needle, like a knitting needle, but cast in gold and with one end shaped into a handle.

Krikri seemed to take great pleasure in SchrummSchrumm's stupefied expression. He made him test the tip of the needle with his finger to feel how sharp it was.

"Let's begin. Name and identification number?" he said, looking mockingly at Alfred.

"I am Alfred, number one hundred forty-seven sixty-three."

"Good! Birth?" demanded Krikri, jotting down each of Alfred's answers in a notepad as he gave them.

"I was born at ten o'clock today. I belong to Colonel Red-Bartlett, who sent me to convey an urgent summons to excursionist SchrummSchrumm," Alfred said politely.

"Very good," said Krikri, closing the notepad. "Are you ready?"

"I am ready, absolutely and entirely ready," said Alfred. "Am I going on my pleasant journey, Mr. Krikri?"

"Yes."

Krikri was growing more and more enraptured.

"Just look at him!" he said to SchrummSchrumm. "They're incredibly alert, you know. And so obedient!"

"Are you going to tell me what all this is about?" asked SchrummSchrumm, certain now that something unpleasant was brewing.

"After! After!" laughed Krikri. Then, to Alfred: "Approach!"

Alfred made a graceful little leap that ended in a curtsy. The guard had abruptly stopped chuckling; his face was now deadly serious, and a strange rictus twisted his mouth as he swiftly raised the arm in which he held the needle. SchrummSchrumm tried to intervene:

"You're not going to do that, Krikri! You wouldn't deprive yourself of such an obedient servant!"

But before he fully knew what was happening, Schrumm-Schrumm was pushed aside by the guard, who raised his arm high and plunged the needle into Alfred's navel. The act was skillful and precise, the product of long experience. He plunged the needle in and drew it out again. Alfred was already making a frightful face and rapidly deflating, while the following words escaped his lips: "Ah! We have loved life!" The air escaping from his navel continued its awful sound for a few seconds more, and then there was nothing left of Alfred but a rubber film which was quickly disposed of.

"Allow me to present you with this little-obese-nudie-piercing needle," said Krikri, proffering the implement.

SchrummSchrumm refused it with a horrified gesture that was not lost on the guard. His forehead was dripping with sweat.

"My God!" said Krikri. "Your sensitivity does you credit, but still! You have to understand that no one attaches the slightest importance to the illusory and fleeting existences of these little obese nudies. They're just sacks of air."

He explained that the little obese nudies were factory-produced. They were delivered ready to use. All you had to do was blow into their navels until they were fully inflated. They obeyed orders promptly and had perfect recall. Most often they were employed as messengers, but occasionally they were given other tasks. For the sake of convenience, as well as for tracking and statistical purposes, it had been agreed to give each newly programmed unit a name and identification number.

This product was reserved for Misunderstanding's top brass, all of whom had several hundred tucked away in sterilized pouches for their personal use. Senior officers always carried two or three in their pockets in case of emergency.

The only restriction the Regulations placed on them concerned the duration of their lives. It had to be extremely short, on the order of two to three hours. This was because, no matter how well programmed they were, they had an annoying habit of forming attachments to people who were friendly to them. Once an attachment was formed, they didn't obey orders as readily and displayed an unwillingness to have their navels pierced. It had even happened that little obese nudies had altogether refused to be killed and had gone into hiding in Misunderstanding. Needless to say, this was an eventuality everyone preferred to avoid, since it meant having to hunt them down and kill them from a distance with arrows.

This was why, though only people of rank had the right to *create* little obese nudies, all guards had not only the right but the duty to pierce them as soon as they completed their missions.

". . . And now, it's time we paid a visit to the colonel," said Krikri.

For the first time since being sequestered on the fourth floor with the other greens, SchrummSchrumm left the hotel. It was deserted, at least what he could see of it—they went out the back. He thought they were going to catch the electric train in some luxurious underground station and he'd get to have a drink and look at pornographic etchings as they sped toward their destination. But after going down several spiral staircases, their route diverged from any he'd known before. They walked along a perfectly straight, brilliantly lit, apparently endless corridor. Iron doors lined either side. Above each door was an electric bulb and above each bulb a series of numbers. An armed guard stood sentry at each door, too, and all of them seemed to be either asleep or in a waking dream, because their vacant stares registered no flicker of reaction when SchrummSchrumm and Krikri walked past. They simply—and no doubt instinctively—stood a little straighter, and at each of the sentinels' regulation heel-clicks Krikri's face lit up with an immense but well-contained joy. The sergeant often pointed out, with an intelligent comment, some detail SchrummSchrumm wouldn't have otherwise noticed. As soon as his attention had been drawn to it, this detail considerably modified, if not the atmosphere of these corridors per se, then at least their obscure significance. For example, the cell doors were all painted in bright colors or else had a bouquet of flowers or a fish tank in front of them. What was the purpose of this ornamentation? SchrummSchrumm couldn't guess. But it transformed the long walk into something more like a leisurely stroll. Next, they passed through a portion of the long hallway with no sentinels at all, though there were still iron doors. Then, unexpectedly, the hallway made a ninety-degree turn. There was a second turn, a third, then another and yet another. SchrummSchrumm felt his head begin to swim. At the same time, the electric bulbs were becoming increasingly sparse and the light was growing dimmer and dimmer. Then darkness. They were now at the threshold of a vast, hemispherical room. Around its periphery were the murky outlines of corridor entrances identical to the one from which they'd just emerged. There was no clue as to the nature of these corridors, nor any apparent means of distinguishing one from the next. But Krikri's knowledge of the premises was undeniably astounding. He didn't hesitate for a second. He marched, at a fiercely resolute pace, down one of the narrow passageways. SchrummSchrumm shuddered: Krikri was no more than a couple of meters ahead of him, he could hear him breathing, but he couldn't see him. His forehead struck a wall and he moaned, frightened:

"My God! Krikri, where are we?"

"This is the Labyrinth we're crossing. Make one mistake here, take one wrong corridor, and it's certain death," answered the sergeant as he tugged sharply on SchrummSchrumm's sleeve to stop him heading down the passageway just beside the one they wanted. SchrummSchrumm began shaking uncontrollably.

"Don't abandon me, Krikri," he begged. "This place is terrifying."

"Dearly beloved friend and companion, little child, little lost brother, never fear! Just follow me." These were the words SchrummSchrumm heard close to his ear. At the same time, the guard unbuttoned his shirt, slid a hand over his chest, and pressed his lips to the nape of SchrummSchrumm's neck in a burning kiss. But all this was done very quickly. SchrummSchrumm could still feel the sergeant's breath on his face when the latter took him firmly by the hand and spoke soothingly once again:

"Never fear! Just follow me, I won't let go of you."

Krikri guided him. His hand was strong and reassuring. SchrummSchrumm progressively lost his sense of time and space. All he knew was that in this terrible tangle of corridors full of sharp and unexpected angles, of bifurcations and no doubt horrifying traps, Sergeant Krikri walked with sovereign ease. Finally they spied a glimmer of light at the end of their nocturnal tunnel, and when they came out into another hemispherical room—identical to the first, except that it was lit and instead of corridors there were some twenty closed doors around its circumference—the sergeant pointed out an old bench:

"Have a seat," he said gently. "We'll rest awhile. But no noise!" he added, putting a finger to his lips and indicating one of the doors with a crack of light underneath. "No one must know we're here."

SchrummSchrumm nodded and plopped down onto the bench, still panting. Krikri did the same. His breathing was normal. No hint of anxiety or fatigue.

"How did you come to learn the layout of these awful corridors so well?" SchrummSchrumm asked when he'd recovered his breath.

"I understand your amazement," said Krikri, "but there's really nothing very extraordinary about it. All my colleagues who hold the rank of sergeant or above know the Labyrinth as well as I do. We're specially trained in it over the course of several years' relentless study at Guard School. You can't earn your diploma until you pass a series of tests, including a very daunting field trial. They drop you into the Labyrinth—without a light, map, provisions, compass, or any other survival gear—and you have to find your way out on your own. Those who don't pass are never seen again: either they die of hunger and thirst, or they go insane down here. Nevertheless, I think this practical trial is a great thing, because a purely theoretical education, which is what you'd otherwise risk getting at Guard School, just isn't enough."

"You certainly learn the hard way! But even if all guards-in-training follow the same core curriculum, I imagine there must be various specialties corresponding to different disciplines."

"Right you are," said Krikri. "To each his allotted role, and to each according to his aptitudes and abilities. Misunderstanding gives every one of us the chance to fulfill his potential."

"What's your specialty? Your real one," asked SchrummSchrumm, surprised at his own boldness.

"I'm not allowed to say," murmured Krikri after a brief pause. "But maybe you've guessed?"

"Honestly, I'm not at all sure. While we're on the subject, there's something I've been wondering since the day I met you. The guard's uniform suits you to a tee, so I can easily believe that you might have been drawn to the undeniable prestige that comes with wearing it, and also that you might have been attracted—more broadly speaking—by the career of a guard. What's more, the assuredness with which you've just navigated this underground Labyrinth—to cite one of many examples—demonstrates your keen intelligence, and you must have graduated near the top of your class . . . But that's just what's gnawing at me. With your background and natural gifts, you could have succeeded just as well, or even better, in a more rewarding field. Do the exceptional perks that come with being a Misunderstanding guard really outweigh the sacrifices it demands? I don't mean the lack of entertainment options, obviously, though that is an important consideration, especially when you're young. I'm talking about the inability to work toward a specific goal, which seems like a malady endemic to the guards in Misunderstanding. A malady that I'm sure is not unrelated to the fact that your whole life you remain voluntary prisoners, or as good as prisoners, in this city . . . It's true, however, that this is only a theoretical argument, because in order to suffer from imprisonment, you have to have first known freedom."

Krikri listened politely to all this. But SchrummSchrumm's expectations for the talk had been too high. The drift of their conversation had taken an unusual turn, yes, but it would go no further.

"You don't need to worry about me, Mr. SchrummSchrumm," said Krikri lightly, unconsciously abandoning the informal pronouns they'd been using with each other since SchrummSchrumm had begged not to be abandoned. "Instead consider this, because I'll have to leave you alone for a minute: Do you see these doors? You may open them. All except those two," he added, pointing to the one with the light underneath and a second door nearby, just like the others but with a little black rectangle above its frame marked with a diagonal red slash. "Don't forget! Entering either of those two rooms is strictly forbidden."

"Why are they forbidden when the others are open?"

"There is always and everywhere *something* forbidden," said Krikri sententiously. "Anyway," he added with a mischievous twinkle in his eye, "that doesn't mean they're locked. Quite the contrary: they're as open as the rest. You're just not allowed to enter . . . I'll be back in a few minutes."

SchrummSchrumm nodded and shrugged. Once alone, he wandered idly over to see what lay behind the doors he was permitted to open. There was nothing. The rooms were empty. He opened nine or ten doors in this way and then stopped short: above the tenth (or eleventh) door was the fateful black rectangle with the red slash. "So this one's off-limits!" he thought with a smile. He'd put his hand on the knob, purely on a whim, just to see what it felt like to touch the handle of a forbidden door. As soon as he did so—though he hadn't pushed or turned it—the mechanism unlatched and the door swung open noiselessly.

SchrummSchrumm's first instinct was to shut it again and hurry back to his bench. He was about to do just that, when it dawned on him that Krikri would be gone for several minutes more. With this thought in mind, he could no longer resist the goadings of his curiosity. He stuck his head through the doorway: this room, too, was empty. There was nothing of interest about it, unless you counted the fact that it had been recently painted and that there was pink gravel in place of the regular floorboards. Simultaneously relieved and disappointed, he stepped into the room and what he saw there made him utter a strangled little scream, but it was too late to retreat. In the corner of the room not visible to someone peeking through the doorway, which is to say the corner one could only see by stepping fully into the room, there was a sort of lighted glass display case, and in this case was a basket of exceptionally splendid fruit. *What an idea*, thought SchrummSchrumm as he moved closer, *putting a fruit basket in a display case*. He felt a sudden, irresistible urge to sink his teeth into one of those superlative fruits.

He glanced around. There was a second door, but it was shut. Also a cupboard, but it seemed to be empty and there was no key in the lock. He opened the case, which offered no resistance, took out a magnificent apple, and raised it to his lips.

At that same instant, the cupboard door gave a creak as if it were being pushed open from inside. Behind it was the silhouette of a man sitting on a little stool specially built to fit the confined space. SchrummSchrumm saw that it was a false cupboard; it had been converted into a sentry box where a man was keeping watch. The sentinel had now opened the door all the way and was looking at SchrummSchrumm, laughing heartily and slapping his thighs.

"Who are you?" stammered SchrummSchrumm.

The man stopped laughing.

"I'm the Keeper of the Apple," he said in a deep voice.

"I beg your pardon," said SchrummSchrumm, his heart still thumping wildly. "I thought this room was unoccupied and this fruit basket had been left behind. So when I saw this Apple in the basket—so round, so lovely, so perfectly ripe—I couldn't resist the temptation. You understand, don't you?"

"Of course I understand; I'm the Keeper of the Apple."

"Please stop kidding around," said SchrummSchrumm. "It's obvious you don't spend all your time in that cupboard guarding this Apple. The truth is, you and Krikri got together and decided to play a practical joke on me."

"I'm the Keeper of the Apple," the man repeated a third time. "And I can assure you this is no joke. Listen here: you were forbidden to enter this room and you entered it anyway, isn't that so? Then I'm obliged to do my duty. With regret, because I don't think the punishment fits the crime. But I'm only a cog in the machine, no one takes my opinion seriously."

"What's the punishment? What are you going to do to me?"

"Nothing, for the moment," answered the Keeper. "You're going to sign a deposition in which you acknowledge the facts of the matter, and later you'll be summoned to see His Excellency the Director, who's the rightful owner of this fruit basket."

"To see His Excellency? But the Holy Director is dead!"

"Don't play the fool. It won't do you any good," warned the man.

"Is there truly no other way? Nothing we can work out?"

"Nothing at all, believe me! Now sign your deposition," said the man, handing him a fat notebook.

SchrummSchrumm read with growing amazement:

"I, the undersigned, excursionist first class SchrummSchrumm, do hereby affirm the following facts: While on my way to visit Colonel Red-Bartlett in answer to a summons, I took advantage of a moment when Sergeant Krikri, who was accompanying me, left me unsupervised, to gain access to a room I had been strictly forbidden to enter. My dazzled eyes immediately perceived a marvelous display case behind the gem-encrusted door, in which reposed a solid-gold basket containing the most extraordinary fruits I had ever seen. The basket was wreathed in a halo of diaphanous light and the fruit appeared to me, I repeat, utterly magnificent. In particular, there was an Apple—so round, so lovely, so perfectly ripe—that the temptation came over me to steal it for the purpose of consumption. Granted, I had just violated a formal interdiction and was fully cognizant that I would be aggravating my offense by unlawfully stealing a piece of fruit, but I seemed to see a bevy of naked young beauties around me; they were dancing and undulating provocatively and eating an Apple just like the one I so fervently desired. I heard the sound of their teeth crunching into the sweet, succulent fruit-flesh; I saw their expressions of gastronomical ecstasy. At the same time, I heard the devil whisper to me, softly and insistently: 'This is the fruit of happiness, pluck it from the basket! You'll become like a bird, light, light! You'll become the handsomest, strongest, most admired, in short, the greatest of all excursionists!' Oh, the awful temptation! From that point on, I could no longer resist. I ran to the display case, I seized the Apple, and I prepared to become the handsomest, the cleverest, the greatest of all excursionists.

"Alas, at that very instant—as the devil disappeared in a puff of sulfurous smoke and the naked beauties evaporated with shrieks of laughter—the Keeper of the Apple, namely the watchman Illustrious, emerged from his observation post and apprehended me. After hearing my defense, considering my tender age, and deeming that I no longer possessed a sound idea of good and evil at the time I committed my heinous act, Illustrious humbly implores His Excellency to be merciful toward me in this unhappy affair.

"Signed in Misunderstanding, the . . . day of . . ."

The deposition had been handwritten on a left-hand page of the notebook. The Keeper of the Apple had already signed it.

SchrummSchrumm noticed that the right-hand page contained the same text with a blank for the guilty party's name.

"Well?" said the Keeper, handing him a pencil. "Are you going to sign, yes or no?"

"What a pathetic joke!" grumbled SchrummSchrumm. "How could you imagine I'd put my name to such hogwash?"

"Something wrong?" asked the Keeper.

"Many things are wrong. This text was written out in advance. Not only that, but I see an identical text already prepared for the next culprit. This is extremely degrading, since the way it's been done refuses to take into account all the little details that go to make up the personality of whoever commits this infraction—little details that individualize the infraction, if you prefer—and that give it an original character different from all others, showing that this is not the same culprit even if he committed the same offense. It's a question of the guilty party's pride, Mr. Keeper. Also, this text is beyond belief in terms of its exaggerations—I say this without impugning the craftsmanship and unquestionable literary talent of whoever had a hand in drafting it. Couldn't these things have been described in simpler terms? Meaning as they actually happened, which is—to my mind—a sensible solution? All this business about the devil talking to me and naked women dancing voluptuously around me, it's very imaginative—once again, hats off to the authors—but it's silly. I just wanted the Apple, that's all. Look, Mr. Keeper, I'm sure we can reach some kind of compromise on this, because it's not the substance of the deposition I object to, only the form. Let me bring one last detail to your attention. I'm grateful to you for putting in a good word for me, but would you mind also noting that this Apple, though arguably stolen, was definitely not eaten? There's a big difference, you have to admit, between a stolen but uneaten Apple and an Apple that has been both stolen *and* eaten.

"Where is the Apple?" asked the Keeper.

"Right here!" said SchrummSchrumm. He was not half pleased with his speech. By insisting on the inclusion of one or two phrases underscoring that it was he, SchrummSchrumm, who had committed this offense and not just any random person coming down the pike, he knew he was giving voice to the conviction held by everyone who had signed a similar deposition before him, as well as all those who would have to sign after him.

"What do you propose, then?"

"I suggest the two of us draft a new deposition: more sober-minded, more nuanced, and rigorously accurate."

"Draft a new deposition!" echoed the man, as if he couldn't believe his ears. "Are you crazy? Or rather, are you really so stupid you don't understand that everything in this deposition holds symbolic meaning? That these words were composed by the greatest legal practitioners, the greatest theologians, the greatest poets? That it's not some 'pathetic joke' but an esoteric text? In short, that the details have been deliberately heightened and embroidered in order to give the event a transcendental significance? Come now, sign it with no more bellyaching or I clobber you!"

"Well!" muttered SchrummSchrumm to himself. He took the quill the man proffered, dipped it in the inkwell, and signed and dated the form.

"Good lad!" said Illustrious. With that, he adroitly snatched back the notebook and tucked it away in a corner of the cupboard. Then he began to clap his hands and dance around the room. His joy seemed genuine enough, but it was perfectly incomprehensible.

At a certain point, his dancing brought him—for the first time—fully into the light. SchrummSchrumm started.

"Are my eyes playing tricks on me?" he said, moving a step closer. "Have you been 'Keeper of the Apple' very long?"

"What do you mean?" asked the man, and came to a standstill.

"I remember you, you old rascal!" continued Schrumm-Schrumm, dropping into the informal pronoun. "No, I'm not mistaken. Don't you remember me? Take a good look."

"You *are* mistaken," said Illustrious. "I don't know you and you don't know me."

"Oh, yes I do!" said SchrummSchrumm. "Let me refresh your memory. You're the bus driver who drove us to Misunderstanding three weeks ago. And a sorry excuse for a driver you were, too; you nearly sent us plummeting into a ravine."

The watchman decided to switch tactics.

"It's true," he admitted, "I used to work as a bus driver, and I took my retirement three weeks ago. I was getting too old to drive, so they gave me this thankless job. But none of my former colleagues knows about it. If they did, I'd never live it down. What price are you going to demand for your silence? That's your plan, isn't it?"

"You guessed it," laughed SchrummSchrumm. "I want the whole truth. I want answers. What's the meaning of this charade? Why did Krikri invent a flimsy excuse to leave me to my own devices? Why did he specifically point out this room? Why were you hiding in that cupboard? Out with it!"

"OK, OK," said Illustrious. They were squashed together side-by-side on the little cupboard seat, and SchrummSchrumm, because the idea struck him as funny, pulled the door closed on them.

"I'm the assistant Keeper of the Apple," he whispered to Illustrious. "Shhh!"

Illustrious shrugged to indicate that he would never understand the ways of excursionists. Then he went on:

"It's all owing to the Regulations that these things happen," he began, in a tone of sincerity. "The Regulations foresee everything. You excursionists, poor dumb innocents that you are, think you're doing what you please. Not so! Open your eyes. Here's the truth: each and every move you make has been predicted in advance, right down to the smallest detail; there are no chance occurrences; everything happens at the exact time set out in the Regulations, in the exact way set out in the Regulations. My job is to write up all the excursionists who—one after another, some a little sooner and some a little later, but always without fail—enter this room as you did today and attempt to steal the Apple. My work is precise and timed out to the minute. I had to rehearse my role as 'Keeper of the Apple' for a solid week. They taught me every answer I was to give, they put me through courses in dramatic acting and diction, they went over every detail with me until I was letter-perfect. Even the faces I made and the sound of the door opening were planned. Can you believe it? I have to polish the Apples, because they need to be surpassingly shiny to attract each and every excursionist, without exception, who enters this room. But that's not the most important part. Everything's planned out in advance, like I was saying. That's why, when I came into work today, I knew you'd be here to steal my Apple at this specific time. I wrote up your deposition this morning. And there will be four more Apple-stealing excursionists coming in after you!"

SchrummSchrumm swallowed several times, with difficulty.

"My dear Illustrious," he croaked at last, "it's hard enough to believe that the Misunderstanding civil service would pay an employee to do such a task. But that all the excursionists in Misunderstanding should enter this room at the precise moments foreseen by the Regulations, to steal this Apple you've been charged with watching? That, I'll never believe!"

"The fact remains," retorted Illustrious with unnerving calm, "that your own entrance happened right on schedule, as has everything else for the two weeks I've held this post. Also, the man I replaced, who's now permanently retired, did this job for twenty years and said he never saw the smallest deviation!"

"Stuff and nonsense," muttered SchrummSchrumm. "You and Krikri could have easily arranged this whole joke between the two of you."

"Now it's a joke again!" Illustrious said scornfully. But he added, in a kinder voice: "Would you like further examples?"

"It would certainly make your story more convincing."

"Well, there's a sequence of events that happens like clockwork to all excursionists at the beginning of their stay in Misunderstanding. These events, which I'm sure you'd remember, must've happened to you, too. All you need to do is listen and correct me if I'm wrong . . . As early as the day after your arrival, you entered your hotel's library thinking you were breaking the rules. There, after having found a hiding place thanks to the apparent (but only apparent) sympathy of the second monitor, you were reprimanded and beaten by the monitor-in-chief. Next, you met with the spy, Leopold. That same day, just a short time later, you witnessed a dispute between an excursionist and several guards. The excursionist claimed to have heard a train carrying passengers away the night before. The guards, naturally, denied the existence of any train. That's when you intervened to back up your companion's assertion, saying that you, too, had heard the noises in question. You were so adamant that you were taken to the 'Acoustic Room for the Production of Artificial Sounds' where, in your presence, they simulated a train departing from the valley nearby, preceded by the sound of feet marching in step, whipcracks, stifled groans, and so forth. This must have put you into a state of extreme confusion and distress. Your distress increased when, a few days later, they brought you three iron-banded wicker trunks, which an officer from the Dispatch and Receiving Department said belonged to you. Initially you refused to accept these trunks. Nevertheless, after a heated discussion, you did accept them, and this was due to a photograph you found in one of the trunks (a photograph of Allright, according to you; a photograph of the Holy Director, according to the hotel manager, a distinguished archaeologist and graffiti expert). This discussion was followed, after a lapse of several days, by the discovery of the Original Pissoir. From that point on, your distress must have transformed into outright panic. You entered first Eden, then Nastarz City. You were chased on foot and saw a table laid for a ritual feast. You were subsequently called in to see Mr. Burns. There you met the President of the Investigating Committee, Mrs. Martha, and the two big dogs with the placid stares, Tobias and Tobias. Next up was—"

"Enough!" said SchrummSchrumm. "You're well informed, I'll grant you that. But it proves nothing: you've could've gathered all that information after the fact. The only truly convincing evidence would be telling me my future."

"Your future . . ." repeated Illustrious. "As it happens, I do know your future, but I can't tell you what it is."

"I would've been astounded if you could," said SchrummSchrumm triumphantly. "You're a lying scoundrel, my dear Illustrious."

The remark seemed to roll right off the former bus driver's back.

"Listen," he said, "I'm sure you realize I probably didn't tell you all this just to be sociable. I did it because these explanations, too, were prescribed by the Regulations, there's the long and the short of it. So don't go getting any big ideas, and don't get cocky. That, for what it's worth, is the best proof of good faith I can give you, because I shouldn't have told you that last bit, according to the plan. Make of it what you will! In any case, you have to clear out, because my next customer's due in any minute (I need to give my Apple a polish so it's as appealing as possible) and Krikri's probably looking for you by now."

"I forgot about Krikri. What am I going to tell him?"

"He'll act like he doesn't know you were in my room," said Illustrious kindly. "It'll be fine. Go on, now, scoot. So long!"

"So long," said SchrummSchrumm.

Just then, Krikri's voice rang out: "Where are you, Mr. SchrummSchrumm?" The sergeant was noisily opening and closing doors, making a deliberate show of looking for him in the places he wasn't. SchrummSchrumm stepped back out into the huge hemispherical chamber. He saw that the first room—the one Krikri had said was also off-limits, with a strip of light under its door—was now open. Even more astonishing: though earlier Krikri had made it abundantly clear that they were supposed to be keeping their presence discreet, he was currently standing in the doorway of this room motioning for SchrummSchrumm to join him.

"What's going on? I thought this room was off-limits."

"Don't worry," said Krikri. "The man inside's a friend of mine. Come and see."

SchrummSchrumm did as he was bid, though somewhat cautiously, since the Apple incident had made him wary of walking into another trap. He was immediately relieved. Not because the room was ordinary and innocuous-looking—if it had been, he would still have feared some misadventure—but because it really was occupied: by a radio operator, to all appearances, who was sitting before a gleaming radio set. His back was to them, he seemed preoccupied, and he was wearing headphones. All of which explained why he hadn't heard the door open or noticed his two visitors. Not that they'd made much noise. Suddenly, the apparatus emitted a monotone whine. The needles on the dials swung back and forth and the man turned a knob: the whine thrummed even louder. It was like a voice from a distant world. Its inflections were sorrowful, sometimes heartrending. After a while it became almost intoxicating, and SchrummSchrumm closed his eyes as if spellbound. Then the hum abruptly stopped, and when SchrummSchrumm opened his eyes again he found the sergeant and the operator staring at each other.

"Hey, buddy!" said Krikri casually. "How's it going?"

"Who the hell are you?" the man demanded, addressing himself less to SchrummSchrumm than to Krikri. He looked genuinely confounded. It was obvious the sergeant had been trying to give SchrummSchrumm the impression that he knew this operator personally. And the operator, either because he didn't want to compromise himself in front of an outsider, or—more likely—because Krikri really was a stranger to him, had involuntarily exposed the deception. This left Krikri struggling for a moment as he considered how to avoid losing face. He looked pointedly at SchrummSchrumm and then went over to the operator, who had by now removed his headphones, and whispered something in his ear. SchrummSchrumm watched their every move: now that he'd caught on to the guard's ruse, he found the situation extremely funny. He saw Krikri straighten up and give him a smug grin, as if he were sure his colleague would play along from here on out. Instead of which, the operator glowered and his face went purple with rage.

"Are you out of your mind?! Bringing an excursionist in here? What branch of the service do you belong to, anyway?"

"Staff Sergeant Krikri of the private guard," Krikri answered testily.

"I don't give a damn. No one's allowed in here!" said the man. Nevertheless, he was clearly a little overawed by Krikri's rank. He scratched his nose and gave SchrummSchrumm another look. The sergeant took this opportunity to seize the man by his collar. As SchrummSchrumm had already discovered on one or two previous occasions, Krikri possessed a formidable physical strength that his use of makeup and generally effeminate appearance belied.

"Imbecile!" he said through clenched teeth. "Do you know what people get for talking to their superiors like that? Well, I'm going to teach you!"

SchrummSchrumm could tell they were about to come to blows. He rushed over, grabbed Krikri's arm, and pushed him away. Krikri was stunned by his audacity. Now it was the radio operator's turn to take advantage of his opponent's distraction. SchrummSchrumm saw a glint of malice in his eye and realized the man was looking around for an object to use as a weapon.

"Enough, Jacques!" ordered SchrummSchrumm, having no idea whether this was operator's name or not.

Incredibly, these words worked like magic on the two antagonists. The operator burst out laughing, and Krikri, somewhat uneasily, followed suit. SchrummSchrumm breathed a sigh of relief.

"Are we all friends again?" he asked.

"If you say so!" said Krikri, shrugging. He went so far as to accept the cigarette "Jacques" offered him. Meanwhile, a curtain covering the entrance to an alcove moved, and there appeared the last thing SchrummSchrumm expected to see: two young women. They were very young indeed, both with long blonde hair. Though they hadn't taken any particular care with their dress, they were exceedingly pretty, and their aprons were not unbecoming. On emerging from the alcove, they'd pulled aside the curtain and SchrummSchrumm could see that they'd been doing laundry during the dispute. There were two enormous washtubs and various articles of clothing hanging on lines.

"Oh!" cried the taller of the two girls, overjoyed, when she saw Krikri. "Here's my handsome sergeant!"

In her excitement, she'd dropped her companion's hand. She made a gracious curtsy to SchrummSchrumm.

"My name's Vera," she said. "And this is Marie. Who are you?"

"I'm SchrummSchrumm, excursionist first class."

"This one's handsome, too," murmured Marie as she took Vera's hand again. The girls stood mutely before them. Then, as if unable to hold back any longer, the lovely Marie fell to her knees in front of SchrummSchrumm and began fervently kissing his feet.

"My dear, dear excursionist!" she said, interrupting her kisses every so often to gaze up at him in admiration. Krikri and Jacques looked on with frowns of disgust. Vera hadn't moved. Schrumm-Schrumm was paralyzed. Luckily, a strident sound erupted from the radio equipment at that moment. The operator picked up his headphones but didn't put them on.

"It's the first warning," he said to SchrummSchrumm, apparently to excuse his lack of haste.

Then, with no transition, as the warning signal blared louder and louder, he tapped his temple in a meaningful gesture.

"You two are crazy," he declared flatly. "The duty officer might have caught you. Now get out of here!"

Marie was clinging desperately to SchrummSchrumm's ankles, but Krikri gave her a brutal kick in the midsection and she fell back, moaning. Krikri dragged SchrummSchrumm toward the door.

"Goodbye," said SchrummSchrumm. Vera curtsied. Marie sobbed and clutched her stomach.

They were once again in the hemispherical room.

"Why did you kick that girl?"

The sergeant shrugged and began to whistle, evidently to cover his embarrassment.

"I suppose we have a lot more walking to do?"

"We've traversed the Labyrinth. We're almost to the colonel's superintendents."

Two minutes later, they stopped at a door at the end of a hall. Krikri lifted a heavy bronze hammer with both hands and let it fall with a deafening racket. The door opened. Krikri steered SchrummSchrumm inside. The door closed. SchrummSchrumm found himself face to face with thirty or more of the hairiest, most repulsive men he had ever seen.

XI

They were sprawled on Roman-style couches around a table laden with food that stretched nearly the entire length of the room. The chief superintendent, at one end, presided over the feast. He was busy manhandling a fat woman he'd forced onto all fours, and whose buttocks he was viciously biting. His colleagues cheered him on with excited hurrahs. A spirit of frank and open camaraderie prevailed. To put it a better way, everyone was drunk. "Don't move a muscle," instructed Krikri. The two stood there and waited to be noticed. Hanging on the walls was an eclectic assortment of objects: binoculars, torture devices, diplomas in dusty frames, medals. Two other women—dancers—were performing rhythmic contortions in time to a flute and tambourine being played by dwarf musicians. At the opposite end of the table from the chief superintendent was a vacant couch luxuriously upholstered in panther skin. Krikri explained in an undertone that this couch belonged to Colonel Red-Bartlett himself, who, whenever his schedule allowed, liked nothing better than to join his subordinates in their bacchanals.

Finally, the superintendent who'd opened the door to them managed to get the group's attention. The musicians stopped playing, the dancers stopped gyrating, the other superintendents stopped clapping along. All the men imitated their chief and turned their flushed, oafish faces toward the two intruders. Krikri, fortunately, knew exactly how to handle himself. He took advantage of the lull in the festivities to introduce SchrummSchrumm and present the reason for their visit, all in terms of the most servile humility. The chief acknowledged his speech with a grunt and said the visitors would have to wait. One of the superintendents had already climbed onto the table—he was staggering around with a bottle of wine—and had launched into the opening stanzas of a military song, when the bronze hammer clanged again.

"Can't we get a moment's peace around here?" grumbled the chief. "We're literally drowning in work." And to show what kind of work he meant, he finished off the contents of a wine bottle to general applause. Notwithstanding the chief's comment, the superintendent upon whom the task devolved went to answer the door, and there found a second guard bringing in a second excursionist. This new guard was shorter than Krikri. Fatter and older, too. He was escorting a man of about fifty with blue disks sewn on his chest and back. The man's clothes were in tatters and he seemed at the limit of exhaustion. The guard had to hold him upright, without which he would almost certainly have collapsed to the ground. The superintendents looked over the new arrivals and burst into violent tirades against the trials and tribulations of the service. Krikri and his counterpart had approached one another and made their introductions. Everything seemed to be going smoothly until, after a few words of small talk, a fierce argument flared up between the guards. Krikri was claiming priority: SchrummSchrumm had arrived first and should therefore be the first to see Colonel Red-Bartlett. The other guard said he didn't give a fig for Krikri's priority, his own excursionist was here on a matter of the utmost urgency. To which Krikri retorted that the Regulations contained no provision for his quote-unquote urgency. This exasperated the other man, who suggested that Krikri forget about the Regulations for once in his life and try using his brain for a change, if he had one . . . They wound up shouting so loudly that the superintendents offered to mediate. Krikri reacted as astutely as he had before. He declared himself greatly honored by the offer. His colleague, on the other hand, was apparently much less adept. For a start, he hadn't introduced his excursionist to the group the way Krikri had SchrummSchrumm, which seemed to have rubbed the superintendents the wrong way, as it clearly went against custom. And when the chief demanded to know the reason for this behavior, the guard replied almost insolently that his reasons were none of the chief's business. This was too much. He was seized, tossed into a small closet, and shut inside. Krikri gave SchrummSchrumm a knowing wink and he replied with a quiet "Bravo, Krikri! Well played." The chief superintendent cried "Enough!" and there was silence.

"Who're you?" he barked at the new excursionist. "You'd better try and answer, because if you don't . . ."

"I'm the grade-crossing gateman of Misunderstanding's older brother," was the man's prompt reply.

"Then you're not an excursionist! Why are you wearing a blue disk?" exclaimed SchrummSchrumm.

He felt like biting his tongue as soon as he'd said it, but the question was so pertinent that no one seemed to begrudge him having asked it. They all waited for the man's reply.

"Yes, I am an excursionist," he said. "But before I became an excursionist, I was the grade-crossing gateman of Misunderstanding's older brother."

This answer set off a firestorm of debate. "What grade-crossing gateman?" "What grade crossing?" "What rail line?" Some maintained that the rail line existed but the grade crossing didn't.

Others denied the existence of everything: grade crossing, gateman, and rail line. Someone sparked a fresh volley of opinions by asserting that all the gatemen had left their jobs years ago. "Is that true? How does he know?" But another superintendent broke in: as a matter of fact, he did happen to know a former gateman who had an older brother. To bolster his claim, he said he'd had a drink with him and the Bavarian-lager deliveryman only last week, after which they'd gone to see the lamplighter—the one who set up the paper lanterns at the funfair. "What funfair?" someone shot back. "What lamplighter?" And the discussion was off and running again as they argued over whether the funfair in question had actually taken place and the lamplighter in question actually existed, whether the fair had been held in such-and-such a location or such-and-such other location, and whether the man alluded to was lamplighter X or lamplighter Y. The debate raged on for quite a while. Eventually, when most of the men were hoarse from shouting and the remainder were pausing for breath—in other words, during a rare moment of calm—the chief called for everyone's attention.

"You wouldn't be acting under orders from Leopold, would you now?" he asked in an insinuating tone.

"I beg your pardon?" said the man, his eyes alight with extraordinary animation. It so happened that SchrummSchrumm had been noticing a gradual transformation over the course of this discussion in the demeanor of the other excursionist, the older brother of the gateman and ex-gateman himself: he'd been steadily gaining confidence. This impression was confirmed when, after the superintendents had conferred privately one last time and come to an agreement, they called the man over: he shot SchrummSchrumm a smug, self-satisfied look, as if he thought he'd won the game. What happened next, therefore, surprised Krikri, SchrummSchrumm, and the self-satisfied excursionist: the same superintendents who had flung the guard into the closet now grabbed the excursionist by the collar and, over his outraged protests, heaved him in with his protector. The superintendents had a hearty laugh all around. SchrummSchrumm and Krikri laughed, too; they had taken care to stand well back and not intervene during the heaving, and the sergeant had even pulled SchrummSchrumm into a corner to be further out of the way.

"Now your turn!" called the chief.

"Me?" said SchrummSchrumm. He was all the more frightened because Krikri had swiftly stepped away to make it clear that he did not want his fate to be bound up with SchrummSchrumm's.

"Yes, you! You're that famous excursionist, the renowned SchrummSchrumm, aren't you?"

SchrummSchrumm tried to disavow his celebrity, aided in these professions of humility by the comings and goings of several superintendents; they were pushing the table aside and moving the couches to clear a space in the middle of the room where the floor was paved in slate flags. The chief shrugged. A cardboard box had been placed beside him. He took a folding ruler from his pocket and set about measuring distances from certain reference points. Using these measurements, he chalked three parallel lines on the floor, all under the watchful eyes of his colleagues.

"Here's the Great Iron Gate," he said, indicating the first of the chalk lines to SchrummSchrumm. "And here's the Enchanted Poplar Forest," he added, indicating the last line. "You, SchrummSchrumm, are in the middle."

A chorus of approval greeted these bizarre remarks. They sat SchrummSchrumm on a chair and set it on the middle line. The chief then produced from the box a sort of bishop's miter with ass's ears hanging down in place of lappets. He placed it on SchrummSchrumm's head and threw a red cape over his shoulders. The miter was fairly light, made of the same cardboard as the box that had contained it. They put a gold-painted wooden scepter in his hand. The carved fingers on the scepter were frozen in an obscene gesture.

"SchrummSchrumm! Excursionist first class Schrumm-Schrumm!" cried the chief superintendent. "By virtue of the powers invested in me, I proclaim thee King of Misunderstanding and Prince of the Quicksands. King thou be, and King do I proclaim thee."

More exclamations and hoots of laughter. The superintendents approached him one by one and bowed low before him. They said: "Our gracious lord, protect us!" or: "SchrummSchrumm, King of the excursionists, look out on your right!" or even: "King, fair King, give us a kiss!" As they did so, they kicked, slapped, and whipped him repeatedly. These taunts continued for some time. Krikri made no move to help him. When at last they'd had their fill, they took away the miter, the crimson cape, and the scepter, and shoved him unceremoniously into the closet. He found himself on a dirt floor. Outside the door he could hear them roaring with laughter, talking over the incident, and singing, but it was hard to make out any words amid all the ruckus. So SchrummSchrumm, once his eyes had adjusted to the dark and he could see the two men who had preceded him into the room, took comfort in knowing that they couldn't possibly have discerned the nature of the treatment that had been inflicted on him. The guard was snoring. The other man ignored him; he simply struck a match and lit a small candle. His face appeared in the glow of the flame. He was perhaps not quite as old as SchrummSchrumm had initially thought. The stink rising off him, however, was almost unendurable. A curious thing: in spite of his half-starved appearance, the man, on seeing himself observed, haughtily thrust his hands into his pockets. Even as he was putting on this outward show of nonchalance, he was laboring to conceal the gaping hole in his shoe from which fragments of rotting sock hung out on either side and from whose center an incredibly filthy toe projected. SchrummSchrumm found this detail touching rather than comical, and he decided to make the first overture.

"You really threw those superintendents into a tizzy," he said. "They don't know which way is up anymore. Boy, are they furious with you!"

"I'm not surprised," replied the man. "You know, they don't much like Misunderstanding's former grade-crossing gatemen around here." Did "they" mean everybody, or did it—as events might lead one to suppose—apply mainly to the superintendents? It was difficult to say.

"Why don't they like you?"

"Oh, please! I am Hermann Occursus, sir," answered the man in a voice that implied his name said it all.

"And I'm SchrummSchrumm, excursionist first class," answered SchrummSchrumm, smiling. "But what are you, really: excursionist, gateman, or spy?"

This rejoinder had its desired effect. Hermann Occursus gave him a sidelong glance and said, in a tearful voice entirely at odds with his previous attitude:

"Please don't mock me, Mr. SchrummSchrumm. It's only through a series of particularly unfortunate occurrences that I've been reduced to the miserable condition in which you now see me. But through it all, despite my many misfortunes, there's still nothing in the world I want more than to help excursionists who find themselves in a bind. May I offer you my counsel? I'm a wily old fox with more than one trick up his sleeve. If you need a scheme, a scam, or a stratagem of any type, I'm your man. I know all about Colonel Red-Bartlett."

"Thank you very much," SchrummSchrumm answered coldly, pinching his nose to block out the odor of Occursus's feet. "Forgive me for being blunt, but I'm a very conscientious excursionist and I don't go in for schemes and scams. It's hard to see how you could help me, anyway, since even I myself don't know why I've been summoned to Red-Bartlett's office."

"There's only one reason you could have been summoned," cut in Hermann Occursus. "An investigation is underway and proceedings have been opened against you."

"An investigation! Proceedings! Do you think they could delay my departure for the Quicksands?"

"Now we're getting somewhere!" laughed Hermann Occursus. "Trust me, Mr. Excursionist-First-Class SchrummSchrumm, you'd best avail yourself of my advice. Give me one measly banknote—just one!—and I'll tell you things that will astonish you and that you'll find well worth hearing."

SchrummSchrumm, though marveling that anyone could still be concerned with money in Misunderstanding, carefully weighed the proposition all the same. He handed over a banknote and stretched out on the floor to hear what Occursus had to say. Occursus, however, had started blinking as if he were suddenly in need of sleep.

"You aren't nodding off, are you?" said SchrummSchrumm.

"I beg your pardon," yawned Occursus. "In truth, there are a great many things to tell you, but given the present turn of events, it will probably be easiest to start with this: investigations and proceedings can in no way delay an excursionist's departure. On the contrary, in many cases they hasten it. Two assertions that are doubly contradictory, you'll say. First, because if a judicial procedure can hasten one's departure, by the same token it should also be able to retard it. Second, because an investigation—which, by definition, takes up a lot of time—ought naturally to have a retardative effect. That's what you're thinking, isn't it?" he asked, raising one finger pedantically. "Alas, such objections, though perhaps compelling in theory, have no merit in Misunderstanding. Misunderstanding is not the domain of logic, any more than it is of justice or morality."

"Enough of these pointless generalities," said Schrumm-Schrumm irritably. "Tell me about my situation."

"Patience, Mr. SchrummSchrumm. I have to start by laying a groundwork of generalities or you'll never understand a word of what I'm about to tell you. Have you noticed how numerous are the excursionists awaiting departure in proportion to the tiny number who actually leave? Answer me that!"

"Of course I've noticed."

"Good! Some of them, in fact, have been waiting four, five, even six months. And that's not all. There are others who've been waiting far longer, but those excursionists are never seen, because the Misunderstanding authorities keep them isolated in a special hotel—*prison* would be a more appropriate term—for fear they'll spread despair through the ranks of their comrades. And do you know why there are so many of them? Because they're *never* going to the Quicksands, that's why."

Hermann Occursus had delivered this last sentence very gently, but it echoed ominously in the cramped space. SchrummSchrumm, taking care not to betray any emotion, scrutinized his odd companion. Was he joking, or was he serious? In a skeptical tone, he asked:

"If what you say is true, why don't they let them return home instead of locking them up in a prison?"

"I knew you'd ask me that," said Occursus with a smile. "The answer is quite simple: they know too much to be allowed to leave. During the six months or more they've spent in Misunderstanding, they've learned all there is to know about the city—if they have eyes and ears, that is. And especially because a long wait tends to sharpen men's powers of observation. No, no, it wouldn't be at all prudent to let them return home."

"It sounds like you endorse their policy," remarked Schrumm-Schrumm. But he immediately amended his tone: "Assuming for the moment that things really are done this way, I still have to ask: what does this have to do with my situation?"

"We're coming to that," said Occursus, unruffled. "All those excursionists who want to go to the Quicksands but never will, do you know *why* they won't, when some of their fellow excursionists leave two weeks after their arrival? Because they haven't performed satisfactorily on the tests. That's it: the tests! The city could have arranged the order of departure using the traditional system, which happens also to be the only fair and logical one, namely by assigning the excursionists sequential numbers as they arrive, and then—as a function of this sequence, together with the availability and frequency of departures—giving first priority to those excursionists whose numbers are lowest, and so on and so forth, departure after departure. But no! As I said before, Misunderstanding is neither the domain of logic nor of justice. You'll see for yourself in this very example. In place of the old, time-honored system, they've instituted the test system. Here's where it will become clear how all of this applies to you, by the way. Under the old system, it was possible to modify your departure order. For example, by offering a large sum of money to the bearer of a number whose departure was imminent; or by having your connections pull some strings for you; or, easier still, by approaching the man in charge directly. In other words, under the old system, if someone wanted to leave for the Quicksands right away, there were ways of making it happen. The test system, however, is a different animal. It's 100 percent tamper-proof. Now do you understand me?"

"I understand you, but at the same time I don't understand you," SchrummSchrumm admitted. "It's true that the numerical system seems more logical. But the test system isn't as unfair as you've made it out to be, since it seems reasonable to prioritize those who are in good shape, meaning those who aren't at risk of suffering an accident on the excursion. It's equally true, on the other hand, that I don't know the specific tests they're using to determine which excursionists qualify, so I can't really speak to whether they're fair or unfair."

Hermann Occursus frowned, nodded sagely, and clucked his tongue in acquiescence.

"My dear Mr. SchrummSchrumm, you're quite right. The key question is indeed what qualification tests they use. I think you've already gotten your money's worth," he added, crinkling the bill between his fingers. "There are so many things of which you're so very ignorant! For another little banknote like this one, I'll tell you what the tests are."

"Here." SchrummSchrumm offered a bill of a higher denomination than the first. Hermann stared at it in wonder and, dancing around the closet, began to sing: "Thank you, thank you, noble SchrummSchrumm, my generous but uninformed excursionist!"

"Stop fooling around," said SchrummSchrumm, afraid the guard would wake up.

"Understood," said Hermann, sitting down again. "I'll explain. But first, I'm sorry to say, I'll have to set out another general principle, that which determines the choice of one test over another. Let's take a simple example. You recall, no doubt, having to go to a teller window where some officials were supposed to give you your green disks?"

"Certainly. The officials were particularly cordial to me. They let me jump the line, they offered me coffee, and the head official even promised to have his friends intervene on my behalf to get my departure date moved up. Which, between you and me, seems to contradict your earlier assertions."

"Just so! Just so! What a monstrous error you've fallen into! I hate to disillusion you, but that was all a ruse designed to put you in a certain frame of mind. You were given no advantage whatsoever: every excursionist receives the same 'preferential treatment.'"

"Don't be silly! I saw my companions; I was served before they were. I even felt a little guilty about it."

"An error! A monstrous error!" repeated Hermann. "The people ahead of you in line were merely stand-ins: guards dressed up as excursionists for the occasion. Think back. You didn't recognize any faces, did you? That must have struck you as odd."

"It's true, I didn't," SchrummSchrumm admitted. "Do you mean to say this disk distribution, which in no way resembled a test, actually was one, while the swamp pier training, for example, which was presented to us as a test, actually wasn't?"

"Bingo! Now you're getting it," said Hermann, a strange light glimmering in his eye. "The real test—one of the main ones, anyway—was your interaction with the disk-distribution officials. Follow me closely now. The official at the window—the test administrator, if you will—underwent special training to enable him to render a definitive verdict on the person tested. He makes an autonomous decision on whether or not you're fit to go to the Quicksands. So far, so good. But here's where things get a little more complicated. Before this test, you were put through other tests. And in each of them, the test administrator, who would be just as qualified as all the other administrators, made his own autonomous decision. Which means that, at the moment you stepped up to the disk-distribution window, if you'd been previously judged unfit for the excursion, then even if the distribution official had judged you fit, you wouldn't be going anywhere. In other words, if you'd been accepted, it would have been useless to try and hasten your departure, because the process would already be moving along as quickly as possible. Likewise, if you'd been rejected, it would have been equally useless to try and pull strings. So now you see why a minute ago I said that the proceedings opened against you couldn't possibly delay your departure. Investigations and proceedings only delay the departures of those who will never depart. Which means, paradoxically, that they don't delay it. On the contrary, I tell you these proceedings will surely move your departure date forward. Indeed, since it's necessary for them to maintain, if not logic, then at least a funhouse-mirror parody of logic, we know that when proceedings are filed against someone marked for departure, they do their best to ship him out even quicker, that is to say, before the proceedings have time to do their work."

Hermann Occursus accompanied these final arguments with vehement gestures. Was this dirty little man lying? Though he had a gut feeling that Hermann had just given himself away, SchrummSchrumm still had to hand it to him: his analysis had been cogent. Hermann, in any case, hadn't noticed his suspicions.

"Well?" he said. "Have I proved myself useful, or haven't I? You've got to admit it was a lucky thing you ran into good ol' Hermann Occursus."

"Even supposing you're right," said SchrummSchrumm, "there's still something about your account that doesn't add up. How can the test administrators be sure they're not making the wrong call, even with all their special training?"

"Fair point! Fair point!" Occursus grinned. "Because you're a noble and generous SchrummSchrumm, I'm going to give you the best proof yet of my good faith and expertise. Your objection, however fair, won't hold up under scrutiny, my dear young man. Let us say, for the sake of argument, that errors of judgment do in fact occur—the officials are, after all, only human. Even so, it would make no difference. They have an absolutely infallible criterion to guide them, namely: the reason an excursionist gives for wanting to go to the Quicksands. If the reason is valid, he's accepted. If not, he's rejected. And you have to admit, this criterion was well chosen. Going to the Quicksands has come into vogue recently; people set off at the drop of a hat. It's almost a status symbol! If someone's interested in tourism or sightseeing, they can go elsewhere. They need a valid reason to travel to the Quicksands; the trip has to be a necessity for them—as I'm sure it is for you, fortunately, Mr. SchrummSchrumm. Besides, you also have to admit, having had some experience of Sunday excursions, that the Ultimate Excursion would be meaningless if just anybody could go on it. Trips to the Quicksands have always been, and will always be, of extremely limited availability. They say there's a threshold percentage—a percentage established by eons of statistics—that must never be exceeded, lest the excursion lose its purpose and significance. There's nothing to say to that!"

Here he stopped, having talked himself out of breath. SchrummSchrumm noticed that the guard had woken up during this rant and had been listening to them for some time. He was blinking and squinting his eyes into focus. Occursus, too, noticed the guard. His transformation was instantaneous. He put on a dull-eyed, woebegone look; he resumed his character of a poor, beaten-down excursionist, sickly and a little dimwitted. Nevertheless, it was to him that the guard, after looking thoughtfully at SchrummSchrumm, addressed his remarks:

"Aren't you ashamed of yourself, Hermann Occursus!" he scolded. "Come now! Look at me!"

"No!" said Hermann, staring stubbornly at the ground.

"Fine then," said the other quietly. "Unbutton your putrid, reeking shirt and show this excursionist the mark on your neck."

Hermann complied immediately and bent his head to reveal something at the base of his neck. The guard had picked up the candle and was holding it higher to aid SchrummSchrumm's examination. At first he saw nothing. He had to choke back waves of nausea triggered by the odors of grime rising from the depths of the man's shirt. Finally, however, he spied a small tattoo in red, yellow, and green. It was fairly distinct, even against the dirty skin, and about the size of a shirt button. It showed a length of barbed wire *gules* and carbine *or*, intercrossed on a field *vert*.

"What do you see?"

"There's a tattoo."

"Exactly," said the guard. And to Hermann: "Rebutton your shirt and tell him what it means."

"This tattoo signifies that I am a stinking slave. Fouler smelling than the most foul. It means I have renounced my former faith. My only purpose is to dutifully serve the Sunday Quicksands Excursion Company. My only master is the Holy Director. My only god is Misunderstanding the Great. By this indelible and dreadful sign, all the world can see that I have sold my soul."

"Fascinating," murmured SchrummSchrumm.

"Mr. Excursionist," said the guard, "before I explain the motives for my behavior, let me first tell you that I have the same tattoo at the base of my own neck. All Misunderstanding employees—the Holy Director excepted—bear the mark. Thus, there are sixty-seven thousand seven hundred and seventy-seven employees in Misunderstanding, as there are in every seat of every Sunday excursion, and all of us are marked with this same indelible sign showing that we belong to Misunderstanding, body and soul. Now you can better appreciate my disgust for this little creep. This man, this Hermann Occursus, has—as we all have—solemnly forsworn all future excursions for himself and his family. This vow is a prerequisite to undergoing our initiation. His mission, which he carries out very incompetently, is to prevent excursionists from leaving for the Quicksands."

"Really?" said SchrummSchrumm. "Then why tell me? If he really is a suborner, I think his lies are honed to perfection."

"Don't you believe it! Don't believe that, whatever you do!" said the guard, affecting to be deeply upset. At that moment, Hermann looked up and showed his face. There was no trace of the shame SchrummSchrumm had assumed he would find there. Instead, he was laughing so much that tears were streaming down his cheeks, and he tugged at the guard's sleeve to get his attention.

"Yes?"

"Cross my heart and hope to die, stick a needle in my eye," recited Hermann, locking eyes with the guard. SchrummSchrumm tried to think back: where had he heard those words before? In any case, the result was unexpected: the two men burst into spontaneous laughter and threw their arms around one another.

"Ah! It's a tough profession! It's tough, isn't it?"

"You said it! A tough profession!"

"Let us press each other to our bosoms, friend, in this lonely seclusion."

"Yes, let us press each other to our bosoms in this lonely seclusion."

These ridiculous, lyrical outpourings went on for some time.

"Nice work, don't you think?" said Hermann to the guard at last.

"Yes, nice work," he agreed. Then he went to the door and began pounding on it as hard as he could.

"Hey! I'm hungry!" he shouted. "I want to eat! Hey! Superintendents!"

"Quiet down," someone replied from the other side of the closet.

He pounded even louder. Hermann Occursus, after a moment's hesitation, joined in.

"This is barbaric!" cried Hermann. "I can't breathe! Help! I'm dying in here!"

Someone swore at them from the other side, and one of the superintendents opened the door.

"Are you finished?" he asked Hermann and the guard.

SchrummSchrumm thought the superintendent was reprimanding them for making a racket, but he was doing nothing of the kind.

"Done and dusted! Piece of cake!" answered Hermann, and the guard added, in a lower tone, but not so low that SchrummSchrumm could avoid overhearing:

"He's a moron, just like all the rest. Total moron!"

"Good," said the superintendent. He turned to SchrummSchrumm: "You, moron! Follow me!"

Out in the main room, the revelry had ended. The men were now sleeping off their drink. Following the superintendent on duty, SchrummSchrumm stepped over unconscious bodies and made his way to a niche in the wall. The superintendent spoke Schrumm-Schrumm's name into a small intercom mounted at the back. He listened to the response, which SchrummSchrumm, though straining his ears, could not decipher. "Very good," said the superintendent. Still in the lead, he guided the excursionist down a hall. At the end of this hall was a closed door. To one side was a niche with an intercom just like the first.

"Toto!" said the guard into the speaker. A brief pause, and then: "Excursionist first class SchrummSchrumm is returning to his hotel."

"What does that mean? I'm not going to see Colonel Red-Bartlett after all?"

"Your appointment has been postponed until tomorrow. The colonel can't see you today," said the superintendent as the door opened automatically.

"Isn't Krikri going to accompany me? How will I find the hotel?"

The superintendent didn't answer, only pushed Schrumm-Schrumm through the door and closed it after him. Krikri was there, waiting. SchrummSchrumm had been literally quaking with fear at the thought of navigating the Labyrinth alone, but Krikri quickly reassured him. They'd be riding back on the little electric train, "because we never take an excursionist through the Labyrinth more than once." They'd use the same mode of transportation tomorrow, the sergeant assured him.

The hotel seemed as deserted as it had at the beginning of the afternoon. SchrummSchrumm looked for his companions, but with no luck. Shortly after his departure, said Krikri, four more little obese nudies had arrived bearing four more summonses to Colonel Red-Bartlett's office. The other greens hadn't returned yet . . . and still hadn't by the time SchrummSchrumm finally turned in for the night.

XII

The room in which Red-Bartlett received SchrummSchrumm was reminiscent of the superintendents' hall, only more refined. An imposing desk dominated the far end, along with a few leather chairs and some ultramodern filing cabinets. At the opposite end was a panther-skin couch on which Red-Bartlett was now reclining. The air was heavy and close. The place must have been drenched in perfume. A black woman was swinging a censer, another fanned the room with a palm frond. The colonel was wearing a candy-pink kilt cinched around his waist, leopard-skin ankle boots, and had retained his traditional uniform jacket. The jacket was unbuttoned, and the same carroty hairs that covered his legs formed a thick, furry pelt over his chest and bulging gut.

"Ah!" he said with a smile. "Here's my savior. Come sit next to me, and please help yourself."

Assorted fruits, beverages, and miniature meat pies were laid out within easy reach. SchrummSchrumm sat gingerly on the edge of the couch. The combination of smells—incense, perfume, the women's sweat, the lingering odor of the furs, the meat pies—was almost unbearable. A pair of guards stood sentry at the entrance. Like the black women, they gazed on the scene with vacant impassivity. While SchrummSchrumm took some refreshments, Red-Bartlett struck a bronze plate and a small Chinese man appeared. He resembled the Chinese men depicted in old engravings, with a close-fitting blue cap and a long queue. When he reached Red-Bartlett, he kowtowed before him, smiled inscrutably, and unpacked a pedicure kit.

"I need to have my whitlow tended to," explained the colonel. "This will only take a few minutes. Then we can chat."

The pedicurist, scalpel in hand, was already busying himself about the patient's toes. When he lanced the whitlow, a gush of nauseating pus spurted out practically into SchrummSchrumm's face. Red-Bartlett emitted a groan and let his head drop onto his chest. One of the black women hurried over to console the poor colonel, calling him her "big, gold-braided honeybun" and her "repulsive pumpkin." She sucked on his nose, his ears. The pedicurist, finishing up the dressing, seemed to approve of this therapy. He assumed an expression of beaming hilarity, kowtowed several more times, and left the room. Red-Bartlett shoved the black woman aside and, in a dignified manner—bare-legged, kilt around his waist, uniform jacket undone—conducted SchrummSchrumm to his modern desk, where they sat across from one another.

"My dear Mr. SchrummSchrumm," said the corpulent colonel, "before we get down to business, I'd like to take this opportunity to tell you once again that you saved my life during that training exercise and I haven't forgotten it. I wanted to remind you of this so that, whatever transpires, you know you can count on my sympathy and, above all, on my clemency . . . That being said, I must inform you that an investigation into you was opened three weeks ago. I summoned you here so we could clear the matter up. Several indictments have been brought against you, the most recent dating from only yesterday. I'll give you a summary reading," he added, taking a paper from a file folder. "You gained illegal entry into Eden and the Original Pissoir. Worse, during the aforementioned trespass, you penetrated as far as Nastarz City, where you accosted our Holy Director before fleeing the scene. You contrived to witness the setting for a ritual feast while concealed in a cupboard. Finally, the indictment that was brought to my attention this morning states that you were guilty of the attempted theft of the Apple of Good and Evil, this larceny having been perpetrated yesterday. Is that correct?"

"Correct," said SchrummSchrumm without flinching. "As it happens, though, one Hermann Occursus—who represented himself as an excursionist, but who is, in my opinion, a spy—told me a great deal about the reasons and meanings behind the acts you've just enumerated. Furthermore, his statements strangely corroborate the confidential information imparted to me by the Keeper of the Apple, one Illustrious, the former bus driver who drove me to Misunderstanding. I did a lot of thinking last night and came to the conclusion that there's a sizable grain of truth in what Occursus and Illustrious told me. In other words, I'm now firmly convinced that I am not responsible for the offenses imputed to me. For, as you surely cannot help but be aware, I was in some sense forced to commit these blameworthy acts. Those among Misunderstanding's leadership who oversee the excursionists' activities have carefully orchestrated each and every one of these events. In still other words, all the acts for which I'm now being denounced are part of a plan devised by all-powerful beings: I've done nothing but follow their blueprint to the letter, and the leadership can't punish me for it, because then they'd have to punish themselves!"

Red-Bartlett met SchrummSchrumm's eye without showing the slightest hint of surprise. He simply laughed lightly, as if excusing himself for a faux pas.

"You're an intelligent young man, Mr. SchrummSchrumm. Very intelligent, in fact. How is it possible that, even while giving such a brilliant demonstration of your acumen, you can, in the same breath, commit such a grievous error? Listen to me. First you prove to me, in an irrefutable manner—but irrefutable only to me, please note, because, though I know you're right, you yourself have had to extrapolate your conclusions from the hearsay (premeditated hearsay, no less) of this Occursus and Illustrious; you prove, I repeat, that you can't be held responsible for any of the blameworthy acts imputed to you, because they were laid out in a plan conceived by the highest echelons of Misunderstanding's leadership. Which amounts to a claim that you had no free will when you committed these offenses. Where there's no free will, there's no offense. That's what you're driving at, yes? Well and good. Up to this point, anyway. How can you not see that you're drawing a ridiculous conclusion from a remarkable hypothesis? Or, at the very least, that you're drawing a conclusion which implies the negation of either the hypothesis or the conclusion itself? To put it in other terms, how can you not see that you have, in fact, raised no real objection to my statement? Because it is I, my dear young man, who have put those words into your mouth! This, for the very excellent reason that it's the job of Colonel Red-Bartlett—a man whose life you've saved, and who won't forget it—to be one step ahead of your objections, to place you in a set of circumstances such that you could not have responded otherwise than you have. As you spoke, you were congratulating yourself on your cleverness and believed you were backing me into a corner. In reality, before you even opened your mouth, I knew, verbatim, what you were about to say. Note, too, Mr. SchrummSchrumm, that I'm not taunting you. I take no pride in having maneuvered you into my trap. As I said, it's my job. An unglamorous job that demanded a long and tedious course of study before I was finally able to elicit the intended objections and provide for all eventualities. Moreover, my task is facilitated by the detailed program I'm given of all the acts slated for each excursionist, and therefore, being in possession of all the relevant information on the past (predicted and accomplished) and the future (predicted and inevitable), it's impossible for me to go wrong . . . The inescapable conclusion is indeed the one at which you've already arrived: an excursionist has no free will. But you must apply this theorem more broadly, and conclude that the plan—or the Regulations, if you prefer—always knows everything, and that its predictions are always borne out. Your logic was therefore faulty, in that you presumed, during the course of our conversation, that you were temporarily escaping from the plan's predictions. Not a bit of it! You were conforming to them as usual, because there are never any exceptions."

SchrummSchrumm frowned in acquiescence. He picked up a liquor bottle and poured himself a drink. The alcohol did him good. He needed it.

"The way you've laid out your case is awfully convincing, Colonel. All the facts seem to be on your side, and I can tell you're not lying. But I can't accept your argument. I'm already in great confusion and distress. If I conceded this point, I'd go insane."

"Strong words!" said Red-Bartlett good-naturedly. "Others have gone down this road before you. They withstood the ordeal well enough . . ."

"May I ask a question?"

The colonel made a gesture of encouragement.

"Illustrious swore to me that his predecessor as Keeper of the Apple, during the two decades he served in his post, never witnessed a single deviation from the plan. Which would mean, if we extended this principle, that for all the countless years excursionists have been coming to Misunderstanding, they've all had the illusion of free will even while they were fulfilling the plan's predictions in every particular. Is that right?"

Red-Bartlett nodded.

"Can you tell me what would happen if, one fine day, an excursionist *didn't* conform to the predictions? Hypothetically, of course."

"That outcome is strictly impossible. Why plan for what can never occur? The predictions are based on an ancient and infallible science dealing with the behavior of excursionists immersed in the distinctive environment of Misunderstanding. We adjust our predictions as we go. To this end, we've compiled massive amounts of observational data and statistics. We make no decision lightly. The plan is drawn up by the greatest experts in both general behavioral psychology and the behavioral psychology of excursionists in Misunderstanding. It takes into account an excursionist's weaknesses, vices, virtues, aspirations, fears, and cowardice. No, we cannot and do not make mistakes . . . I'm giving you all this in layman's terms, of course—I'm not a Programmer, and I know how these things work mainly because the Planning Department Head is a close friend of mine. I can see very well what's worrying you, though, and so I'll tell you that I had a talk with my friend only yesterday. He explained to me basically this: he said the programs do go so far as to envisage the possibility you raised, but they consider it a feature rather than a bug. To put it another way—if I've understood him correctly—they deliberately provide excursionists with what appear to be serendipitous opportunities to deviate from the program. So much so that this possibility only serves to reinforce the plan's infallibility, because do what you will, you always return to the fold of its predictions.

"I see," said SchrummSchrumm, trying to hide his excitement. For the first time since the conversation began, he had the feeling that there might be a flaw in the colonel's seemingly airtight reasoning. He still had to find it, however.

"Let me run another theory by you," he said. "Suppose an excursionist, realizing the impossibility of contravening the plan as long as he acts logically, and having come to this realization following explanations given to him intentionally and in conformity with this same plan, suppose that this excursionist (me, for example, as soon as I leave your office) from that point forward refuses to follow his habitual mode of conduct and begins to act in a systematically irrational manner. What then?"

"Another impossibility!" Red-Bartlett said with a nervous little laugh. "An excursionist's goal is to depart for the Quicksands as soon as he can. Why would you work against your own interests? Why would you indulge in stupid behavior that might result in your departure being delayed, perhaps indefinitely?"

SchrummSchrumm didn't answer. He was deep in thought. He felt increasingly certain that he'd found the chink in Red-Bartlett's armor. But the colonel reclaimed his attention:

"Mr. SchrummSchrumm, I know exactly what you're thinking and where you're going with this idea. In order to avoid a lot of pointless explanations, I'll tell you this (I hadn't quite made my mind up to this, but since you're so insistent, I'll have to bite the bullet): what you do or don't do—all of which remains within the ambit of the predictions—is really of only relative importance. The truly important thing, according to what is perhaps one of the guiding principles of the plan, is that to which you yourself attach importance, whatever it may be. We'll make sure you experience it to the fullest, right down to its furthest ramifications. Take the role of our spies, for example. It's up to them to tell us what significance you attribute to all the events, both large and small, set out in your daily agenda. If you're afraid, then believe me, you'll be given good reason to feel afraid. If you decide to behave stupidly—in a 'systematically irrational manner,' to use your phrase—then believe me, you'll be provided ample opportunity do so: 'as soon as you leave my office,' as you say. Even, paradoxically, this free will—which you are wrong to boast of, since thanks to the plan and its projections you have none—even this will be restored to you, in a sense. Your most secret intentions, the ones you aren't always aware of yourself, have been scrutinized and uncovered by the plan, and will be actualized—or, at the very least, the plan's provisions will give you the means to actualize them. I'm sure this is hard for you to accept. But that's how it works. This free will, which you have so little use for in Misunderstanding, you relinquished to us by the mere fact of signing up for the Quicksands excursion. We restore it to you by making you act in accordance with the plan's prescriptions. For the plan obliges you to do, not what *we* want—as it may seem at first blush—but what *you* truly desire. Only you're not always capable of realizing this, because most of the time you're ignorant of your most secret intentions."

"Mr. Red-Bartlett," said SchrummSchrumm slowly, "you've gone to a lot of trouble to demonstrate to me that I'm just a poor excursionist, ignorant and alone, who has never and will never understand anything about the symbols of this excursion. You've succeeded. I'm convinced."

"You haven't understood me," retorted the colonel in a bored tone. "I did, indeed, try to demonstrate to you that every move you make has been, and will continue to be, predetermined. If I've managed to convince you, I'm glad, because I believe it's for your own good. But don't go thinking you've been treated unfairly or singled out for special persecution. I, like you, am subject to a number of laws that are infinitely beyond me. What we need to do is persuade ourselves that our acts are not thereby rendered arbitrary. Such an idea would be inherently foolish, in any case: nowhere, least of all in Misunderstanding, does anything happen to anyone unless it—that precise thing, and no other—*must* happen. Everything is therefore wonderfully exact. That which, because of ourselves, has to happen to us, does happen, and happens necessarily. And nothing happens that isn't both inevitable and fully justified ... I do admit, however, that I enjoy a certain advantage over you in the sense that you're seeing the plan from below, if you'll allow me the metaphor, while I see it from above. In other words, because you're forced to live out the plan on a day-to-day level, the driving mechanisms of Misunderstanding—and, more broadly speaking, of all the Sunday excursions—may appear nonsensical from your perspective. Actually, it's only in the details that one finds these mechanisms tending in an apparently illogical direction. Seen from a little further up the food chain in terms of knowledge, they form a much more orderly and structured system. Hence, the plan is more perfect from my point of view than from yours. And so on all the way up the hierarchy. The Holy Director is at once completely free and completely a prisoner, in the sense that he doesn't have the luxury—predicated on a comparative stupidity—of even a single moment's belief that he might have acted differently than he has. All in all, the Holy Director's knowledge of the excursionists could be called demiurgic, because it's comparable to a creator's knowledge of his creations."

With that, the colonel stopped talking and raised himself ponderously to his feet. SchrummSchrumm realized he'd finished off half the bottle without noticing. The interview seemed to be at an end, but the colonel told him to stay seated.

"We still haven't dealt with the most important question, my dear Mr. SchrummSchrumm. Today, as it happens, is the day I must reveal to you the Secret—either in whole or in part, it all depends. Do you recall the explanation given to you the day of your arrival by the representative of the Cigarette Smoke-Ring Blowers?"

SchrummSchrumm said that he did: the Secret was the sum of Misunderstanding's accumulated knowledge, symbolically expressed in the seven rings of cigarette smoke. The meaning of this design could be inverted, depending on whether you went from the innermost circle (ruled by the principle of Abocketaback) toward the outermost (the kingdom of nothingness) or the reverse. As a corollary, the principle of Abocketaback was either applicable or inapplicable, depending on whether you went in one direction or the other, in which case Abocketaback would replace the nothingness or vice versa.

"Precisely," said Red-Bartlett. "And did you notice this diagram behind my desk?"

It was a picture of seven concentric circles with a dotted-line radius. The line connected the center of the innermost circle to a point just beyond the outermost.

"Look closely. This is a map representing the visible portion of Misunderstanding. Imagine we're leaving from the center of the city and going all the way out to the Quicksands. The nucleus of Misunderstanding is, as you know, the primordial house of Nastarz, which is therefore the center of the innermost circle. Moving outward from this center, you have to pass through seven obstacles, or circles, to reach the Quicksands. These obstacles are, in order: the first circle, namely the swamp surrounding the primordial house; the second circle, the garden around the swamp; the third circle, the wall enclosing the garden which forms the boundary of Nastarz City. Around this wall are Eden proper, the city walls of Misunderstanding, the barbed-wire entanglement, and the Poplar Forest—the fourth, fifth, sixth, and seventh circles that make up Misunderstanding and its outer frontiers. The eighth, imaginary circle isn't depicted here. That's the Quicksands. With me so far? Good. Let's leave that for a moment. You'll notice that this dotted line connects the primordial house and the Quicksands to an indeterminate point beyond the seventh circle. This line is, both literally and figuratively, a road. More precisely, it's the Way of Misunderstanding, imagined here complete with its extensions to the center of Misunderstanding at one end and the Quicksands at the other. So, in theory, the Way of Misunderstanding links Nastarz City with the regions beyond the eighth circle. I say 'in theory' because, though this will surprise you, we know absolutely nothing of the Outer Regions."

"No one has traveled the Way of Misunderstanding far enough in the direction of the Quicksands to know what's out there?" said SchrummSchrumm, who was indeed surprised. "But isn't that the route the excursionists take?"

"No," said Red-Bartlett, "and I'll tell you why. This being very late in the cycle, and things being what they are, the Way of Misunderstanding, which in less troubled times would be 'open'—meaning it would normally allow access to the Quicksands—is currently 'closed.' And so the excursionists have to take another route, the so-called 'arduous' route, as opposed to the Way, or 'easy' route."

"What is this route?"

"We don't know. We don't accompany the excursionists on the final leg of their journey."

"I don't understand. Even assuming people can no longer cross the Quicksands by following the Way, the fact remains that all the excursionists you approve and deem qualified succeed in making the crossing. You could do the same. Why not go after them? Or, even simpler, ask them to supply you with the information you lack?"

"Unfortunately, it's not nearly as simple as you say, Mr. SchrummSchrumm. The Excursion is governed by two ironclad principles. The first concerns the excursionists themselves: those who enter the Quicksands never return to Misunderstanding. We don't see them again and we can't get any information from them. Let me be clear: even if they wanted to, it would impossible for them to return. That's just the way it is. The Ultimate Excursion is aptly named: there's no going back ... The second principle concerns Misunderstanding's public servants. We're forbidden from attempting the excursion, which is the exclusive privilege of the excursionists. Later on, I'll have occasion to point out a few consequences of this piece of legislation. For now, I'll simply say that it's because of this restriction that we know nothing whatsoever of the Outer Regions. We've sent several expeditions along the Way of Misunderstanding. None has ever been heard from again: all were lost without a trace. We're therefore reduced to speculations and hypotheses."

"I'm enormously interested in all this," said SchrummSchrumm, laughing. "Won't you tell me what's awaiting me on the other side of the Quicksands?"

"That's what I'm here for, Mr. SchrummSchrumm. It's part of my job. The hypotheses in question number only two. The first is based on a strictly orthodox interpretation of the Gospels. I want to emphasize this one because I know from firsthand experience how disinclined excursionists are to take it seriously. According to this first hypothesis, beyond the eighth circle there's nothing at all: nothingness, if you prefer."

"Nothing at all?" repeated SchrummSchrumm, furrowing his brow.

"Nothing," said Red-Bartlett with an indulgent smile. "Once outside of Misunderstanding, time, space, and phenomena in general become sparser and sparser, until total nothingness reigns—if you'll permit me this term—in the regions beyond the eighth circle."

"That would certainly explain why neither excursionists nor expeditions have returned," quipped SchrummSchrumm.

The colonel did not appreciate this flippancy.

"My job is to reveal the Secret, not to convince you. At any rate, I'm sure you'll find the second hypothesis more appealing. According to this theory, those who cross the Quicksands reach the kingdom, not of nothingness, but of peace and freedom. That being said—and the Secret having now been revealed to you in its entirety, I'd like to point out, Mr. SchrummSchrumm—I'll confine myself, again as a favor to you, to a certain number of further considerations, and let you make of them what you will.

"You'll find, depending on whether you feel more drawn to one or the other of these two hypotheses, that the hypothesis of your choosing will soon come to seem ever more plausible, and you'll start finding many additional proofs in support of your choice (often the same ones in both cases)—to the extent, of course, that we can speak of 'proofs' in such a matter. You can easily verify this for yourself. One of two things must be true. Either nothingness reigns beyond the Quicksands—but it's incongruous to imagine nothingness as the end goal of the excursion, since one can't go from 'something' to 'nothing'—or great happiness reigns beyond the Quicksands. But then Misunderstanding, as the departure point of the excursion, would have to reflect this great happiness in some fashion, however imperfectly or paradoxically. And it's safe to say that this does not appear to be the case. So you find yourself facing an irreconcilable contradiction. Instead of which, if you see that the difference between these two theories rests solely on how you envisage the Outer Regions—as a reward in one case, a respite in the other—the contradiction disappears, and whether you call the Outer Regions 'Nothingness' or 'Happiness' amounts to the same thing.

"Here, incidentally, are two brief remarks that might help to clarify things for you. Remember what we said about the Way of Misunderstanding, which crosses through the seven circles in what one might call seven privileged locations. You cross the swamp on the pink bridge. You exit (or enter) Nastarz City through a garden gate. You access Eden through the Original Pissoir. You enter and exit Misunderstanding through the Great Iron Gate. We can therefore discern a number of analogies: between the Nastarz City swamp and the Quicksands; between the garden gate and the Great Iron Gate; between the Nastarz City walls and Misunderstanding's walls; between Eden and the Poplar Forest. There's a one-to-one correspondence. Just as a pink bridge spans the Nastarz City swamp and provides access to the Primordial House, a pink pier greets you at the Quicksands at the end of your journey. After that, we know no more, because we can go no farther. But the analogy holds up, and a pink pier provides access to the Outer Regions. Is it mere accident that an excursionist can only get into Eden via the Original Pissoir, while the officials of Misunderstanding can easily go there by other, less disgusting and degrading routes? Wouldn't it make more sense if there were a very good reason for this that remains for you to discover? Conversely, isn't it odd that any excursionist can travel to the Outer Regions, while we, the public servants responsible for organizing the excursions, can't?

"This brings us to the second group of considerations I want to highlight for you. You must surely have heard about the reform doctrines circulating in Misunderstanding, doctrines sanctioned and promoted by the Holy Director himself. And you must no less surely have heard something about the issue of prostration. It's true that this issue served as a convenient pretext for getting the reform movement rolling. But the real roots of the movement go much deeper: they consist of a desire to protest the interdiction against public servants in Misunderstanding attempting the excursion. An interdiction which is practical as well as theoretical, since every city employee, no matter his rank, is required to swear an oath renouncing all future excursions for both himself and his family. Don't you see the close link between these apparently disparate phenomena? On the one hand, you have the difficulties excursionists encounter when they try to penetrate the mystery of the symbols (difficulties which find their expression, analogically and anecdotally, in the various ordeals both moral and physical that they have to undergo to enter Eden and Nastarz City); on the other hand, you have this outlandish rule forbidding Misunderstanding employees from turning excursionist. Let's return now to what we were saying earlier about the golden age. During that happy time, the Way of Misunderstanding—the 'easy' route—is not only open but freely accessible to all and sundry: excursionists as well as employees. It's only in the cycle's decline that the Way closes up and the employee initiation comes to include this silly oath. Consequently, proponents of the reform movement have had solid grounds for saying: 'Just as the excursionists get around the Way's prohibition and reach the Outer Regions by a different route, so we public servants can and should get around the prohibition that forbids us from attempting the excursion.' Their success is all the greater because there's undeniable justice to their claims. Things have gotten to the point that a sanitized, toned-down version of the Gospels called the 'Apocrypha' is now being disseminated, which aims to give these claims textual justification and a theoretical footing."

"Do you mean some Misunderstanding employees go on the excursion in secret?" asked SchrummSchrumm, breathless.

"Not yet, Mr. SchrummSchrumm, although that day is almost certainly coming . . . But that's beside the point. We need to wrap things up. Suffice it to say that the principle of Abocketaback, which governs Misunderstanding—the law of paradox and absurdity—renders all arbitrary classifications null and void. It lends a flavor of legitimacy to the most diametrically opposed aspirations, and, looked at another way, it justifies the excursionists' attitude as well as that of the employees, the spies, and anyone else caught up in the gravitational orbit of the Quicksands. When you come right down to it, everything that happens in Misunderstanding—and this brings us back to what we were saying earlier—even if it seems aberrant or nonsensical to some, will seem justified to others; everything contributes to an order that transcends comprehension. An order in which, like it or not, you participate to the extent of your abilities, just as I do, and as everyone who lives here does."

"Hmm!" said SchrummSchrumm. He'd lost the thread when Red-Bartlett began talking about Abocketaback.

But whether he'd understood it or not, the interview was now definitively over. The colonel sank heavily back into his chair, tossing aside the ruler he'd been holding. The room, which SchrummSchrumm had put entirely out of his mind during this curious conversation, now reappeared to him in all its eccentricity. One black woman was fanning her palm frond, the other swinging her censer. The two sentries were daydreaming. The incense burned on, the women sweated on. The liquor bottle was empty; SchrummSchrumm had drunk every last drop. At that moment the sentries seemed to rouse themselves from their waking dream; the office door opened and a panting lieutenant stood at attention. He ran over and whispered something in the colonel's ear. The colonel rose and hurriedly threw on his uniform.

"Farewell, Mr. Excursionist," he said with a faint smile. Then, turning to the lieutenant: "I'm right behind you." One of the sentries came over and laid a hand on SchrummSchrumm's shoulder. He steered him toward a second door. When they reached it, the guard uncovered a niche in which there was an intercom.

"Toto!" he barked into the receiver. A brief pause, and then: "The excursionist SchrummSchrumm is about to enter the educational promenade area."

"What does that mean?" asked SchrummSchrumm. "I'm not going back to the hotel?"

The door swung open automatically and the guard just shrugged. He stepped aside to let SchrummSchrumm pass through alone.

"Isn't Krikri going to accompany me? How will I find the hotel?"

The guard didn't answer, only pushed SchrummSchrumm through the door and closed it after him.

XIII

A beautiful inner courtyard lay before him. Porticos—thick with shadow despite the early afternoon light—surrounded a spacious, carefully manicured lawn. In the center was a fountain, or rather a disused well converted into a fountain, but it was dry. Close beside it stood a wooden platform resembling an open-air stage. A profound stillness reigned over the whole scene, broken only by the chirping of birds. All things considered, it should have been relatively reassuring to find himself in such a calm, peaceful setting. Yet SchrummSchrumm was far from reassured. If only Krikri were here; Krikri would have affectionately taken his arm and protected him, just like he always did. But at this hour and in this place, SchrummSchrumm was alone, entirely alone. He realized too late that he shouldn't have stood around gawping: people were now swarming out from beneath the porticos. Perhaps they'd been watching for him, hidden in wait behind the colonnades. What did they want with him? Dozens of them were converging on SchrummSchrumm from all sides in such serried ranks that they forced him into the middle of the courtyard. There they stopped. They'd formed a circle around the fountain and its adjoining platform. A path had been left clear leading to a narrow wooden door, which was tucked beneath the porticos and more visible now that SchrummSchrumm was closer. The crowd was quiet but seemed to be awaiting some imminent event with barely controlled impatience. No one was the least bit bothered by his presence; that had just been his imagination playing tricks on him.

Suddenly the narrow door was flung open and two oddly dressed men appeared. They were clad in red tights and their faces were concealed by ski masks of the same color. Deer antlers, painted blue, were attached to the forehead of each mask. One of the men gave the crowd a friendly wave before murmuring something confidentially to his companion.

"No! No! It's no use!" said the other man stubbornly. At the same time, however, he raised his voice enough to be heard by the throng and made motions of his head as if encouraging his friend to continue insisting.

"Now look here!" said the first man. "You can't keep them waiting any longer." And, addressing the crowd in a knowing tone: "Aren't you all getting impatient?" The question drew roars of assent, and the crowd begged the man to hurry up and get started. By this point it was clear that the dialogue between the spectators and the men in red was a conventional call-and-response and that everybody around SchrummSchrumm knew exactly what it meant.

"Oh, very well!" said the man, as if giving in to the exhortations. "I'll tell the men to begin . . . Hey, fellas!" he shouted into the doorway, "Are you playing cards back there or what? Let's shake a leg! Folks are waiting!"

"We're coming!" was the reply.

A gratified hush fell over the crowd as the men emerged. There were eight of them in total. A clown in a Pierrot costume led the way. Then, marching two by two, were four men in yellow tights, yellow ski masks, and black antlers. Behind them was a lone man. Bringing up the rear were two guards, outfitted in green for the occasion: green helmets, trousers, boots, and gloves. These colors, however original, were nonetheless in terrible taste and greatly displeased SchrummSchrumm, who was becoming less and less amused by the sartorial whimsy so prevalent in Misunderstanding. Once they'd stepped up onto the platform, the seven new men and the two in red tights began berating the lone man who'd been walking in the middle of the group. He might have been about thirty—almost a young man—but he was unshaven and stared wildly out at the crowd like a hunted animal. They gave him a hard shove and he fell to his knees without protest; no one seemed to pay any further attention to him. SchrummSchrumm couldn't get a good look at his face.

"Who are those two men in red?" he asked a man standing near him.

"The executioners!" said his neighbor, not taking his eyes off the stage.

"And the four in yellow?"

"The executioners' acolytes, who do you think?" he answered, glancing at him in surprise.

SchrummSchrumm hesitated a second before he spoke again.

"And the blood-spattered man in rags they've just forced onto his knees?"

To this, he received no answer. Only: "Where'd this guy come from? What a moron!" After saying which, the man looked at him with a combination of scorn and bewilderment before backing away as if he were infected with plague. Luckily, no one had overheard their exchange; SchrummSchrumm had timed his questions to coincide with a murmur of satisfaction that was just then rippling through the crowd. He looked to the stage. The clown had taken a step forward. The unknown man was still on his knees, the others standing at attention. The two executioners in red, off to one side, were chatting to each other as if not yet involved in the events underway.

"Tralala and tralalay! Whoooooo am I?" the clown asked the audience.

"Our friendly clown!" several voices replied.

He thanked them with a series of comical faces. Then he mooned them, clapped his hands, and a baby chick fluttered out from between his thighs. The spectators shrieked with laughter. But he put a finger to his mouth and, pretending to stifle himself, said: "Shhh! Shhh!" The crowd went quiet.

"This is the very veracious story whose final scene our talented actors are going to perform for you today," he continued. "Once upon a time—toodle-dee-dize and eyes on prize—there was a semi-wholesaler in small hardware supplies. A lying, hypocritical, vultureous vexation. At Lickety-Split Station, he climbs into a train with no reservation, and after some acceleration, arrives at Misunderstanding's location. Deployed in formation is a triple array of barriers to cause hesitation: the tangle of barbed wire with razor-sharp points to snag your feet; the grenade-, mine-, and booby-trap zone where everyone's dead meat; the ramparts you can't climb and the Great Gate locked up neat. What's more, prowling in the shadows, tireless and fleet, of training so elite, the Smoke-Ring Blower guards are there to bring the heat. But what's that sound? The rascally semi-wholesaler is around, leaping over barbed wire, mines, and ramparts in a single bound, displaying agility and strength to earn renown. Portentous is his stride, terrible is the shadow of his misshapen hide, and the man won't turn aside. He's a fright, I must confess, but arrested nonetheless. He's foiled and despoiled. The things they find on him would make your blood boil: he's a despicable huckster—those people are a blight. He's acting all polite. Says semi-wholesaling's his career, he travels far and near, a mere salesman is what he tries to appear, but it's clear he's here to interfere, smuggling into Misunderstanding, across the great frontier, banned books—the 'Apocrypha' to be quite clear. The knave is tried and he's condemned. The penalty's severe. Now this bandit insincere, this dirty profiteer, stands . . . here!"

The clown paused to gauge his effect. People were clapping and shouting "Bravo!" and "What next?" But they were not to hear the end of this pitiable story. One of the red executioners looked at his watch, swore, and said to his yellow acolytes: "It's time! We're behind schedule. Get a move on!"

The four acolytes began running helter-skelter. The executioners stayed put. SchrummSchrumm quickly realized, however, that each of the acolytes knew exactly what moves to make, and that this scrambling around was just an act. They were actually very well organized.

Two of the acolytes ducked back in through the wooden door. They returned, each with a large box which must have been quite heavy, because both were bent double under the weight. They set down their boxes—the first on the stage, the second beside the well—and ceremoniously opened the lids. From the box on the stage, one acolyte extracted a bulky apparatus which grew, as accessories were added to it, into a large receptacle mounted on a sturdy tripod. A long pipe was affixed to one side. From the second box, the other acolyte drew out various small objects which he placed around the rim of the well. SchrummSchrumm, despite his best efforts, couldn't see at first what these objects were. Finally, though, they revealed themselves to be metal figurines representing naked little girls, pigs, birds; there was even a plucked and decapitated chicken, as well as a female torso with the tips of its breasts painted scarlet. These dolls, each about the size of two fists, were fastened onto a mechanical contraption that could rotate freely around a fixed axis. Basically, a miniature carousel. They joined the free end of the pipe to a knob at the center of the carousel. This done, the two acolytes heaved a sigh of relief and lit cigarettes.

Meanwhile, the two other acolytes had been busying themselves with the kneeling man. With a great show of politeness—exaggerated for the purpose of humiliating him—they asked their victim to please rise. They brought out a clothes-brush and vigorously brushed down his torn, blood-stained garments; they combed his hair and hung a slate around his neck on which the day, month, and year were written, tying it behind his back. Why this formality? Why have a pipe connecting the outlandish receptacle on the tripod to the doll carousel? SchrummSchrumm didn't understand. In any case, most of the preliminaries seemed to be over with, at least as far as the yellow acolytes were concerned. The prisoner had been pushed back down to his knees so that his head rested on the receptacle—what for?—and the four men had taken up positions at places assigned by whatever protocol they were following. The first two stood on either side of the prisoner; they'd each put one hand under one of his armpits and planted the other firmly on their hips in a very martial pose. The third acolyte held the man's head inside the receptacle. The fourth pointed at the slate. All four looked extremely stupid.

It was now the green guards' turn to swing into action. Just as the acolytes had done, they ran back to the doorway, disappeared inside for a minute, then returned, each carrying a large ceremonial knife on a fancy embroidered pillow. They presented the first and second executioners with their respective knives.

SchrummSchrumm began to get the sense that something unpleasant was coming. Until now, the crowd's upbeat mood and the merry antics of the clown—who, during all this hustle and bustle, had been goofing around and making corny jokes—had persuaded him that the worst was not to happen. Now, however, there was little room for doubt. Especially once the two red executioners and the others began the ritual questions and responses.

"Are you ready?" asked one of the two official executioners.

"We are ready!" said the four acolytes, who hadn't moved.

"Are you ready?" repeated the other executioner.

"We are ready!" echoed the guards in green. The clown had stopped making faces and had withdrawn into an inconspicuous corner. The guards set down the cushions and stepped forward with a typewritten sheet.

"Proceed to the reading of the act," came the order.

The guards put on reading glasses and perused the text, no doubt to avoid forgetting a line. Then they shut their eyes, threw back their heads, and sang in duet, one taking the tenor part and the other bass:

"I, the Lord High Executioner,

"In the name of the Holy Director,

"King of the Excursion, Lord of Misunderstanding and the Quicksands,

"In view of the fact that the rabble-rouser here present,

"(Conniving, hypocritical, disloyal, and dumb)

"Practicing the profession of semi-wholesaler in small hardware supplies,

"Has been guilty of deceptions, sacrileges, abuses, and other presumptive acts (all prejudicial)

"Do hereby ordain that he shall this day have his neck severed with an ax.

"Likewise shall his chest and belly be slit open with a knife.

"Likewise shall his heart be thrown to the two large, black, placid dogs

"And his entrails partitioned into seven steaming piles on which shall be planted seven pink flags called 'inviolable.'

"His blood be upon us and upon the little spinning objects!

"Proclaimed in Misunderstanding, the . . ."

The day, month, and year written on the slate followed.

The crowd was buzzing with excitement. The semi-wholesaler in small hardware supplies hadn't said a word during the reading, nor during the preparations that preceded it. He now emitted a kind of monotonous moan. He looked up, and for the first time SchrummSchrumm saw him clearly.

"Hey!" he cried. "I know that semi-wholesaler! He's my neighbor, a respectable young man who's never done any harm to anyone!"

"Your neighbor?" someone echoed.

They demanded an explanation. SchrummSchrumm obliged. The semi-wholesaler lived in the same building he did, back in Mahasky. He had a spotless reputation.

"Mahasky?" someone echoed.

A man stepped forward who seemed to have the authority to settle the matter. He spoke calmly. Mahasky, he said, did not exist. Mahasky was a mythical city. SchrummSchrumm's mistake likely stemmed from the fact that, like so many excursionists, he had projected onto this Mahasky the whole of his desires and aspirations. The phenomenon was well known among Misunderstanding's leadership: SchrummSchrumm had convinced himself that he'd been born in Mahasky, though in fact it was merely a place he would have liked to go. In other words, SchrummSchrumm was taking his desires for realities, and because he couldn't go to Mahasky in the future, he'd decided that he'd lived there in the past . . . Ergo, SchrummSchrumm had no grounds for interfering with the execution of this semi-wholesaler in small hardware supplies, an execution that was both just and necessary.

Having said his piece, the man disappeared back into the crowd. The semi-wholesaler moaned a second time but no one attached the slightest importance to it. He was being held fast. The two executioners nodded at one another.

"Are you ready? Absolutely and entirely ready?" they asked.

"We are ready!" said the others.

It was all done very methodically. The two executioners, after taking up their knives, put their tongues between their teeth and gave several loud whistles. Then the first knelt down beside the condemned man, whose head had been pulled back. The executioner gazed at him affectionately, as if wanting to apologize for his role in this drama. Delicately, with the tip of his blade, he sliced open the prisoner's shirt and seemed to be taking the measure of his chest and belly. "Poor, poor little child," he crooned. His colleague came over and joined him. They gave each other one last look and nodded. "Avaunt! Avaunt!" they shouted suddenly. They pushed the man's head into the receptacle. No sooner had his throat been cut than the second man made a lengthwise motion from the man's thorax to his pubis. He parted the skin and pulled on the flesh as if it were cloth. By rummaging around with his left hand and making supplementary cuts with his knife, he finally managed to pull out what looked like a hunk of bloody meat. Two large black dogs had just appeared; they were yelping excitedly and wagging their tails.

The executioner tossed them the heart, which they gobbled down with horrible gulping noises. During this time another container had been brought over, and the entrails from the slit belly tumbled into it. These were swiftly divided into seven piles placed at points around the stage. The two executioners smiled in satisfaction. They had good cause to be proud of their work: they'd acted with extraordinary precision and had finished in record time

"Hurray!" cheered the crowd. The dogs licked their chops. An impromptu saraband was begun around the fountain, whose mechanism SchrummSchrumm now understood. The little metal dolls had been set in motion. From the central knob, warm blood was spilling down. First it inundated the pigs, the little girls, the plucked chicken, and the woman's torso with its scarlet-tipped breasts. Then, from the receptacle end, one of the men made an adjustment and the blood gurgled out faster, splashing onto the dancers. Many of them, in a kind of frenzied ecstasy, smeared it on their faces. SchrummSchrumm, now spattered himself, felt he was about to faint.

"You OK, mister?" asked one of the people who'd joined hands with him in the saraband. Soon others had gathered round. One spectator, who might have been a doctor, took his pulse; another slapped him several times across the face.

"He must've had a bad spell," someone said. "That always happens with people who aren't accustomed to it."

"It's nothing," protested SchrummSchrumm. The people around him, meanwhile, were having a grand time. Several were discussing the execution in conversational tones. There was still some agitation up on the platform and in the area surrounding both platform and well, but it was a happy agitation, like when the stagehands come to strike the set and clean up after a play.

"What's going on now?" asked SchrummSchrumm. He was torn between morbid curiosity and the belief that it would be better not to ask.

His impromptu nurses looked abashed.

"How silly of us! Would you like to see? Of course you would, it's only natural! This will put you to rights . . ."

With extreme affability, they took it upon themselves to part the ranks of the remaining spectators. "Make way! Make way for a young excursionist who's feeling unwell and wants to see the finale," they cried. SchrummSchrumm was moved up to a place in front.

Three crews were hard at work: the washers, the packers, and the undertakers. The washers and packers worked in tandem. As the pipe, receptacle, chopping block, and carousel components were disassembled and cleaned, they were put back inside the two boxes. These were then closed and taken away. The washers immediately turned to their main task, equipped with brushes, mops, buckets, and large bars of soap. All were jovial, pink-cheeked lads. They started splashing bucketfuls of water over the stray pools of blood. Some soaped the boards, others gave them a vigorous scrubbing. As icing on the cake, a loudspeaker was now playing music that might have been a tango. It was like the end of a day in the country, after a funfair. The men worked with cheerful enthusiasm. The corpse had been tossed into a wheelbarrow and the entrails cleared away. If he hadn't been able to see, here and there, a few traces of red missed by the washers, and if he hadn't been bloodstained himself, SchrummSchrumm could easily have believed that what had just taken place was only a bad dream. Alas, it was no nightmare. He attempted a feeble gesture: he put his hands over his eyes. In vain, because the two men holding him up, mistaking his meaning, thought he was having another weak spell and so pried away his hands and grasped them firmly, gazing at him with friendly concern.

"Are you excursionists?" he asked his caregivers.

"Of course! We're all excursionists here."

"Real excursionists? Not stand-ins?"

"Absolutely not!" they answered, shocked.

"Then I don't understand at all. Tell me, friends: what happened to you?"

Several heads had already turned to hear the speaker, but he was interrupted.

"It's him all right," said one of three newcomers, and SchrummSchrumm recognized the man he'd questioned about the executioners, their acolytes, and the semi-wholesaler.

"It's him all right," agreed the second, and SchrummSchrumm recognized Leopold the spy, the man who stank and hopped like a mountain goat.

"Good," said the officer with them, and SchrummSchrumm recognized him, too. It was the lieutenant who'd come to see Red-Bartlett an hour earlier. The officer asked the two others to leave him to it. When they were gone, he steered SchrummSchrumm toward the courtyard exit.

"Believe me, Mr. SchrummSchrumm, I'm as sorry as you are that you had to witness this execution. It was an error, a monstrous error. It wasn't part of the plan!"

"Can I go back to the hotel?" was all SchrummSchrumm asked.

"Right away," said the lieutenant.

Krikri, in fact, was already walking toward them. Before SchrummSchrumm was quite out of the courtyard, he took a final look back at the scene. One of the two executioners, leaning against a colonnade, had lit himself a cigarette. He was smiling vaguely while his right hand, as if inadvertently, caressed his privates, which formed a prominent bulge beneath his red tights. He and SchrummSchrumm locked eyes. Neither his smile nor his movements stopped. The smile wasn't ironic, or even mocking. It expressed only satisfaction in a job well done. Krikri and the lieutenant followed SchrummSchrumm's gaze.

"Alas, Mr. Excursionist," said the lieutenant, "these acts of onanism are regrettable but more or less inevitable. Especially at moments like this! We have to turn a blind eye. The executioner's vocation is a thankless one. Not only docs it demand exceptional professional skill, it requires a very particular cast of mind. Which means these two executioners are, frankly, irreplaceable. We must excuse their little peccadillos."

SchrummSchrumm nodded.

"What's he mumbling?" he asked. The man was indeed mumbling something, and also keeping time with his foot.

"He's reciting an incantatory phrase required after executions."

"I see. What's the phrase?"

"'Happy are the pigs, methinks, that go to make the sausage links,'" said the lieutenant, looking embarrassed.

They left the courtyard.

XIV

O glorious day! SchrummSchrumm was told that he'd been granted special permission to go wherever he pleased within the city limits. When they signed his pass, they asked only that he return before nightfall. The sky above was radiant; the very atmosphere was radiant. So intoxicating was the sense of freedom that he made little, if any, effort to keep track of where he was going. He crossed countless flagged courtyards surrounded by buildings, then yet more flagged courtyards surrounded by buildings. His footsteps echoed awfully, drawing people to their windows wherever he went. These people didn't seem surprised, nor did they appear to bear him any ill will. On the contrary, they made signs to him, shaking their heads or knitting their brows as if wishing to communicate some message. But they did so silently, without speaking a word. At length, these strange dumbshows began to annoy him. Where was he, anyway? What time was it? He no longer had any idea. He spotted a small door in the corner of a courtyard and, after debating with himself for a moment, he knocked, determined to ask where he was. He had his pass ready in hand, just in case.

"Yes?" growled someone from inside. The door was promptly opened. There was a chair beside a small cot. The light now flooding the windowless room threw the man's inordinately distorted shadow against the far wall.

"Well, what is it?"

"I beg your pardon for disturbing you. I just need a little information."

"Come on in," said the man, sounding somewhat startled. He shut the door carefully and rubbed a hairy hand across his bald head. "Who are you? Are you from the Exterior Hygiene Department?"

"No," said SchrummSchrumm.

"The Interior Hygiene Department, then?"

"Neither Exterior Hygiene nor Interior Hygiene."

"Now look here, sir. I know you're connected with the hospital in some way. If your suit jacket can be relied upon, that is—the jacket's seen better days, but it unquestionably came from the Hospital Clothing Service. The cut is unmistakable."

SchrummSchrumm replied that he was surprised to hear it, since he'd had this jacket for ages and had bought it in a place far removed from Misunderstanding. The man shrugged, stepped closer, and, flipping over one of the jacket's lapels, showed him the lining near the collar. SchrummSchrumm saw the little Misunderstanding crest and read: "Quicksands—Misunderstanding, Hospital." The man sat down and considered him.

"So you're in no way connected with the Hospital, you say! How do you explain that Hospital suit on your back? And what brings you here at this hour?"

"I'm an excursionist."

"Excursionist!" spat the man. "A likely story!" He scrutinized SchrummSchrumm even more intensely.

"Why are you so convinced that I must be with one of the Hospital Departments?"

"Because this is the Hospital anteroom."

"Do you work in the Hospital?"

"No."

"Are you the Hospital tailor, then?"

"No. I'm the former grade-crossing gateman of Misunderstanding. Have you ever heard of Misunderstanding's grade crossing?"

SchrummSchrumm said that yes, as a matter of fact he had. But the existence of a grade crossing seemed very improbable to him. The man concurred:

"I know, no one believes me. Back when I was a gateman, everyone respected me. Now that I've lost my job, I haven't a friend in the world, and even the people who once fawned on me when I was a gateman refuse to admit the fact." SchrummSchrumm gave a tired shrug. He didn't care. Was there any story he'd balk at now, even an outright impossible one?

"I've met your older brother," he said to demonstrate his friendly intentions. "Hermann Occursus, isn't it? What's your given name?"

"Franz," said the man. Then, seeming interested: "What's become of that old devil Hermann?"

"You haven't seen him for a while?"

"We lost touch after the grade crossing was automated. Before that damned invention came along, times were good and we were getting along just fine, him and me. We sold sandwiches and bottles of beer to excursionists on the trains coming out of Misunderstanding. We'd actually worked out a little side deal with the conductors: we gave them a cut of our take, and they stopped their trains for a few minutes in front of our house."

"Where was this grade crossing?"

"At the edge of the Great Park," said Franz Occursus. "That's why we made such good money. In those days the park was still open to all and you could wander wherever you liked. The excursionists would step off the train for a while to enjoy the cool shade. They could pick wild strawberries. The denser thickets were furnished with feather mattresses for young lovers. There were orchestras playing slow-dance music under golden bandstand pavilions . . . In short, things were going along swimmingly and there was something for everyone. Between trains, we'd kick back and make our sandwiches. Then one day some people from Misunderstanding showed up. Oh, not all at once! In fact they were so sly about it we didn't even notice at first. They started by closing the park. It was a heavy blow, but they did offer us a tangible compensation: they built a recruitment center for Misunderstanding guards next to our house . . . then again, they also sent in engineers to set up that stinking automatic grade crossing."

"How long ago was this?"

The man thought a moment.

"I don't remember exactly," he said apologetically, "but a good long while. That was when Hermann and I decided to go our separate ways. We were forced to move out of our house. Naturally! We had nothing to do there anymore. I capitalized on my former title and, thanks to my connections, found a little work here in town. But for Hermann, things were tough. He took to drink. He'd watch the passing trains that didn't stop for us anymore and the sight would depress him. He stayed on in the house until the three-month deadline they'd given us to vacate the premises was up. Toward the end, those trains were really messing with his head. One night when I went over to visit, I found him falling-down drunk. He told me the train cars coming back from Misunderstanding were loaded with iron cages filled with men pleading for help. He claimed the Misunderstanding bigwigs had used the automatic grade crossing as an excuse to get rid of us so we wouldn't see the cages. Pure hooey! He ended up enlisting in a spy regiment. Not because the work appealed to him, but just to have done with it, if you ask me. Said he wanted to look into some things."

SchrummSchrumm listened to this story with rapt attention.

"I don't know what it was like when you and your brother had to leave your grade crossing," he said, "but the last time I saw Hermann, he was in full possession of his faculties."

Franz agreed, rather fatuously:

"Sure!" he said. "Sure he was!"

"Also," SchrummSchrumm insisted, "I've heard other people talking about iron cages, too. It's not outside the realm of possibility that they might actually exist."

Franz agreed again:

"Sure," he said. "I had a hand in recording that 'record for the artificial production of sounds simulating the passage of a train through the valley, a group marching in step, the moans of shackled excursionists, the cursing of guards, the creaking of numerous iron cages, etc.' It's that damned record that's got everyone fooled."

At this moment there came a knock at the door and two men entered. One was about thirty, with an elegant derby hat and a malacca walking stick. SchrummSchrumm saw the dazzling brightness of his teeth; he was smiling. The other, dressed all in white, wore a surgical gown, scrub cap, and steel-rimmed glasses. Franz Occursus greeted them respectfully:

"Good evening, Doctor."

"Good evening, Franz," replied the doctor, and made an inquiring gesture toward SchrummSchrumm.

"He's an excursionist," said Franz.

"An excursionist! You don't say!"

"I have a pass," interjected SchrummSchrumm. "My papers are in order."

The doctor took the pass, examined it carefully, and returned it.

"Perfect! I'm Dr. Hell. This is Dominic. Why don't you come with us?" he said, caressing SchrummSchrumm's cheek. His fingers were long and immaculate, his hand perfumed. SchrummSchrumm dropped his eyes. The other man, Dominic, said in a half-whisper:

"I'm leaving, actually. See you in a bit."

Dr. Hell nodded, though SchrummSchrumm had the distinct impression the words had been addressed to himself. Whatever the case, they all left—the young man in one direction, Dr. Hell and SchrummSchrumm in the other. They ascended a staircase, went down a hall, and stopped in front of a double swinging door with a dim night-light above it. The hall was dark. No windows, complete silence; anyone would have thought it was the middle of the night. A faint smell of ether hung in the air.

"Welcome to my little domain," said Hell, pushing open one of the doors. SchrummSchrumm saw a long room with some forty beds lining the walls on either side. At the far end was a steel door equipped with a superabundance of bolts, crossbars, and padlocks. The door itself was behind a sturdy metal grille that spanned the width of the room. Between the grille and the door stood an armed guard who saluted the doctor. The latter was already busy showing off his patients to his new visitor. They were lying spread-eagle as if literally being quartered. A leather strap had been wrapped several times around each wrist and passed through a ring cemented into the wall, the arm being stretched to its uttermost limit by a weight on the opposite end. Since this system couldn't be used for their ankles, they had simply been lashed to the bedposts. But the straps were so tight that their feet, which could be seen sticking out from beneath the covers, were purplish-blue. SchrummSchrumm was stupefied. His view of the room was indistinct because the night-light offered scant illumination—once again, there were no windows—but it was clear nonetheless that the poor wretches had been completely immobilized and looked more like torture victims than patients. Dr. Hell went ahead of SchrummSchrumm and lifted a blanket here, a sheet there. As if it were a great gag, he pointed out the knots that were tied too tightly and gave one or two men a friendly slap across the face. Or he'd pinch his nose in a "P.U." gesture, because as soon as the bedclothes were lifted, a horrible reek of excrement would fill the air. These patients said nothing, didn't even groan, just stared with burning eyes. A few pulled back their lips as if they wanted to bite, revealing rotten teeth.

"No chance of them wandering off," said SchrummSchrumm, nauseated.

The doctor grinned.

"Can't be too careful, can we?"

By now they had reached the metal grille. The guard had presumably pushed a button somewhere, because the portcullis raised itself and the door slid open noiselessly.

"You can go in," said the guard. As SchrummSchrumm walked past, the guard pinched his bottom. He must have been a little tipsy. The doctor stepped in:

"None of that, Abdullah! You know better."

"Yes, doctor," replied the guard meekly.

Without wasting another glance on the man, who was now relocking the grille, the doctor brushed SchrummSchrumm's cheek once more:

"Let's go, my dear little excursionist. Pay no attention to such behavior, these men are brutes!"

"Where are we going?" asked SchrummSchrumm. The doctor's touch made his skin crawl.

"My place," said Hell.

They crossed a small room where a male nurse was dozing on a makeshift bed. There were a few medical jars, a syringe; the sleeper was clutching a carbine rifle to his chest. More staircases. Another hallway. Then the doctor pushed open a door:

"Here we have my office, control center, and living quarters."

The room they'd just entered couldn't have been part of the office, much less the living quarters. Two of its walls were covered by vast panels of electronics; the other two were floor-to-ceiling windows. On the panels were green, blue, and orange lights, all blinking away. They blinked off here and on there, some brighter than others. Beside an apparatus loaded with switches and buttons was a sort of piano keyboard topped by an intercom. In front of it was a stool. Hell sat down and ran his fingers over the red and black keys. At the same time, with a motion of his chin, he invited SchrummSchrumm to watch the wall panels. After a few seconds, two new lights appeared, one blue and one yellow. They shone much brighter than the rest. Almost simultaneously, two numbers appeared on a little monitor: 1125 and 11033.

"These instruments enable me to locate any of my patients within seconds," said Hell proudly. "The two lights that have just appeared correspond to patients eleven-hundred twenty-five and eleven zero double-three. Look out the windows, you can see for yourself."

SchrummSchrumm obeyed. The doctor's control room overlooked a courtyard some six or seven meters below. This was no ordinary courtyard. It was enclosed by a tall chain-link fence and had a lookout tower at each of its four corners from which guards with machine guns kept watch over the strange patients milling around the yard. These patients were connected to a kind of free-spinning central hub by chains long enough to allow them to pace in a circle around it. More guards were down among these poor souls, cracking jokes and laughingly pointing Tommy guns at them. And what sort of dangerous maniacs were these patients? Nothing but pathetic invalids.

"Pay attention now!" said the doctor excitedly. "Eyes peeled!"

He counted "one, two, three," and on *three* SchrummSchrumm saw two of the patients jerk into the air and fall writhing and screaming to the ground. Neither the guards nor the other prisoners seemed surprised; the latter had stopped circling around the hub and the guards whooped and laughed.

"The men who just fell are patients eleven-hundred twenty-five and eleven zero double-three. I administered a powerful electric shock to both of them. It's quite effective!"

He glanced up at SchrummSchrumm, who had jumped as well, recoiling from the windows. The doctor chuckled as his perfumed hands fondled imaginary forms with suggestive movements of the forefingers.

"I have to leave you for a moment. Guests await. I'll have the trusty Kronos conduct you to the sitting room … Kronos!" he snapped into the intercom. "Kronos! Get in here on the double!"

A few minutes later, a guard walked in. He wore a metal cuirass over his black leather uniform—the first time SchrummSchrumm had seen this particular accessory.

"Kronos," said Hell, "you're going to show this nice excursionist into the parlor. Take good care of my friend. No roughhousing! Understand?"

The guard grunted.

"Will you do me the pleasure of coming to see me when I've finished with my guests?" Hell asked.

SchrummSchrumm nodded. He wasn't sure whether to take this as an invitation or an order. Either way, this hospital tour must have some purpose behind it, which he'd discover sooner or later.

"Let's go!" said Kronos. He led SchrummSchrumm to a framed door. He knocked, opened it, and after putting a beefy finger to his lips to indicate that silence was imperative, disappeared through the doorway. SchrummSchrumm followed and found himself in an attractive parlor that must once have served as some kind of anteroom. He sat down and waited in the semi-darkness. He felt at home here. The silence, the dimness, the furniture that looked like it came from an old-fashioned, middle-class house—everything, down to the slight sound of scuffing slippers he heard now and then, reminded him of the parlor of the house he'd grown up in, back in Mahasky.

How long did he sit in his armchair? He wouldn't have been able to say. The sound of conversation woke him. The next room, under whose door a ray of light showed, was occupied.

Dr. Hell's voice rang out above the rest:

"Madame Rose, would you be kind enough to bring in the meat course?"

At the same moment, the door opened. A short, round woman shuffled past and exited through a second door, leaving the first ajar. Dr. Hell and three guests were in a dining room, sitting at supper. They were all in formal attire, the room was brilliantly lit, forks clinked against plates, and wine glugged out of carafes. SchrummSchrumm's mouth watered. A middle-aged butler was furtively offering the guests something from a silver platter, and when he stopped silently behind each, he seemed to watch his face for some sign of gratitude or complicity. The little woman reappeared. SchrummSchrumm had the impression she was looking his way. She bent down to murmur something in the doctor's ear.

"Good Lord, that's right! I completely forgot about him. Tell the young man to come and join us. If he doesn't mind contenting himself with our leftovers, that is."

The dinner guests tittered genteelly and the little woman opened wide the door between the rooms. They gazed at him with friendly interest and motioned for him to come in. But he didn't dare sit at this sumptuous table amid such elegant guests. He hung his head sheepishly.

"Come! Don't keep the doctor waiting," urged the little woman, pulling at his sleeve.

He found himself sitting at the table with a place-setting laid before him.

"I'm afraid I've put you to a lot of extra trouble," he said, his head still down.

These words were greeted with polite murmurs. "It's nothing. Please, eat, Mr. SchrummSchrumm," said Hell, making benevolent, protective hand gestures. The man seated beside the doctor looked up from his plate.

"Why, it's Mr. SchrummSchrumm!" he said with manifest delight. "Do you remember me? Basil, the industrialist."

"Yes indeed," said SchrummSchrumm. "I recognize you now. I'm glad to see you in such good company. How is Mr. Broadway?"

"Very well, very well," replied Basil, seemingly embarrassed. Dr. Hell was chatting to the guest on his other side. They were paying no attention to Basil and SchrummSchrumm. By contrast, the third guest, a young man—he had the voice of a young man, anyway—joined in their conversation with vehemence, as if it were his designated role to defend Basil's presence at the meal.

"Mr. Basil is one of our leading industrialists. He does business with our Holy Director, who's ordered special steel for his factories. It's quite natural that he should be treated with favor."

SchrummSchrumm had no answer for this. He was flustered. It was the young man, once again, who broke the silence by suggesting that SchrummSchrumm take his meal in the pantry, where he might feel more at ease.

"I think that would be the most convenient thing," SchrummSchrumm agreed. And without quite knowing how, and still not fully awake, almost as if he were in a dream, he found himself seated at a different table, a pantry table. Victuals, salads, and fruits were piled around him. He ate voraciously, opening his eyes long enough to grab a piece of food and closing them again to chew; he was half asleep. The sound of a pot clanking made him start. A young girl was warming a sauce on the stove. She glanced over at him, and, seeing that he was looking her way, smiled. He smiled back. She had an ugly, swarthy little face and beads of sweat were running down her forehead. She mimed some gestures and made faces as if she wanted him to understand something, but what? Then she burst into a fit of giggles and scampered away, leaving the sauce unattended.

"Look here," said Madame Rose's voice, "it's time to take your leave of the doctor. Come now! Wake up!"

SchrummSchrumm made a supreme effort. The little woman was studying him with kindly curiosity. He followed her, saying: "I'll be fine. Thank you, madam." The guests had lit after-dinner cigars. They were engrossed in a lively discussion.

"My dear Constanzi," the doctor was saying in a professorial tone, "they're all sick. That's not the point. The point is that some of them know it and others don't; there's the crucial difference. Those who admit they're sick are already half cured. But those who refuse to accept their condition often turn dangerous. Therefore, we must take appropriate measures to render them harmless . . ."

He paused, made a friendly but lofty gesture to Schrumm-Schrumm, and continued:

"We treat one and only one malady at this hospital . . ."

The others hadn't taken their eyes off the doctor. "Let's go now! Come along!" said Madame Rose. "Only one malady, my dear Constanzi!" cried Dr. Hell. The next thing SchrummSchrumm knew, Madame Rose was pushing him outside. He watched her walk away; she was dragging her slippered feet like a wounded animal, leaning against the walls and clinging to the hangings so as not to topple over. He took a few steps and breathed a sigh of relief. Dusk was falling. Lights were burning in a few of the windows. A bell somewhere tolled seven. But perhaps he could still find his way back before he became completely lost.

XV

He walked for some time. He thought he was retracing his steps, recrossing the same endless succession of echoing courtyards toward the hotel. It was therefore not without a sharp pang of anxiety that he found himself facing the courtyard surrounded by porticos where he'd witnessed—how many days since?—the semi-wholesaler's execution. He looked at the rim of the well and the hole where they'd attached the pipe that supplied fresh blood to the little carousel of metal figurines. It was now fully night; the porticos were inky black. Two silhouettes were advancing on him. Had he been expecting them? In any case, he felt no surprise.

The first was the dapper young man, Dominic, who'd come to Franz Occursus's house with Dr. Hell. The second figure seemed even younger, though because he was hanging back a few paces SchrummSchrumm didn't have a clear view of his features.

"Good evening," said Dominic. "What a splendid night! Don't you find it so?"

At that same moment a floodlight came on above them and SchrummSchrumm saw Dominic's companion. He really was quite young, with a bit of downy fuzz on his upper lip; he'd filled in this proto-moustache but had done a bad job of it, and the pencil marks were clearly visible.

"Who are you?" asked SchrummSchrumm. He wanted to know who he was dealing with before he said anything. This attitude seemed to suit the two young men. Though Dominic didn't bother introducing himself—there was no need—the stranger stepped forward and bowed.

"I am he whom one encounters on the eve of the excursion," he said. His voice was extraordinarily beautiful, warm, rich, and persuasive, though somehow both lilting and monotone. This magnificent voice caught SchrummSchrumm so much off guard that he neither heard nor listened to the rest of the sentence. Where had he heard these familiar and awe-inspiring tones before? But of course! It was the voice that read passages from the Gospel of Misunderstanding over the bedroom loudspeakers and gave the responses to the ritual questions during ceremonies.

The young man had to repeat himself. He did so with a touch of self-satisfaction; he was obviously proud of his instrument, enjoyed exercising it, and relished speaking. As a result, SchrummSchrumm began looking at him with amusement rather than awe. The young man's lips quivered with rage and his blue eyes became almost transparent:

"I am he whom one encounters on the eve of the great journey," he said.

"You're pretty young for such a grown-up job." SchrummSchrumm couldn't bring himself to use anything but the informal *you* when addressing the young man, as if he were talking to a boy.

"I'm old enough," retorted the young employee, lifting his chin in an adorably childish way. "Moreover, I have a task to fulfill. Before I do, I must nevertheless inquire as to whether you have any particular wishes that might be satisfied prior to your departure."

"Are you here in an official capacity?" asked SchrummSchrumm. The term "official capacity" seemed to give the kid pause. Despite already knowing the answer, SchrummSchrumm teasingly repeated the question:

"Is your role here an official one? Is it your task to take down the excursionists' last wishes? I'm asking you because I'm surprised that you would be informed of my departure before I was. Are you sure I'm due to leave?"

The boy replied, now also addressing SchrummSchrumm with the informal *you*:

"Tomorrow is Sunday. I am certain you are leaving tomorrow and I can assure you that I am acting in an official capacity."

He stood at the ready, seemingly waiting for SchrummSchrumm to express his last wishes. But SchrummSchrumm had no desires left. He said as much to the young man, who, throwing open his arms in a fatalistic gesture, replied: "Very well! Very well! In that case . . ." He was about to continue when Dominic interrupted. Though until that moment he had shown himself elegant, aristocratic, and aloof, now he was looking alternately at his own feet and at SchrummSchrumm's, for all the world like someone who was terribly embarrassed. Tucked under his arm was a long black box tied with a blue ribbon.

"This is for you, Mr. SchrummSchrumm," he said, proffering the box.

"For me? What is it? Should I open it?"

Dominic nodded. SchrummSchrumm untied the ribbon, opened the box, and took out a magnificent rose.

"Good God! Who sent me this?"

"This flower is presented to you by the personnel of Misunderstanding. It was Sergeant Krikri's idea, actually. We took up a collection to get you this rose, which is the solitary rose from a rosebush planted and cut at midnight. We all join together as one, Mr. SchrummSchrumm, in hoping you'll attain the goal you've set yourself. In short," he concluded, stammering with emotion, "we all wish, from the bottom of our hearts, that you'll find peace and happiness."

"Thank you. It's … it's a very beautiful rose," spluttered SchrummSchrumm, who was just as moved as Dominic. But the younger man cut short their effusions:

"Well? May I begin? Have you finished your silly blubbering?"

"You may proceed," said Dominic.

"Proceed," said SchrummSchrumm, amused by the kid's serious expression.

What he saw next wiped the smile from his face.

A crowd of people emerged from beneath the porticos. They numbered about fifty, they were holding hands, and they came forward dancing a farandole. SchrummSchrumm knew them all. Everyone he'd spoken to or had personal contact with in Misunderstanding was there. Mr. Prestige, the President of the Inquisitorial Investigating Committee, Lieutenant Medullus, Mr. Burns and his wife were there. So were Lucette and Lulu, Leopold the spy, Coctus, the library warden, and Director Bushido. Even Red-Bartlett, the ticket-window official, Krikri, and the two executioners, Jules and Jim. There was the spokesman for the Cigarette Smoke-Ring Blowers, the two Occursus brothers, the handsome Colonel Negas—Adelaide's fiancé—Dr. Hell, and Abdullah. Everyone was there. Stranger still, the two little obese nudies (Joseph and Alfred), and the semi-wholesaler in small hardware supplies—in the flesh—were dancing along with the rest.

Standing off to one side was a group of spectral beings wreathed in a kind of mist. These were people SchrummSchrumm had known even longer ago: friends, relatives, former fiancées, teachers. He approached the group.

"Who are you? Are you living beings? Are you dead? Are you ghosts?"

"We are those you have loved, those you have known, those you have hated."

"That can't be. My father, my mother, and, generally speaking, my whole family are dead. I have no more friends, no more teachers. My former girlfriends have all forgotten me and married other men."

"It doesn't matter. We've come to wish you a happy excursion. Goodbye and good luck!"

They vanished. In the meantime, the others had formed a dancing ring around him. The kid had clearly been charged with overseeing the details of this farce and was keeping a watchful eye on the dance. He gave a brief order. The dancers stopped.

"You may continue," he said quietly. Then, in a much louder voice, he read from a paper he took from his pocket:

"Tests one, two, and three. The case of the library; the case of the Acoustic Room for the Production of Deceptive Sounds; the case of the three trunks from nowhere. Executors: the library warden; Coctus, Head of the Acoustic Room; Lieutenant Medullus, Head of the Reception Department, Doubtful Trunk Dispatcher. Step forward!"

The warden, Coctus, and Medullus each took one step forward. They made the following declaration, speaking in turns:

"Mr. SchrummSchrumm, you have successfully passed psychological aptitude tests one, two, and three. We thank you for your kindness, your initiative, and for the considerable aid you gave us in performing our difficult and delicate roles. Goodbye, Mr. SchrummSchrumm. We wish you the very best of luck and a happy excursion."

They stepped back. SchrummSchrumm had just opened his mouth to ask what all this meant, but the young man didn't give him the chance:

"Psychological aptitude tests four and five," he announced. "The case of the aberrant double photograph of our Holy Director, aka Allright, aka Nobody; the case of Nastarz's garden, which garden was a misleading fake. Executor: Bushido, hotel director, distinguished archaeologist, specialist in graffiti and old family photographs. Step forward!"

The little old man, his yellow beard neatly combed, stepped forward and thanked him in the same manner and the same terms as the first three. This procedure was repeated until the young man had called forward everyone present. SchrummSchrumm learned that he had successfully passed psychological aptitude tests six, seven, eight, nine, ten, eleven, twelve, thirteen, and fourteen. "The case of the Golden Apple of Good and Evil; executor: Prestige." "The case of the semi-wholesaler." "The case of the feast room" (executors: Jules and Jim, "our two respected executioners"). "The case of the hospital" (executors: Dr. Hell and Madame Rose). "The case of Occursus." "The case of the little obese nudie Joseph." And so on.

When they had all thanked him and recited their little speeches with conviction, SchrummSchrumm was left tongue-tied. Another order was given. The dancers joined hands once again and the farandole swept them away just as it had swept them in. The kid had taken up the dance along with them and was also gone.

"Wait! Come back!" cried SchrummSchrumm. But no one listened to him.

"The madness of it all!" he muttered, baffled and disconcerted. And, with his head in his hands, he repeated it so loudly it seemed to echo through the whole city of Misunderstanding:

"The madness of it all! The sheer madness!"

Dominic, who hadn't left, furtively brushed away his tears before saying gently:

"It'll all be over soon, Mr. SchrummSchrumm. One last formality, and it really will all be over."

Seated on a little stone bench in the corner of the courtyard, which is to say directly under the light, two elderly people were smiling at SchrummSchrumm. He walked over. The old man held a suitcase and the old woman a cradle. She had green hair under a black scarf; her eyes were red, her teeth black. She gripped the cradle tightly. Her hands were green, with red nails and black veins. How strange was this cradle! It was pink, decorated with stencils of black death's heads. How horrible the infant inside the cradle! It was dead. Its tiny skull oozed fluid onto the finely embroidered pillow. The smell was horrendous.

SchrummSchrumm shuddered.

"Good evening," said the old couple, rising from their seats.

"Gracious!" said SchrummSchrumm. "I'm delighted to find some people I know here. How have you been?"

"Ah, me!" said the old woman, stifling a sob. "Then you haven't heard the news? We've lost our eldest son, our little Fernand."

SchrummSchrumm stammered out his condolences.

"And how are things in Mahasky?" he asked.

"Good, good. The neighbors have missed you since you've been gone. They ask about you all the time. And we should tell you that the semi-wholesaler—you know, the one who commuted to Acupuncture every day—well, he disappeared. They've rented his apartment to a new tenant. Yours too, come to think of it . . . Apart from that, the Sunday Excursions bus stops regularly in front of the building now. Your initiative set a precedent, one might say. A lot of the younger people in the building have sent in applications; the Quicksands Excursion is a great success."

"I'm not so sure that's a good thing," muttered Schrumm-Schrumm. "By the way, what brings you two here?" he asked, realizing that he'd forgotten to ask this crucial question.

"Bah!" said the woman. "It's an old story. We get the call to come out here every so often. We both have a background in vaudeville. Maybe you didn't know that? So we get called out here. We go to this forbidden park. In the park is a path, also forbidden. The path leads nowhere. We go down this path anyway; first we pass some little cottages belonging to retirees with carefully tended gardens. We keep on going. The houses begin to thin out, then there are no more houses. A strong wind starts to blow; we hear the ticking of tremendous clocks. Black birds of an unknown species are screaming in the sky. There, in that deserted place, not far from a dismal pond, and not far from a barbed-wire entanglement, is a house whose doors and shutters bang open and closed with a clatter. In that house lives a sort of guy, our employer. We wait for him, and we have to go through the same routine every time. He calls to us; we come. Then I do a striptease version of the 'dance of Salome.' We finish with a magic trick that requires some particularly challenging sleight of hand: my hubby pretends to cut off my little Fernand's head and offer it to me on a silver platter while the man runs off screaming. And there you have it, that's it."

"Ah, me!" lamented the old man. "Now that our little Fernand is dead, we can't do the act anymore. We're out of a job."

As if to highlight her despair, the old woman began crooning a quaint old love song that SchrummSchrumm had heard often in his childhood. Its meaning, however, had been twisted around; the words were obscene and the crone emphasized the worst of them with repulsive leers. The old man elbowed her sharply in the ribs. She stammered: "Oh! I beg your pardon! I'm always forgetting that it's not the time for that." The old man added, speaking to SchrummSchrumm:

"She's still getting used to the idea that we're not doing our routine anymore. You can understand, can't you?"

"Yes, certainly," said SchrummSchrumm. "But tell me, is this dead baby another bit of vaudeville artifice?"

"Ah, yes! Of course!" said the old man. "What must you think of us? Show him!" he ordered his wife.

She hesitated for a moment, and then—after first taking one withered teat from her blouse, no doubt from force of habit—showed him the baby. It was a doll, but an ingeniously realistic one. You pressed a button and blackish pus seeped from its eyes, ears, and mouth. Press a different button and a horrendous odor was diffused. There were a number of other buttons, too. Everything worked to perfection.

"Would you also like me to do the dance of Salome for you?" asked the old woman. A lingering hope was still detectable in her voice.

"No! No!" SchrummSchrumm quickly interjected. "I don't have time. One last thing, if you don't mind: what happened to little Fernand? Was there an accident?"

"Precisely," said the old man. "A terrible accident. My ax slipped and 'chock!' the head of my poor little Fernand really did fall onto the silver platter."

"Hm!" said SchrummSchrumm. "Well, good night."

"Good night," said the old couple. They walked away, she pushing the sinister cradle in a handcart, he carrying the suitcase. The floodlight was switched off. Dominic had laid his hand on SchrummSchrumm's.

"There now," he said. "It's over."

"Dominic," said SchrummSchrumm, "do you by any chance belong to the reform movement?"

"Yes, it's true. I read the 'Apocrypha of the Semi-Wholesaler' assiduously. Never fear, it will all go well."

"What will go well?"

"Why, the excursion, Mr. SchrummSchrumm, the excursion! You'll succeed in crossing the Quicksands. I'm firmly convinced of it now."

"Do the Quicksands really exist?" replied SchrummSchrumm. "I've started to wonder. It's said, isn't it, that excursionists set out from home happy and confident. They think they'll be returning soon. But a whole slew of absurd, unforeseeable events intervenes. They wait for months, years. And at some point during all that time—all that *lost* time, you'll note, Dominic—they forget why they left home in the first place. Did they even have homes? Ah, they don't know anymore! So much so that when they're finally told: 'Excursion day is here. You're to depart today. Go now! Depart!' it's too late. Having forgotten their names, their professions, and their homes, prisoners of time and of overlong waiting, benumbed and miserable, they wander through a strange country, exhausting their energy on vain questions, until every last one of them is dead, good and dead."

"I'll walk back with you," said Dominic after a pause.

SchrummSchrumm accepted the offer. He would have been incapable of finding his way alone. They walked side by side, making no haste. Every now and then they came across guards bustling busily about. One let out a curse because visibility was poor and he'd missed a step. "You need to soak your wick better, brother," said a voice: some other guard must have been lighting a pipe; then silence redescended. SchrummSchrumm would have willingly strolled through Misunderstanding for hours in the company of this helpful young man, listening to the strange, faraway sounds. But presently they arrived at the hotel.

"How's this for stupidity, Dominic," said SchrummSchrumm morosely. "All I know of Misunderstanding is a series of paved courtyards and a string of awful underground passages called the Labyrinth!"

"You'll see Misunderstanding tomorrow," Dominic promised. "Farewell, my dear Mr. SchrummSchrumm. And know that I envy you."

"Farewell," said SchrummSchrumm. He waited until Dominic was out of sight before going in. He saw immediately that something important had happened, or was about to happen. The main lobby, which he hadn't set foot in since the day they'd walled off his floor—when he and his green companions had been separated from the others—was now packed with people, just like at the beginning of his stay in Misunderstanding. He didn't recognize any of the faces, but all the excursionists present were greens. Two or three minutes later, someone opened the door.

"Here's the list!" he shouted, waving a sheet of paper.

He read aloud the names of those who would be leaving for the Quicksands the next day. SchrummSchrumm listened with half an ear. As their names were called, the happy elect gave shouts of joy and grabbed each other by the arms. They danced or hopped in place. Finally, he heard his own name spoken. It was the last, and a deep hush fell over the crowd. The man who'd read the list took his leave, saying that if anyone had any questions they could see the official who had been placed at their disposal in the next room.

SchrummSchrumm stood at a window and let his eyes wander aimlessly. Krikri came over to slap him on the back and congratulate him, giving him a hug. The evening meal had long since been served. This meant SchrummSchrumm wouldn't be eating, so he joined the others who were going up to bed now because they wanted to be bright-eyed and bushy-tailed for the morning.

XVI

He was awakened by the crackling of the ceiling loudspeaker. "Rise and shine, rise and shine," intoned the voice. "Today is Sunday, and our thoughts are with those who are about to depart for the Quicksands. For them and with them, we shall first recite the Excursion-Morning Prayer:

"He spoke to friends of his beloved's face,
"of his beloved's smile,
"of his beloved's breasts;
"and in the depths of their cesspool, the friends dreamed of her.
"But when she came, plainly dressed,
"they cried out:
"Is this the Princess of whom we dreamed?
"And they were disappointed."

Somewhere in Misunderstanding, a bell tolled five. The loudspeaker crackled again. SchrummSchrumm pricked up his ears:

"We shall now hear a passage from the Holy Gospel of Misunderstanding.

"The Flood came, and most men perished. They alone survived who, being weighed down with neither desire nor regret, rose to the surface of the troubled waters. At last they took refuge on a high place, called from that day forth 'The Mountain of Forgetting.' And when the rains had ceased, they looked about them. The waters had abated from off the face of the ground. They saw that all the former buildings, all the writings, and even the very memory of man had been washed away. And so they set about making rude shelters for themselves and going in quest of food for their womenfolk and children. Among the survivors was a young man named Nastarz; his wife was with child. This man was he whom the prophets had foretold would accomplish the absurd and spectacular undertaking: he would build Misunderstanding. Nastarz lived, unrecognized by his people and ignorant of his destiny, until the day the magnitude and urgency of his task were revealed unto him. Thus, he abandoned his companions and proceeded on foot to the country of the Quicksands. And lo, he began to build Misunderstanding. He built rooms without windows, rooms of darkness in which to pen beasts and human-beasts. He dug passages beneath the earth in which the proud would lose themselves. He devised soundproof rooms in which the cries of the tortured would not be heard. He fashioned rooms for rape, rooms for lies. He erected concentric walls to remove from men's hearts all desire to take themselves for gods. He made golden cages in which to exhibit those who were lunatic, the most bastard of all bastards, the monsters. And he ordered Misunderstanding according to the principle of absurdity, that despair might flourish there and root out impudence. Lest there come another flood. And for the pure of heart, he invented the excursion . . .

"Many years passed. Nastarz was old and his children's children grown. Misunderstanding was finished at last. And so he sent his people far and wide over the earth to spread the good tidings. Men had once again been fruitful and multiplied, yet had become like errant wayfarers wandering in a dark wood where but few lights shone out here and there. The children of Nastarz conducted them all to Misunderstanding. And when the men arrived at the Great Iron Gate, they shielded their eyes, for lo, they were dazzled. They looked with much amazement, one man to another, and lifted up their voices in a hymn of praise. For Misunderstanding was like unto a great sun which warmed their bruised and battered hearts. And they were content to be forever penned like beasts, to be monitored and despised . . ."

There was a moment's silence; the voice announced:

"You have just heard verse three, chapter seven of the Holy Gospel of Misunderstanding. Meditate on these words, little children, beloved brethren! Because on this beautiful June day, many among you will be attempting the Ultimate Excursion. May our prayers be with them during their labors in the Quicksands."

Another silence: the static stopped crackling and the loudspeaker died. The prayers and Sunday Meditations were over. Shortly afterward, Krikri made his appearance. He was full of emotion. He rubbed SchrummSchrumm's body with the precious and immaculate balm of the martyrs, helped him into his excursioning outfit, and began gathering up all the personal effects scattered throughout the room, drawing up an inventory of them as he did so. When he came to the precious photograph of Allright, SchrummSchrumm asked if he might be allowed to keep it. Krikri apologized: no, it wouldn't be possible. He chewed his pencil, a sign of deep reflection:

"How should I describe this photo in my inventory?"

"Easy. Write: 'Old photograph of Allright flanked by two companions, taken on a rise overlooking the Mahasky city walls.'"

"Out of the question," said Krikri. "This photo isn't of Allright flanked by two companions on a rise overlooking the Mahasky city walls, it's of our Most Holy Director flanked by our two executioners, Jules and Jim, on the knoll in the middle of the Nastarz swamp, in the center of Eden."

"Krikri," said SchrummSchrumm quietly, "don't tell me you've been given official instructions regarding this photograph."

"But I have. Very precise instructions, as a matter of fact. Listen, Mr. SchrummSchrumm," he said tenderly, "there's no point in lying anymore, now that you're leaving for the Quicksands. We both know the truth."

"Explain yourself, please."

"It's quite simple. Your theory was run through the lie-detector machine—which is absolutely infallible, as you may already know—and its answer was unequivocal: Mahasky doesn't exist. It is in fact a mythical city, one that very often functions as a projection of excursionists' desires."

SchrummSchrumm dropped heavily onto the bed and sat there. Krikri said nothing for a moment, then seemed to reach a decision. He took out his wallet.

"Here," he said, holding out another photograph.

SchrummSchrumm stared at it, comparing it with his own.

"Am I dreaming? These photos are the same!"

"Precisely!"

"But that's impossible!"

"Listen," said Krikri, putting his arm around SchrummSchrumm's waist. "I did some thinking about this problem when I was given this photo and told what it was. Here's the conclusion I came to. Suppose—for the same reasons you gave old Bushido—that you're correct, and your photo is of Allright, while mine, in this case, is of the Holy Director. I've discovered something that disproves this idea. Look at the clouds above the wall in the left-hand corner of both snapshots. They're exactly the same shape, wouldn't you agree? That means the two photos must be of the same three men, taken in the same location. Though it's possible—just barely—that with the right clothes and makeup the main subjects of these photographs could have been made to look like a person you would interpret as Allright and I as the Holy Director, the fact that the clouds are identical destroys that possibility. Never have clouds in two different locations at two different times been identical. So I'm going to put it down as: 'Photo of the Holy Director, flanked by Jules and Jim, on the knoll in the center of Eden.' Please sign the inventory, if you would."

"My God!" cried SchrummSchrumm. "It never ends!" He signed the inventory and Krikri bade him farewell.

A few minutes later, he and some others were conducted to the covered inner courtyard near the place where those huge, cruel portrayals were pasted on the walls. How large this inner courtyard was! Many excursionists were already waiting here. In an adjoining courtyard, sixty-seven Company buses were parked in impeccable alignment. SchrummSchrumm counted them with a shudder. He also tried counting his excursionist companions, all decked out in their best attire. It made him dizzy. Some were standing in pairs, stamping their feet in an attempt to warm themselves. Two or three were coughing and hacking terribly. But many, seated face-to-face, in groups extending as far as the walls covered with those hideous snapshots, were—surprisingly, astoundingly—asleep, despite the amazing adventure on which they were about to embark. Others, still more numerous, were chattering gaily, brought together in various groups according to their respective sympathies. In their lighthearted, jolly mood they were waving him over, motioning for him to sit down beside them so they could exchange ideas and talk about the families they would soon be seeing again, the inevitable little everyday problems they'd be returning to when they got home. SchrummSchrumm remembered how high his confidence had been the day he arrived in Misunderstanding. Alas, so many days had passed since that afternoon when, still full of illusions, he'd hoped and trusted that he would speedily decipher all the difficult symbols of the Ultimate Excursion. Now, on the dawn of this long-awaited day, he felt no joy. He was indifferent, like the excursionists of legend who died because their hearts had hardened and they'd watched their hope run dry . . .

A commotion pulled him out of these reflections. Those who'd been sleeping now awoke, those who'd been talking fell silent, and those who'd been sitting rose to their feet. A troop of Accredited Drowners had just arrived. They wore black leather trench coats and had on gloves that were also of leather but red. These were apparently the Accredited Drowners who'd be accompanying them to the Quicksands. They were surrounded by an entourage of women in garish makeup, dressed like whores, who were peeling off what skimpy clothing they still had on while clinging to the men and feeling their muscles. "Ooh, those handsome Accredited Drowners!" they cooed, parting their thighs and grinding their bellies against the men's. But the Drowners, indifferent to their advances and seemingly absorbed in their own thoughts, pushed them away. They had to inflict a number of indignities on these ladies, including kicking them and dousing them with buckets of cold water (which seemed to have been prepared in advance for just this purpose) in order to run them off. Once rid of them, the Drowners broke into squads—seven squads of seven men each—and got down to work doing training exercises in a corner of the courtyard. They showed great zeal for the task. Against one wall they'd lined up about a dozen wooden mannequins, whose clothing—picked out in oil paints—was a close match for that of the real excursionists standing nearby. They started with some stretches and warm-ups, taking deep, powerful breaths. Then each squad in turn took up a position some twenty paces from the mannequins. One of their number was posted near the targets, his eyes glued to a stopwatch. "Are you ready, absolutely and entirely ready?" he asked, in the inevitable Misunderstanding phraseology. On getting an affirmative response, he gave the signal by lowering his upraised arm. In a flash, the seven Accredited Drowners' lassos were twirling over their heads faster and faster, in ever-expanding circles. Another signal. They sent their long ropes flying through the air and around the necks of the painted dummies, which, thanks to their ingenious construction, stuck out their tongues to indicate success. When this first stage of the exercise was complete, they snatched up the flexible gaffs lying at their feet and went through the motions of an imaginary Quicksands rescue. They were incredibly dexterous and rarely missed their mark. SchrummSchrumm felt he should have been reassured by what he saw, knowing that these men had been well chosen. They were inarguably solid, strapping lads, and anyone watching them now could put his mind at ease on one point, at least: they'd be capable of pulling even the most corpulent excursionist out of the hazardous Quicksands, should he be careless or clumsy enough to fall in. Nevertheless, SchrummSchrumm couldn't rid himself of the nagging feeling that there was something morbid and unwholesome in the way they were carrying out these exercises. And there were so very many of them! Not just the Accredited Drowners themselves, but others—training instructors, primarily—who continued to swell the already sizable ranks. The training instructors, like the Drowners, busied themselves with their final preparations; some were sharpening their daggers to a razor-fine edge, others were disassembling and cleaning their carbines, making sure all the components were in good working order. It was evident that the officers still weren't here, however: there were no white cords with gold threads to be seen—none among the Accredited Drowners, the training instructors, or the guards—and everyone looked up impatiently each time the little door reserved for personnel opened to admit new arrivals.

That was how things stood, with SchrummSchrumm just beginning to get antsy, when the man beside him nudged him in the ribs. As he did so, he muttered almost inaudibly: "Check out the window on the second floor, but be discreet. Don't let them see you looking." SchrummSchrumm raised his head very slowly. Behind a closed window he spied two small, dark, rather frightening figures. Their faces were incredibly thin, and this thinness was further emphasized by false noses shaped like birds' beaks—specifically, the hooked kind seen on birds of prey. From deep within cavernous orbits, their beady eyes darted back and forth with unnatural rapidity. They were examining the crowd with keen attention. It occurred to SchrummSchrumm that he'd seen these faces somewhere before, but he couldn't recall where or when. For that matter, there was nothing all that extraordinary about their presence. He was just about to shrug off the incident when the two men opened the window. Now he could see them clearly. They were as alike as it was possible for two men to be. One of them grabbed a pair of binoculars and aimed them in a direction roughly corresponding to the far end of the group in which SchrummSchrumm stood. The man's mouth curled into a disturbing smile. He said something to his companion and pointed to the place where he'd been looking. At once, the second man committed one of the most senseless acts SchrummSchrumm had yet witnessed in Misunderstanding. He brought a tube to his lips, slipped something into the end, took a deep breath, puffed his cheeks, and blew out a tiny, dart-like projectile. From the opposite end of the group came a cry, a man fell backward, and people called for help, saying someone had fainted.

"Heart attack. Pulmonary embolism," diagnosed a guard who'd gone over to investigate.

"He's dead?" cried several stunned excursionists.

"As a doornail! The excitement of the upcoming departure must've been too much for him," chimed in another guard, and that was all. They signaled to two stretcher-bearers—no one seemed surprised that they were on the scene as if they'd been told to stand by in case of this very event—and the cadaver was borne away. "What's the meaning of this?" asked SchrummSchrumm under his breath. "Shh," said the man next to him, a finger to his lips. "Now look here!" said SchrummSchrumm. "You saw what just happened as well as I did. Those men might do it again and pick you as their next target!" The other excursionist gave him a wry look. "They won't do it again," he said calmly, and jerked his chin toward the window. It was true. The first thin-faced man had put away his blowgun, the other was taking one last look at the crowd through his binoculars. Then they threw their arms around each other and danced with joy. They were exultant, whooping in triumph and laughing with pleasure as if they had pulled off not only a hilarious practical joke but a difficult feat and a most interesting bit of handiwork. Then they closed the window again and disappeared.

"Those faces … I know I've seen them before!" said SchrummSchrumm.

His neighbor answered right away. Now that the two men were gone, he seemed more at ease.

"No surprise there! That was the Director and the Deputy Director."

"The new Director?" said SchrummSchrumm. "He's off to a fine start."

"No, no," said the man. "The old Director."

"The old Director's dead, I can assure you you're mistaken."

"I know what I'm talking about: the Director's been here for twenty years. I know it for a fact!"

"The old Director died three weeks ago. I saw him die," repeated SchrummSchrumm, becoming irritated.

But another brouhaha interrupted them. The officers had arrived. There were twenty-five of them, all in dress uniform, surrounding a twenty-sixth man whose appearance left SchrummSchrumm agog. The leader of the Ultimate Excursion was young Colonel Negas himself, Adelaide's dashing fiancé. As soon as they saw the officers and the colonel, the training instructors and Accredited Drowners stood at attention and saluted. The officers responded distractedly; they were in the middle of debating something among themselves, and the discussion apparently concerned some weighty matter on which Negas and his general staff were at loggerheads. At last it seemed the former had carried his point, because the rest nodded. An order was issued and the excursionists were asked to board the buses while the guards took roll. The bus doors were then closed and sealed from the outside, as if by judicial order. A private car with Negas and three other officers inside led the way, chauffeured by a black man with huge gold rings in his ears. The twin leaves of the Iron Gate of Misunderstanding opened with a terrible groan; one by one, the Sunday Quicksands Excursion Company buses passed through the monumental city entrance. There was no ceremony of any kind, but all the bus drivers leaned on their horns as they drove through, unleashing a cacophony that should have been enough to make any excursionist not among the fortunate elect tremble. They were hardly out of the gates when the passengers were blindfolded and the heavy metal shutters pulled down over the windows. “Needless precautions! Needless precautions!” thought SchrummSchrumm. Nevertheless, guided by his experience of the first bus trip, he did his best to clear his mind and made an effort to get some sleep. Truth be told, though, the journey wasn’t long. Two hours later their blindfolds were removed, the shutters raised, and they descended from the vehicles.

Before them lay the Quicksands, stretching as far as the eye could see. The landscape surpassed all expectations. The sun was rising: a delicate halo of pink mist like a corona crowned the terrible bogs. These boggy areas formed irregular grids, with the lines between them likely indicating strips of solid ground one might use to cross the mire. But there was no sign of life, no fantastic creatures like those depicted in the courtyard photographs. A complete and absolute silence reigned here. To their right were tall dunes. On the far side of the dunes, the tops of the giant poplars in the Enchanted Forest swayed lazily to and fro in the breeze. SchrummSchrumm, who’d been taking in the view, was snapped out of his contemplation by the officers ordering everyone to line up in front of a folding table, where a man from the Ministry of Statistics checked off names in a big notebook as they filed past. This done, SchrummSchrumm went to sit in the sand with some other excursionists. At regular intervals, a dozen or so names would be called and the group, led by a training instructor, would ascend the dunes and disappear down the opposite side. The atmosphere was fairly relaxed. People were relating anecdotes to while away the time. Colonel Negas wandered over only to play a cruel joke on them. An accident had occurred during one excursion, he said, and everyone had tumbled into the Quicksands. The sole survivor, according to the colonel, had managed to escape what would otherwise have been certain death by using his companions' heads as stepping stones. Terrible numbers were cited, too, either in centimeters sunk according to the victim's height or in seconds sunk according to the victim's weight. For example, an excursionist who stood one meter seventy-five and weighed seventy kilos would sink into the Quicksands at the rate of one kilo per second, which meant he'd need to be rescued within the span of a minute, because in seventy seconds he would have completely vanished. Looked at another way, this same excursionist would sink into the sands at the extremely rapid rate of two and a half centimeters per second.

Finally, a training instructor came to collect SchrummSchrumm and ten of his fellows. The man's name was Leo. He said he'd heard about SchrummSchrumm's exploits and was honored to make his acquaintance. "So how does this Excursion work?" asked SchrummSchrumm. According to Leo, all one had to do was climb the dune and everything would become clear. This they did. The two of them went ahead of the others, who watched them climb with inexplicable energy and zeal. As SchrummSchrumm ascended, his conviction grew that he was doing exactly the wrong thing, the very thing he *shouldn't* be doing. But he was carried away by a sort of passionate fervor. He was the first to reach the crest of the dune.

Thirty meters below him was a stagnant swamp so vast that its opposite shore was lost to view. On the bank at the foot of the dune was a pier—built on pilings—extending into the mire. SchrummSchrumm took in the whole scene at a glance and felt an extreme and immediate repugnance for this construction. There was something grotesquely cartoonish about it. It was a pier, but at the same time it didn't seem like a real pier. A thousand tiny details gave it away. For a start, it was in an undeniably advanced state of dilapidation, despite the great pains that had been taken to conceal the fact—such as securing loose boards with gold thread and repainting the whole thing pink and white. Seen in a certain way, and under different circumstances, this might have lent it a quaint, old-fashioned charm. Instead, its disrepair, the gold threads, and the pink-and-white paint job all seemed highly suspect to SchrummSchrumm, as if the dilapidation had been fabricated at someone's behest, as if the mere fact of having built this pier in this unlikely spot implied some kind of dark, malevolent design on the part of its builders. In short, it was a truly curious pier, and even more frightening than it was curious, because its resemblance to both the pink bridge in Nastarz City and the training pier was a little too close for comfort.

Leo and the others were catching up to him. SchrummSchrumm didn't want to be seen giving weight to such silly considerations, and yet he couldn't help looking the training instructor straight in the eye and grumbling:

"What is that horrible contraption?"

"That's the Bridge of Ultimate Wisdom."

"It's bizarre, don't you think?"

"There's nothing bizarre about it," said Leo in a tone SchrummSchrumm thought held very little conviction.

"Yes, there is," he insisted. Because he sensed that Leo was taking careful note of his reactions, he added: "I don't like the thing at all!"

"Are you feeling unwell, Mr. SchrummSchrumm? Come now, don't tell me you're scared!" said the training instructor, a hideous note of concern and solicitude creeping into his voice.

SchrummSchrumm made no answer. He'd just realized why he felt such repulsion toward the structure. Though it bore an obvious resemblance to the Nastarz City bridge and the training pier, there was also a glaring difference. The Nastarz City bridge had a purpose: it spanned the miniature swamp. The training pier also had a purpose. But this construction seemed to have none: it led nowhere. It ended in the middle of the bog.

XVII

A distant rumor of voices broke the spell of morbid fascination the pier had cast over him. He saw that, absorbed as he'd been in examining that pointless structure, he'd paid no attention to the unrest below. Groups of training instructors and Accredited Drowners were scrambling in all directions. Negas, standing on a shield held aloft by four bare-chested guards in gladiator costume, was barking out orders. The excursionists who'd been with SchrummSchrumm had descended the dune and were now standing or sitting in the sand, waiting for someone to attend to them; a few were already asleep. There was no sign of the previous groups of excursionists. *They've left for the Quicksands already*, thought SchrummSchrumm.

"Your Excellency! Colonel!" Leo called out.

But no one heard him amid the hubbub. He turned to look at SchrummSchrumm and the two of them, cupping their hands around their mouths, tried again to attract the colonel's attention. Again, it was of no use.

"We'll have to go down there," concluded Leo. They ran down the slope. At the foot of the dune, SchrummSchrumm nearly crashed into a tall man staring straight ahead, his hands in his pockets. The man cut an impressive figure; a cord was cinched around his waist—white interwoven with gold threads—and he stood on a broad tree stump, sawn off low to the ground, that formed a kind of dais for him. Beside him was a pretentious little popinjay of a man. He was of the bohemian gypsy type and carried an artist's portfolio, some big sheets of blank paper, colored pencils, and an eraser.

"Who might you be?" said SchrummSchrumm, respectfully addressing the tall man on the stump.

"I," said the man disdainfully, "am the bailiff."

"And who're you?" SchrummSchrumm asked the gypsy type, less respectfully.

"I am the sketch artist," replied the little man in an equally self-important tone. Saying this, he beckoned over a guard and whispered something in his ear, rubbing his hands together in anticipation. The guard shrugged and replied at a normal volume:

"Come now! Have a little patience!"

SchrummSchrumm gathered that in some vague way he was being included in this exchange, when a far more captivating scene grabbed his attention. A group of Accredited Drowners was jogging toward the pier. They were carrying complicated instruments—very small in size, though, as most had just been taken from the men's pockets. Naturally, they were also equipped with their long gaffs and the obligatory lassos on their belts. They lined up single file and paused. The man in front gingerly mounted the steps, signaled to his colleagues that all was well, and then proceeded, with infinite precaution, along the length of the structure. He was surely the most agile and nimble among them; he might even have been a former dancer, because he was not so much walking over the boards as performing a complex ballet. He seemed to be scouting a path. First, he'd stand with both feet together on a board whose soundness he'd tested by experiment. Next, he'd execute a sort of *chassé-croisé* that served no discernible purpose, yet at the end of which, after having placed his right toe on a new board and gradually shifted his entire weight onto it, he'd be balancing on one leg some fifty centimeters further along the pier, in perfect equilibrium and admirably steady. Another *chassé-croisé* and his left foot would be brought forward, planted flat beside his right, and the whole process begun again. Once he had progressed a few meters in this manner, the others followed his example. They performed exactly the same movements, though with none of the same grace, more like giant marionettes. All the while, with the aid of those curious instruments SchrummSchrumm had seen them take from their pockets, they were measuring every hole, noting the degree of rot in each piece of wood, checking the misalignment of the planks, and contorting themselves into strange shapes to avoid falling over, using their long gaffs to brace themselves. They were sweating from the heat and seemed to take pleasure in their work, keeping up a nonstop patter of bantering jokes and laughter.

When they reached the end of the pier, they paused again and bent down to study the perilous morass glistening below them. They must have been satisfied with the results of their examination, because they nodded meaningfully to one another. SchrummSchrumm assumed that they'd now turn around and retrace their steps. But no! They flung a rope ladder off either side of the pier and climbed down. They took up their places as best they could on ten cement cubes almost entirely submerged in the muck, whose upper extremities, rising about fifty centimeters above the surface, provided just enough space to sit down. This was the posture they all adopted. One of them jabbed his gaff into the mire and it disappeared entirely. They laughed. They were in high good humor. A few took out cigarettes and had a smoke. There could be no doubt that they were waiting for something to happen and wouldn't be leaving their posts until it did. What could it be? SchrummSchrumm watched them open-mouthed and had the distinct impression that not only they but the bailiff, the sketch artist, Negas, the training instructors, and the guards were all awaiting the same impending event. Not that there was anything particularly significant or meaningful in what they were doing, except maybe for a mysterious smile or two that flitted across a few faces, and yet SchrummSchrumm remained convinced that something was imminent.

It was no real surprise, therefore, when the man on the stump—the bailiff—began to speak in a loud, clear voice, carefully enunciating each word. His hands were still in his pockets and he was still staring straight ahead, so that his sentence—though apparently addressed to Colonel Negas and the guards standing just behind SchrummSchrumm—seemed to be directed at SchrummSchrumm himself.

"Well?" he said. "Who's going to tell him?"

It was neither the guards nor Negas who answered, but the Accredited Drowners seated on their blocks of cement by the pier.

"He'll come!" they assured him, smiling sadly.

SchrummSchrumm didn't understand the meaning of these sad smiles. Was it because they were afraid "he" might not come after all? Or because whatever was going to happen—provided "he" turned up—had filled them in advance with sincere compassion? He took two steps forward and planted himself squarely in front of the bailiff. He was sure the man wouldn't have the effrontery, now, to continue addressing SchrummSchrumm while giving the appearance of talking to someone else. The man must have seen through his stratagem, however. Swiftly averting his gaze—so swiftly that SchrummSchrumm didn't have time to meet his eye—he addressed, quite unambiguously this time, the training instructor Leo, who'd remained behind in the place SchrummSchrumm had just vacated.

"You there!" he said. "Who're you?"

"Leo," was the quaking answer.

"Approach!" ordered the bailiff.

Leo made an apologetic little motion to SchrummSchrumm and did as he was bid.

"Closer!" the bailiff shouted roughly. The training instructor wavered, then finally worked up the nerve to step onto the stump alongside the towering giant, who resumed the same game he'd been playing before, namely pretending to address Leo while really speaking for SchrummSchrumm's ears alone. He drew a whistle from his pocket and said he was going to explain "the business," speaking loud enough for SchrummSchrumm to catch every word.

He blew a short blast on the whistle and then, counting "one, two, three," said that "he" was to have mounted the steps to the raised deck of the pier. A longer whistle. The bailiff counted "four, five, six, seven, eight, nine, ten, eleven, twelve, thirteen." He explained that at thirteen, "he" was to be at the end of the pier, having crossed the intervening twenty meters "neither running nor dawdling, with no hint of hesitation, but instead proceeding at a resolute, steady pace. Otherwise the whole thing's ruined. Have you got all that?"

Leo nodded. SchrummSchrumm wondered, with a certain degree of amusement, what would come next. After giving one last emphatic nod to indicate he'd understood, Leo turned away, but did an about-face when the bailiff called him back. He must have omitted something from his demonstration; he murmured a phrase in the training instructor's ear. SchrummSchrumm couldn't hear it, but he watched Leo's face. Whatever it was, Leo hadn't liked it, because after a second or two he said "No" quite firmly and shook his head in denial. "No?" repeated the bailiff, incredulous. In effect, things had gone so smoothly thus far that he must have been ill-prepared for this refusal. The bailiff's face darkened. He began cursing Leo under his breath. Then he seized him by the lapels and asked him a rapid-fire series of questions, to which Leo responded only by shaking his head more and more desperately. Finally, the poor training instructor turned white as a sheet, wiped his forehead with the back of his hand, and unbuttoned his collar as if he needed air. The bailiff let him go: he slumped backward with a sigh.

"What's wrong with him?" asked SchrummSchrumm, rushing forward to stop Leo from falling. He had clearly fainted.

"Force of emotion," replied the giant.

This was the first time he'd addressed SchrummSchrumm directly. He instantly realized what he'd done, and with a faint smile said quietly:

"What a slip! I forgot I'm not supposed to speak to you directly under any circumstances."

"Why not?"

"That's just the way it is," he said. "Regulations."

And, perhaps to recover his former composure, he set about giving Leo revivifying slaps on the face. SchrummSchrumm, increasingly amused by the turn events had taken, decided to help him, but was shouldered aside by the sketch artist, who had bustled over with a fresh sheet of paper on his drawing board. SchrummSchrumm asked him what he was doing, and he replied that he didn't want to miss such an opportunity for an interesting sketch.

"No," said a voice. "I don't want to be drawn."

This was Leo, eyes wide open and fully recovered from his swoon, which perhaps had only been feigned.

". . . I'll carry out my task," he continued, speaking to the bailiff.

"Good. Stand up and explain matters to the excursionist."

Once again, the bailiff was staring straight ahead of him. He'd resumed his role. Leo turned to face SchrummSchrumm, trembling and sniffling in an extremely irritating manner. Worse, he covered his eyes with his hands as if he couldn't bear to look at him (though he parted his fingers a fraction and peeped through nonetheless).

"Ah, Mr. SchrummSchrumm, how deeply ashamed I am!" he began.

"Get to the point," said SchrummSchrumm. All this sniveling was starting to grate on his nerves.

"I've been entrusted with a difficult task," continued Leo. "Alas! The goodwill I bear you makes it all the more difficult."

SchrummSchrumm cut short this sickening dialogue. "That'll do! You can go," he said in a voice dripping with contempt, and Leo, without another word, scurried off and disappeared into the crowd of guards.

Then SchrummSchrumm completely lost his head for a time. He began by hopping about on one foot. He soon discovered this wasn't enough. He pulled his mouth wide with his index fingers and squashed his nose with his thumb, making the most dreadful face he could imagine, accompanied by wild howls and sheeplike bleating. He shouted "Hee haw!" and loped around in imitation of a donkey. After each of these ridiculous antics—yes, he knew they were ridiculous!—he stopped for a moment to gauge the reactions of the bailiff, the Accredited Drowners, and the rest. What was he hoping for? The men, perhaps out of pity, had turned away, and the bailiff was examining his feet with uncustomary interest. When he saw that no one was watching, SchrummSchrumm finally realized the inanity of his behavior. He fell to his knees and furtively brushed away a tear of impotent rage. "Just look at him!" said one of the guards with scorn. The affront stung SchrummSchrumm like a lash and he sprang to his feet at once, planted his fists on his hips, and—for the particular benefit of Colonel Negas—opened his mouth to let fly an ordinary human expletive. Imagine his shock, therefore, when at the very moment of doing so he heard a voice much like his own launch into an insane speech. And yet he hadn't said a word; he looked around in desperation to see who was speaking in his place and imitating him so perfectly. Of course it had to be something they'd rigged up together, some ghastly conspiracy along the lines of what he'd witnessed in the "Acoustic Room for the Production of Deceptive Sounds," but no one around him—not the Accredited Drowners, the guards, or the excursionists—seemed to have caught on to the trick; they were all listening to the babble quite attentively, believing it was SchrummSchrumm they were hearing. The voice, with a kind of impassioned eloquence, said:

"Beloved brother excursionists, I have been chosen by the hand of fate: I must show you how to go about crossing this pier, which is, to be precise, the Pier of Ultimate Wisdom you've heard so much about. Once on the other side, we'll be free. We'll be able to return to our homes; every week, we'll have those nice little weekends in the country like we used to, those quiet, easy little excursions ... Therefore pay close attention to my demonstration, follow my example, and show your mettle ... *Viva l'excursion!*"

The voice stopped. SchrummSchrumm observed the men who thought they'd been listening to him. The bailiff had long since forgotten his official instructions: he was gazing at SchrummSchrumm in wonder and admiration. Nearer to him, the long-haired sketch artist had let fall his board in a surge of emotion and was now chewing absently on the end of his pencil. And not just these two, but all the Accredited Drowners on either side of the pier had lost their sarcastic smiles: they seemed simultaneously impressed and deeply moved. The excursionists themselves—though one or two were only half-awake and still groggily rubbing their eyes—were applauding wildly and proclaiming their eagerness to follow his example . . . SchrummSchrumm understood that it would be useless to try and protest. Especially since Colonel Negas, as if sensing SchrummSchrumm's fatigue, was smacking his riding whip smartly against his boots, making the excursionists form a line, hurrying along the final preparations, and issuing curt orders while his alert, resolute gaze darted tirelessly left and right.

"Let nothing more interfere with the Ceremony!" he declared for all to hear.

The guards had lined up on the bank to watch. The excursionists were right behind them. Negas, aloft on his shield, had the best view of all. SchrummSchrumm advanced slowly toward the pier. What he wanted now was for everything to be over with as quickly as possible. But this was not the general view. The bailiff told him to wait a moment: the final formality was about to take place.

"What formality? Is this going to go on much longer?" asked SchrummSchrumm. The bailiff glanced nervously around him, then muttered: "You know very well I can't talk to you! I'm sorry!" and turned away. SchrummSchrumm shrugged and entertained himself by looking at the little artist's sketches. He'd drawn SchrummSchrumm while he was supposedly in mid-speech, and had embellished the scene by depicting him with one hand outstretched and the other laid over his heart.

"Mediocre talent, mediocre artist, don't you agree?" said a voice behind him. SchrummSchrumm turned. It was a little fellow wearing the death's-head singlet so popular among the guards. Yet something in his attitude seemed to say he was no guard. He took SchrummSchrumm's arm and smiled warmly.

"Who're you?" said SchrummSchrumm.

"I'm here to give you your final instructions."

SchrummSchrumm interrupted him:

"I know what to do!"

"I'll give you a good word of advice anyway, dear Mr. SchrummSchrumm," said the man, unperturbed. "As soon as the leader blows his whistle, take those stairs nice and slow, you've got plenty of time. At the last whistle, do just as they recommended: don't rush, and keep count in your head. When you get to nine, pick up the pace, because the course becomes difficult. That way, you'll reach the end just as Negas is saying 'thirteen' . . . It's the only way to avoid displeasing him!"

"Very well. But why the devil shouldn't I displease him?" asked SchrummSchrumm, half-amused by this remark.

"Hold on and let me explain," said the man, moving closer. But at that very instant the fateful preamble rang out:

"Are you ready? Absolutely and entirely ready?" demanded Colonel Negas.

"I am ready," said SchrummSchrumm in a loud, clear voice. And to the little guard beside him he whispered: "Farewell!"

"Farewell!" said the little guard, staring at SchrummSchrumm with a kind of awed tenderness. SchrummSchrumm proceeded to the base of the steps: the look of compassion from this insignificant man flooded his heart like an ocean . . . The first whistle sounded. Like an automaton, SchrummSchrumm began mounting the steps. When he reached the top, the colonel had just counted three.

"Very good!" cried the colonel to SchrummSchrumm. Nevertheless, he kept watching him like a hawk. In order to seem composed, SchrummSchrumm took a hard candy from his pocket, popped it in his mouth, balled up the wrapper, and tossed it at the feet of the Accredited Drowners.

"Bravo! A superb gesture!" said Negas the Magnificent, applauding. Some others also applauded—most likely guards and excursionists—in imitation of the colonel. SchrummSchrumm turned and thanked them for their tribute by inclining his head like an actor. Instantly Negas, no doubt thinking to catch him off guard, whipped out his whistle and, with unexpected celerity, put it to his lips for one final, shrill blast. But SchrummSchrumm hadn't taken his eyes off him. He wasn't the least bit startled by the sound: without running—yet still at a good brisk pace—he began to traverse the fifteen meters of the pier's length. At the count of nine he quickened his step, exactly as recommended by the little man whose parting look had been so kind. Twice he nearly lost his balance. As soon as he faltered, something very strange happened. Hardly had he begun to stumble than two or three Accredited Drowners stood up and shouted "Hup-la!" in resounding but half-hearted voices, and their gaffs grazed his clothing as if they were trying to snag him; he noticed a few of these gaffs were even tipped with very effective-looking barbed hooks . . .

In any case, he succeeded in keeping his feet and reached the end of the pier at the precise moment the colonel counted thirteen.

"Bravo! A thousand bravos, sir!" howled Negas in a frenzy, truly beside himself.

But SchrummSchrumm was no longer listening. The Accredited Drowners, as it happened, had been trying to attract his attention for the past few seconds now with discreet little musical calls; one of them was playing a haunting, sentimental tune on a bamboo flute.

"What do you want?" asked SchrummSchrumm disingenuously.

"Jump!" came the answer. "C'mon, jump! Attaboy!" several of them coaxed.

"From this height?" SchrummSchrumm complained. "I'd hurt myself! For that matter, why would I jump? I can easily go back the way I came."

"No, that's impossible!" they insisted. "You're the leader. You need to set a good example. Besides, you're jumping one way or another!" They had suddenly switched to the informal *you*.

"So I'm to drown?" asked SchrummSchrumm. He was quickly losing heart.

"Don't be silly!" they replied in the tone used to reassure small children. "You know we have our gaffs and lassos. We're here to help you. Our experience is vast. As is our dedication, kind-heartedness, and skill. So stop worrying. We'll get you out of there!"

SchrummSchrumm peered over the edge and looked at his executioners. He felt his courage draining away like sand slipping through his fingers.

"Listen, isn't there some other way we could do this?" he pleaded. "If you like, I could splash a little mud on my face and clothes. Everyone will think I really did fall into the Quicksands . . ."

"No," said the others. "That won't do. You have to jump!"

The flute was softer, sweeter, more persuasive, and more haunting than ever. All the Accredited Drowners made their discreet little musical calls.

"Go on, jump!" came the voice of the sketch artist from the other side of the pier. SchrummSchrumm was startled by the man's proximity. All the more so because he was almost on a level with him, perched on stilts that must have been incredibly long, given that the Quicksands appeared to be quite deep at this point. Horns had sprouted from his temples; his feet were cloven and smoke was curling from his mouth and ears. He was drawing furiously. *Is he going to sketch my miserable writhings?* thought SchrummSchrumm sadly, and he leaned over to see how he had been represented on the sheet of drawing paper. It wasn't what he'd feared. The little man had in fact depicted him as an angel, with magnificent wings and a long white tunic. Graceful, athletic birds swooped around him; the clouds formed a crown of glory above his head, and with his right hand he lightly grasped a scepter, symbol of unlimited power and authority. *I was wrong about him: he's quite a talented artist!* thought SchrummSchrumm. And he leaned out a little further, entranced.

It was his undoing. For, as he was leaning out further to contemplate the image of derisory homage drawn by this strange sketch artist, one of the Accredited Drowners shouted "Hup-la!" in a changed tone and, smartly hooking one of his ankles, toppled him into the muck as SchrummSchrumm uttered a cry of astonishment. He began to sink rapidly. Through his tear-filled eyes, he saw that the Accredited Drowners were now silent while the sketch artist, above him, had stopped drawing and was staring down at him with fixed attention. He also heard someone calling to him:

"SchrummSchrumm!" said the voice. "SchrummSchrumm, excursionist and king! I, on behalf of my master, the Guide, Prophet, and Supreme Lord of all excursions, declare you free and liberated! You are, henceforth, SchrummSchrumm crowned. Your place is among us, we whose hearts you have touched."

Where was the voice coming from? SchrummSchrumm had no way of telling. It continued:

"Guards!" it thundered. "Throw wide the Great Iron Gate! SchrummSchrumm is free! HE IS FREE!"

In an instant, it seemed to him a sweeping parkland had spread out before him—a green, formal park with centennial trees planted along a wide, sandy promenade. The Great Gate was open, and through it he saw Misunderstanding. The sun was rising over that much-desired city. Geometric buildings, their golden roofs encrusted with gemstones, lined the broad avenues. But it was entirely deserted, anyone would have sworn it was a ghost town. There was nothing to disturb the solemn and terrible splendor of Misunderstanding, except perhaps the immense black birds that circled over its rooftops with great economy of effort. On the outskirts of the city, a forest of towering trees swayed gently in the wind. And finally, beyond these, lay the countryside, the ripened fields ready for harvest, the retirees' little cottages surrounded by their lovingly tended gardens . . .

He smiled painfully. The tears were coursing faster than ever down his cheeks. He was sinking inexorably. The mire was now up to his chin. He wanted to cry out for help, but when he did so his mouth filled with mud. The marvelous park, the terrifyingly beautiful city behind the Great Gate, the countryside: all had evaporated. He strained his ears for a call, a distant echo, even a jeering laugh. But all was silence. And so, very deliberately, he closed his eyes.

He remembered an old love song he used to sing with the little girl next door. They would hold hands and watch each other's lips intently so as not to fall out of sync in their duet. *How far away Mahasky is!* he thought in despair. Just then, he felt the Accredited Drowners pushing down hard on his head with their gaffs to make him disappear completely.

Above him—but this was a sight SchrummSchrumm would never see—the sketch artist was feverishly completing his work. The excursionist SchrummSchrumm, the crowned and bewinged excursionist, was taking flight toward the east, without a backward glance, his eyes fixed on the wavering lines of smoke rising from the little cottages owned by sensible retirees down below him, far away, farther still—beyond the barbed wire, the ramparts, the gigantic forest, and the red death's-head signs that marked the impassable frontiers of Misunderstanding.

Paris, 18 October 1965

TRANSLATOR'S AFTERWORD

This translation follows the 2006 Verticales edition of the novel. The original 1968 Pauvert edition contained two additional passages worth mentioning. Fernand Combet left instructions before his death that both these passages should be removed if the book were ever reprinted.

The first is several pages long and occurs in Chapter 5, when SchrummSchrumm is hiding in a cupboard in the guards' dining hall after having been chased through the woods of Eden. In the original, he watches from his hidden vantage point as the hall fills with guards who seat themselves around the table before two little girls in white dresses are led in. In ritualistic fashion, the girls are clubbed, gutted like animals, spit-roasted in the dining hall hearth, and eaten by the assembled guards. There's a particularly graphic description of the spits being rammed down the girls' throats and emerging from between their buttocks. SchrummSchrumm, though nauseated by the spectacle, does nothing to intervene. Because Combet or his executors apparently forgot to correct Illustrious's allusion to the event in Chapter 10, I added a few words to the text to prevent confusion (and not make a liar of Illustrious): the line "You were chased on foot and saw *a table laid for* a ritual feast" actually reads ". . . and saw a ritual feast." A few words were inserted into Red-Bartlett's speech in Chapter 12 for the same reason: "You contrived to witness *the setting for* a ritual feast while concealed in a cupboard."

The second excision, in Chapter 9, is much shorter. It comes in the middle of the Holy Director's dinner speech, as he's describing the pleasures of taking a "tractable" girl out rowing on a pond. The original version had the excursionist forcing her head under the water and holding it there until the bubbles stopped. In the new version, the anecdote ends with her nodding off in the skiff.

K. E. Gormley (1978–) is an American translator living near Philadelphia.